wife number seven

by Melissa Brown

WIFE NUMBER SEVEN

Edited by Pam Berehulke
Cover Design by Regina Wamba
Photography by Heather Bowser

dedication

For my beta readers.

Every single one of you.

For your belief in this book,
your excitement about the story and
your love for the characters.

Thank you.

I am eternally grateful.

prologue

I ALWAYS KNEW I would share my husband.

I was four when my father took his second wife, Mother Peg, and seven when Mother Louise joined our family. He could have stopped then. After all, in our faith, a man could enter heaven as long as he had three wives. But my father didn't stop there. Next there was Mother Rylee and finally Mother Anne.

I should note that Mother Anne, who is only five years older than me, was just nineteen when she became my fifth mother. The exact age I was when I married Lehi Cluff, when I became his seventh wife.

My mother was a first wife and I had dreamed of becoming a first wife, as well. I dreamed of having a husband all to myself, if only for a little while. Some wives, like my mother, were lucky—she had five blissful years with my father before the prophet's revelation that he marry Mother Peg. I wanted that too.

Bliss.

It seemed unfathomable.

Instead, I'm wife number seven. My husband shares my bed one night a week. And although I don't love him, not in the way I'd always hoped I'd love the man I'm bound to for eternity, I find myself dreading the moment he walks out my bedroom door every seven days.

My existence is a lonely one. Lehi relieves that loneliness for the twenty-four hours when I pretend I'm the only one he lays with.

And I do pretend.

Every waking hour.

chapter 1

"BRINLEY, WAKE UP." The raspy voice interrupted my dreams as fingers poked at my ribs. My sister wife Aspen stood above my bed, urging me to wake. My eyes were heavy and refused to cooperate, and the nudging grew more persistent. "You must wake up!"

"What is it?" I grumbled sleepily.

Aspen pulled me to a seated position, and pulled off the covers. "It's happened. They're here."

I glanced at the clock. It was four a.m. . . . way too early for cryptic statements that needed translation.

"What are you talking about?" I yawned, wiping the sleep from my bleary eyes.

"Rebecca's been reassigned."

That word . . . reassigned . . . it woke me up. Completely. My stomach felt heavy, a brick of apprehension weighing it down.

"To Lehi? To us?" I asked, swallowing hard. An eighth wife, one with four children. Not only would I be the only childless wife of Lehi Cluff, but now I would no longer be the last one to enter the family. My lies would catch up to me. Rebecca's reassignment would see to that.

"Yes. The prophet had a revelation."

"And Elder Jameson?" I asked, my fingers trembling as I held them against my lips. I knew what had happened. Burt Jameson had lost one of his wives and four of his children. They would no longer call him Father. They would no longer give him hugs and kisses. Those tokens of affection would be transferred to Lehi, a man who didn't even know their names.

He was their new father and there was nothing they could do about it.

Aspen shrugged, her eyes cold and dismissive. "I guess he'll learn, *won't* he?"

Aspen was the sixth wife of my husband, Lehi Cluff. She was devout, a true follower of the Fundamentalist Church of Jesus Christ of Latter Day Saints, as well as of the prophet and his teachings. Already the mother of three children, she was only one year older than me and had been married to Lehi since she turned sixteen. Since joining Lehi's family, I'd suspected that Aspen was assigned to me—to watch out for me, to keep me in line, and to remind me of the virtues that were expected of me. She was my sister wife, yes, but she was also the closest thing I had to a "friend" in my new family.

We were different, so very different. Aspen believed what she was told; she didn't question things the way I did. She didn't lie awake at night, wondering if there was more to life outside the compound. Aspen was satisfied with her place in this world and never wanted to be a first wife, or to have a monogamous husband. She'd always wanted to be a young bride so that she could bear as many children as possible, as was expected of her.

Aspen was the perfect example of plural marriage.

I, however, was not. As far as anyone could see, I was an obedient, even-tempered, and loyal wife. I helped with the cooking, the cleaning, and the child-rearing. I'd never tried to secretly cut my hair or wear the color red. But I had my secrets. A voice inside told me I didn't belong here, that there was another life waiting for me. And with each passing year, that voice became louder.

"Wake up and get dressed," Aspen urged me. "Rebecca's going to stay with you for the next few days until we can get her settled into her own area." She crossed the room to my small closet, then pushed my dresses aside to make room for Rebecca's things.

"And the children?"

"They're sleeping in the common area with the other boys."

"Are they okay?"

A disgusted huff left her mouth. Aspen stopped and turned to me with a look that radiated superiority. "Brinley, this is not the time. Right now you're needed with Lehi and Rebecca. Now, get *up*!"

"Yes, Aspen," I muttered.

I dressed in my standard garb: long underwear, long-sleeved cotton dress, and shoes. My hair was tousled from sleep and needed to be brushed, but there simply wasn't time. Aspen stood at my doorway, staring at me impatiently. I pushed a few stray hairs back into the messy bun atop my head and followed her down the long hallway to the common area of our large home.

Rebecca, her skin ashen, sat on one of the several couches in the large room. My sister wife Leandra, the first wife of Lehi, patted her knee in an attempt to comfort her. Rebecca, whether by choice or affliction, ignored it as she kept her eyes downcast, her body visibly trembling.

Lehi's graying hair was disheveled, exposing the bald skin of his expanding forehead. Dark circles sat beneath his eyes as he scratched the back of his neck.

I wasn't the best at reading people, but I knew Lehi was overwhelmed. He wasn't sure how to act in a reassignment situation. He was taking on another wife—an unplanned one—and four young children. Those children would now call him Father or Daddy, and would look to him for guidance and approval. His new wife would now share his bed, even though earlier this evening she went to sleep with the only husband she'd ever known.

Rebecca was about thirty years old and was the third wife of Burt Jameson. They had been married for twelve years and Rebecca seemed to adore him. All plural wives in our community were expected to be obedient, loyal, and loving to our husbands, regardless of how we felt behind closed doors. But Rebecca was different; she was one of the few truly in love with her husband. And for that, I mourned the reassignment. I mourned that she had lost her love.

Leandra, the small and demanding first wife, glanced at me as I entered the common room, then returned her attention to her charge. "Rebecca, you'll be staying with Brinley for a few days, dear."

Rebecca nodded at me, her hands quivering in her lap. "Thank you, Miss Brinley," she whispered.

"It's no trouble," I replied. "Aspen has made room for your things in my closet, and the bed is big enough for the both of us."

Except when Lehi was to join me tomorrow evening. But somehow I knew my place on the schedule would be moved. A fluttering in my stomach surprised me—I usually looked forward to my time with Lehi, but knowing Rebecca would be with me instead was a relief I hadn't expected. It was a break from the ordinary. To be honest, I was excited at the possibility to build a friendship with my new sister wife.

Carefully, I sat next to Rebecca on the couch and took her hand in mine. "You will be a wonderful addition to our family."

I said what was expected of me, choosing my words carefully. Much like I did anytime I was surrounded by my sister wives.

An hour later, Rebecca and I were alone in my bedroom. Her children had fallen asleep easily, not entirely grasping their situation. They didn't know they were being reassigned, only that they were at our home for a sleepover. Rebecca was apparently delaying telling them the truth.

She probably didn't want to tell them that our prophet acted according to what he felt was God's will, and no one in our community could question him or what was "revealed" to him by our Lord. It would be difficult to tell them that they'd lost their father, that they would never return to their home, and that their lives had changed forever because the prophet deemed it so.

"I-I understand that this was a revelation, but . . ." Rebecca sat on the edge of my bed, her hand covering her mouth, the skin surrounding her eyes red and puffy. "I love him. I love my husband."

"I know," I whispered, rubbing her back softly with the palm of my hand, attempting to soothe her as best I could. "I could see that you did."

She wiped her nose with a tissue. "He's kind and loving, and . . . and I just can't imagine not *being* with him."

"I understand."

"You do?"

"I think so." I shrugged. I didn't have children yet. And I could certainly imagine a life without Lehi . . . so did I? Did I *really* understand her? Perhaps not.

"I don't know Elder Cluff. I don't know him at all. And now . . . he's to be my husband?"

Reluctantly, I nodded and said what I *should* say. "Lehi's a good man."

She gasped, looking startled. "Have I offended you? I hope I haven't. I just—I don't, I mean—"

"No, no. I promise." I patted her on the shoulder. "I just wanted you to know that you're safe here. That Lehi will take care of you and your children."

She pursed her lips and stared at the carpet beneath our feet. "But I don't love him."

I knew what I was supposed to say. I knew I should tell her that she'd grow to love Lehi, that she'd have a warm and loving relationship with our husband, that she just needed to give it time. But I couldn't.

I spoke the truth.

"Neither do I," I whispered, shaking my head slowly back and forth.

Her lips parted and her chin began to quiver. She collapsed against me and sobbed into my shoulder. She grasped my sleeves as she held on for dear life, revealing her pain, distress, and despair.

A single tear slid down my cheek as I attempted to comfort Rebecca, even though I couldn't quite grasp the idea of losing someone I loved. I'd never been in love. But instead of being comforted by this realization, it caused a knot to form in the pit of my stomach.

As I mourned her broken marriage, I found myself mourning the love that I would never have. Eventually her breathing evened out, and for one small minute, I was jealous of my soon-to-be sister wife. Jealous that she'd shared twelve years with a man she adored.

I'd never adored Lehi, and was pretty certain that I never would.

chapter 2

LAST NIGHT WAS the first time Rebecca fell asleep without tears soaking her pillow. Her boys were doing well with the other children. Some meltdowns occurred, but nothing that seemed to have her worried. She was making her best effort to learn the structure of our home and to find her place.

"Are you nervous?" I whispered as we lay in bed on our last night together in my room, both fighting sleep, knowing that tomorrow brought much change for all of us. She and Lehi were to be married by the prophet, followed by one night away as their honeymoon.

"About the marriage?"

I nodded.

"Not about the ceremony."

"The honeymoon?"

"No one has touched me but Burt. *No one.*"

The room was almost pitch black. I couldn't see her eyes, but knew they must be pained. She was doing her best, but this wasn't what she wanted for herself or for her boys. She missed her family.

"Does he . . . I'm sorry, it's not proper of me to ask."

"You can ask me anything, Rebecca," I assured her. We'd spent the last five nights getting to know each other better. We shared stories; we laughed and cried. She was quickly becoming my best friend. I trusted her, and I wanted her to trust me.

"Does he expect it on the first night?"

I wanted to ease her fears, to tell her that Lehi was a gentle lover who waited until his wives were ready. But that simply wasn't my experience.

"Yes."

She sighed loudly into her pillow, her breathing ragged as she held back tears.

"But . . . it doesn't last too long," I said, and raised one wicked eyebrow.

Rebecca let out a small giggle, clutching her pillow. When she laughed, I felt the tension in the air break apart and I laughed with her. As our laughter filled the air, we covered our mouths to keep from waking our sister wives.

"May I ask something?"

"Yes, of course," Rebecca answered.

I hesitated and then asked, "What do you miss most about him? About Burt?"

Rebecca lay in silence, but I could hear her wringing the fabric of her nightgown between her hands. Another moment in thought passed by.

"I miss his crooked nose and bushy eyebrows when he hadn't groomed them in a while. The way his smile pulled to the left more than the right. The way he smelled after working a day in the summer heat."

I pursed my lips, confused at her words and at her memory of Burt. "He doesn't sound at all attractive."

"He wasn't, Brinley. Not in the sense that women find Lehi attractive. But he was attractive to my heart. And my heart will have no one else."

"Wow." I was amazed by the idea of missing everything about *one* person. It was unfathomable to me. If I were reassigned this minute, I'd miss the security of Lehi, but not much else. He didn't have much of a sense of humor, and he wasn't interested in discussing current events in the community with his wives. He was a man of few words who kept to himself. But he took care of me, and I didn't feel suffocated. He wasn't a watchdog; I was allowed to go into town when necessary, and he also allowed me to visit my parents as often as I wanted. Not everyone could say that about their husbands.

"He loved me," Rebecca added. "Really loved me. I don't believe I'll ever feel that way for Lehi."

"I understand."

"But I'm thankful for you. I didn't care much for my sister wives before. You're different."

"I feel the same way. Aspen and I are . . . it's complicated, but I guess we're friends. I could never tell her the things I've told you, though. And I've known her for years."

"I feel honored."

I reached over and gripped her hand. "I'll do whatever I can to help you feel at home here."

"Thank you. That means so much."

She drifted to sleep still holding my hand. Her grip loosened as her body relaxed into slumber.

I listened to her breathing, knowing I would miss having her here with me. But starting the next morning, she'd have her own room, her own space. And I'd be forced to welcome Lehi back into mine.

Lehi and Rebecca were married this morning by the prophet. Rebecca wore a crisp white cotton dress with a scalloped collar and a bow in the center of her chest. Her hair was styled in the usual way, but a few of the young girls had found fresh flowers for her to place inside the grooves of her French braid. During the short ceremony, her teeth dug into her bottom lip. I'd seen her do that several times since arriving at the Cluff household. She was holding back tears, and nervously clutched at the fabric of her wedding dress.

Leandra was determined to have a bedroom ready and waiting for Rebecca when she and Lehi returned from their night together. She assumed I was missing him (I wasn't) and that Rebecca was ready for her own private space (she wasn't), and felt the best way to make everyone happy was to rearrange the bedrooms to accommodate Rebecca.

"I need someone to go into town," Leandra said as she clipped coupons at the large kitchen table in our dining area.

That statement was my favorite in the world. I craved it and jumped at any chance to leave the compound and venture out into the "outside world."

"I'll go," I said as casually as I could.

Leandra's eyes never met mine. She reached across the table for a white envelope and handed it to me without looking up.

"Get the items on the list. There's cash in the envelope. Don't be gone too long. We have supper to prepare."

"Yes, Leandra."

On my way out the door, I stopped into my bedroom to grab my purse. The frayed denim bag that I hid inside an old shoebox in my closet desperately needed to be replaced, but it served more than one purpose for me. The secret compartment of the bag held something precious, something that must stay hidden at all costs. No one in my family knew, and I intended to keep it that way. It was my secret and would continue to be.

Placing the envelope in my tattered bag, I grabbed a couple of fresh cookies from the kitchen and walked out of our house and through our small gate. The white stone wall that surrounded the property might seem attractive to some, but to me it was ominous, a reminder that I was living in a cage. And even though I was able to leave from time to time when the first wife deemed it so, this was the cage in which I would eventually raise my children, grow old, and in due time, die.

All within the confines of the Cluff property of the compound.

When I reached the edge of the compound, I found the only two men I interacted with on a regular basis: our daytime guards. Samuel and Daniel were a few years older than me and were each on their way to being an important part of the priesthood. They spent their days guarding the compound, making sure outsiders did not peep into our property or break into our temple. Whenever I ventured into town, I brought them fresh baked goods. In return, they were friendly and never asked me where I had been if I didn't return home before sunset.

Even at a young age, I knew that our temple was grandiose. A large, white, hulking structure, it intimidated those outside our compound. But intimidation can still lead to curiosity. Outsiders were fascinated by our hair, our clothing, our way of life. And although it didn't happen often, Samuel and Daniel would sometimes be forced to escort snooping outsiders off the property.

Because of this, many of the homes in our compound were surrounded by walls just like the one that surrounded the Cluff house. It was all I'd ever known, so to me, it was perfectly normal. When I ventured out into the outside world, it fascinated me how people would build their homes so close to a road where thousands would pass by. Didn't they want their privacy? Didn't they feel on display? Perhaps not.

I'd been taught that *all* outsiders, even those who followed the mainstream Mormon church, would burn in hell when they died. We were the chosen people who were truly living as God commanded—within the doctrine of plural marriage. Our husbands would become gods themselves and rule over planets of their own. They would live an eternal life of paradise. But when I ventured into the outside world, I was always surprised at how friendly and kind the outsiders seemed to be.

When you were raised to think that everyone outside your community was bound to an eternity of punishment and misery, it shaped your expectations. I'd always expected to see misery upon their sinning faces. I'd always expected hatred to spew from their mouths. I'd always expected shriveled skin, bags under their eyes, anything that would indicate misery of the body, of the vessel God had created.

But when I went into town to run errands or visit the free clinic, that wasn't at all what I saw. I saw kindness and common courtesy. I saw children holding the hands of their mothers, just as I'd always done. Only these children were wearing different clothes and had shorter hair, styled in all sorts of ways. Some of the girls wore their hair down so it spilled over their shoulders. Some wore clips or bands around their heads. They looked beautiful.

Makeup was forbidden in our community. What you saw was what you got. But in town, the women had lush pink lips and gorgeous lashes that curled seductively from their eyes. They possessed a confidence that I couldn't quite understand.

The prophet's words echoed through my brain, reminding me that all of what I was observing was sin. I knew this. But I couldn't help but wonder what it would be like, even for just a day, to live like they do. To wear makeup in public, to choose my own clothing, to cut my hair short or curl it with an iron. I was fascinated. If Leandra or any of my sister wives knew of my obsession with the outsiders, I wouldn't be allowed to go into town any longer. So I hid it.

Once I'd purchased everything on Leandra's list, I checked the hidden compartment of my bag. Only three days left. It was time.

The free clinic was only a few blocks from the grocery store. As always, my heart raced when I walked through the revolving door of the utilitarian building. I could only hope Tiffany was working today.

Four years ago, my cousin Tiffany left our community to live on the outside. She had become my confidante, the only person in the world who knew what I had been keeping from Lehi since we married. She knew what I needed and made sure I received it. Every single month.

My pulse slowed when I saw her, sitting behind the front desk of the clinic, explaining to a young woman how to fill out the forms properly.

When our eyes met, she smiled and held up one finger. This was our drill. We didn't say much to each other these days. She knew my reason for visiting. When I first started visiting the clinic, she had all kinds of questions about her siblings, her friends, and the boy she'd had a crush on from afar. But not anymore. She'd immersed herself in the outside world and her curiosity had dissipated. But she continued to help me, and for that I was grateful.

The patient in front of me hugged her clipboard and walked to one of the many empty chairs behind us. The way clear, I stepped forward.

Tiffany whispered, “Cutting it close, I see.”

“It’s been busy at home.”

“Give me just a minute. I’ll have it ready for you.”

“Thank you.”

Tiffany walked to the back room, and I listened to the soft music playing through the speakers. That was one thing I looked forward to when stopping by the clinic. Music was forbidden at home, but I loved the soothing melodies that echoed through the clinic. I didn’t know the names of the songs or the people who created them, but I enjoyed them just the same. Every month when I visited it was different, never the same song twice. I wondered how many songs there could possibly be. Hundreds? Thousands?

My mind drifted, remembering the first time Tiffany had helped me . . .

When the prophet had revealed that I was to wed Lehi Cluff, I’d had a full-blown panic attack, although I didn’t know that was what it was called. Worried, my older sister, Jessa, had taken me to the clinic. Tiffany had taken pity on me and led me to an examination room. While Jessa waited in the reception area, Tiffany had sat next to me, taking my hand in hers, rubbing my back with the other.

“You’re having an anxiety attack.”

“What is that?”

“Your body is reacting to something that scares you. Did something happen?”

"I'm getting married."

"Ah." She shook her head. "I see."

"What? I'm not afraid." I frowned at her, drawing away. I couldn't betray my future husband, my family, my prophet.

"Of course you are," she said, her voice soft and comforting. "That's perfectly normal. Do you even know him?"

I shook my head.

"Damn them," she muttered, pursing her lips together.

"Please don't—"

"Listen to me. Are you ready, ready for all of this? You can run away. You don't have to stay there."

"What?" I recoiled. "Where would I go? What would I do?"

"You could stay with me. I have an apartment above the pharmacy."

"No, I—I couldn't do that. I'm expected to marry Elder Cluff."

"Elder Cluff?" She gasped. "He's old!"

"He's not that old."

"Oh, Brinley." She frowned and patted my shoulder. "I can help you. Just say the word."

Two months later, I did return to the clinic, but not for an escape. I was looking for a delay. A delay to the inevitable. I simply wasn't ready for the next step in my commitment to Lehi. But no one would approve of my desire for a delay.

No one but Tiffany.

"Here you are," Tiffany said, interrupting my reverie as she placed a small bag on the counter. Quickly, I removed the plastic disk and shoved it into the hidden compartment of my purse.

"Thank you."

"Any problems?"

I shook my head.

"Good. My offer still stands, you know."

"I'm fine," I insisted, my head still moving in denial that had become automatic.

Tiffany sighed. "If you ever change your mind, tell me. Don't let pride stand in your way."

"Thank you," I said, waving good-bye as I walked out the door of the clinic, and back to the compound.

Back to my home.

Back to my cage.

chapter 3

FOR YEARS I had prayed that sex with my husband would bring me some sort of pleasure, a deeper connection to the man I married. For years I'd asked God to fix whatever it was that was wrong with me, because I knew it must be me. I must be the problem.

Rebecca said she used to "lose herself" in Burt, overflowing with the passion that built between them before they exploded together. Those whispered confessions of hers late at night made my heart yearn to experience that intensity of emotion. I wanted to lose myself in Lehi, to feel something when he grunts, collapses onto my chest, and grows soft inside me.

But I didn't.

All I felt was relief.

When it was over, he would talk to me for a little while and would ask about my week. It was those moments I craved. Those moments when someone asked me about my day, about my life. It didn't happen often . . . only when Lehi shared my bed. When he fell asleep with his arm draped over my belly, I was left alone with my thoughts.

And lately, those thoughts were always about Burt and Rebecca. About their all-consuming love and how desperately I wished I could feel that way for Lehi.

Last night was our first night together since the reassignment. As always, Lehi knocked on my door after making his rounds and saying good night to his other wives. I was sitting, staring into the mirror of my vanity while I touched up my makeup, knowing that Lehi preferred a painted face.

Although makeup was not allowed in our community, Lehi requested that I wear it privately on the nights he joined me in my bed. Once every week, behind closed doors, I dabbed at my nose with powder, applied scarlet color to my lips, and lined my eyes with jet-black liquid eyeliner.

That was Lehi's preferred image of me. The different colors brought out my features and gave me a more exotic appearance. But I didn't feel like me. I was being painted for someone else . . . like I was a prop, a toy, a possession. It made me feel as if I weren't a person with feelings, thoughts, or desires of my own.

"Come in," I said, watching as my husband cracked open the door.

"Is now a good time?" he asked.

Lehi was generally a polite man unless you made him angry, and then he transformed into someone unrecognizable. I'd managed to avoid Lehi's wrath since joining the family, but had witnessed it directed at Leandra several times when errors were made in his weekly schedule, or the family budget was misused.

It was then that he'd raise his voice, his face turning the color of a beet. He'd throw things, punch walls, and then retreat to his study to calm down. Leandra was his first wife; they had a history and a unique relationship that I could never quite know, and most of me didn't want to know. That was their relationship; I was told to focus on my own with him.

"Yes, of course."

I stood up, shifting nervously as I stood barefoot in my long cotton nightgown, hoping that Lehi would approve of my appearance. A grin appeared on his face as he took in the sight of me, and I was relieved to have pleased him. He approached and extended his tanned hand to me, his fingers long and thin, and calloused from hard work. I placed my pale fingers into his palm and he squeezed them tightly, then led me to the bed.

"I've missed you," he said as he ran his other hand through his brown hair, shot through with silver strands.

Lehi Cluff was exactly fifty years old when we'd married, more than double my age of nineteen. He had looked older than his years back then, and even more so now. Deep grooves bracketed his mouth and his skin sagged. Dark smudges ringed his eyes, signaling his exhaustion from balancing so many wives and children.

But I'd listened closely as he'd talked to me late at night when we were alone together. What he *didn't* say was as telling, sometimes, as what he did. He'd never admit that this lifestyle, this gateway to the kingdom of heaven, was aging him at a rapid rate. Lehi was a devout elder of the church who believed wholeheartedly in what he'd been taught all his life. He was determined to please the prophet, maintain his place in the priesthood of the church, and die having lived the life he was meant to live.

Sheepishly, I nodded, knowing Lehi preferred that I allow him to control the conversation until after our lovemaking was over.

"Thank you for your patience. I'm sure this has been quite challenging."

I shook my head and looked at the floor. Guilt consumed me. It wasn't patience that motivated my cooperation; having Rebecca share my room was a welcome break from my time with Lehi. But I couldn't let my husband know that.

"More than anyone, you welcomed Rebecca with open arms. And I appreciate that. As does our Lord. She was meant to join our family. Thank you for seeing that, Brinley."

His fingers cupped my chin and guided my gaze so that it met his. His eyes were kind but detached, as if this was a routine he'd memorized years before. Slowly, he unbuttoned my nightgown and guided it to the floor. I turned my neck, allowing him access. Immediately, he placed perfunctory kisses on my skin, then gripped my braid in his hand and guided me to lie on the bed, under the covers.

Lehi always made sure the covers rested on his back when we laid together, and this night was no different. He nudged my legs apart with his knee and pushed himself inside me. A pinching sensation that I'd grown used to was present at first, but dissipated slightly as I desperately tried to relax and enjoy this time with my husband.

But I couldn't.

Again and again he pushed inside me as I trained my gaze on the ceiling. I crossed my ankles behind his back, and my toes brushed against the crisp cotton sheets. Through it all, his lips never touched mine, his hands never left my neck or shoulders. A need swept over me, a desire to be touched elsewhere, to be wanted by him more, but I didn't know how. As he pushed with all his might, I gripped his back and waited for it to end.

With one final grunt, Lehi sank onto my chest, breathing heavily, his exhales hot on my shoulder. I stroked his hair as his body calmed and within seconds, he'd grown soft again. He pulled away from me and sat up, then moved to sit on the edge of the bed.

"Thank you, Brinley."

"Of course."

I said that every time. Every single time.

One of the responsibilities of being a celestial wife of Lehi Cluff was for me to open myself to him physically. It was my obligation, my duty, my role. And I had accepted it.

But I knew something was wrong with me, something that kept me from enjoying our time together as much as he clearly enjoyed it. Rebecca said that Burt always gave her pleasure in her private areas. She called it a "release." I'd never found a release, not once. When Lehi was inside me, I didn't feel the pleasure that Rebecca had told me about. I didn't feel a buildup of sensations or an eruption of pleasure. Every time he pushed himself inside me, I wondered what to do to make that happen. But I had no idea, which made it all the more clear that I was the problem.

"Maybe that did it." Lehi rubbed the back of his neck. He was, of course, referring to the fact that we'd been married three years and I hadn't yet become pregnant, despite our regular intercourse. There was a reason for that, but it was a reason that he could never know about.

"Maybe," I said with a forced smile, and pulled the sheets up to cover my bare breasts.

"Perhaps Leandra can switch the calendar. I know it's best for us to be together when you're ovulating."

"I know, and I am . . . right now, in fact," I lied.

"You are?" His face lit up slightly and I nodded, lying again.

The only acceptable reason for sex between two people in our church was for procreation. And after three years, I still hadn't given him what was expected of me. Obviously the problem did not lie with Lehi. He had twenty-five children with the six wives who came before me. It was me. I was the problem.

But I simply wasn't ready. Something was holding me back.

"That would truly be a blessing," Lehi said over his shoulder as he pulled his boxer shorts back on.

"Yes," I said.

"Please keep me posted. You should know in a few weeks, right?"

Considering how many children Lehi had already fathered, he knew very little about a woman's cycle. Perhaps it was because he switched bedrooms every night. Or maybe it was because there were many months that two or even three of his wives were all pregnant at the same time, one further along than the next. It must have been hard to keep up, especially considering that sex between a pregnant woman and her husband was forbidden. They'd succeeded in creating a life. Sex was no longer deemed necessary or appropriate once a woman had conceived. Once the baby is born, though, it was business as usual.

"Yes. I will tell you."

Lehi inched closer to me and placed his hand on my cheek. "I'm sure you must be frustrated. But we'll get there. Perhaps we should pray together."

My stomach churned. I hated false prayer. God knew when I was lying. Not only was I sinning by preventing pregnancy with my husband, but I kneeled on the floor next to him, week after week, pretending to pray to God to give us a baby when it was the last thing I truly wanted.

Of course, I'd be less lonely if I had a baby. I could imagine myself with the tiniest of little girls. I'd sew pink dresses for her and knit little blush booties. I'd snuggle her and love her and protect her with everything I am. But not yet.

Together we knelt, facing the bed, our elbows resting on the mattress. I closed my eyes as Lehi spoke for the both of us.

"Dear Heavenly Father, we thank you for this consummation in the hopes that you will allow Brinley to become pregnant. Lord, we pray that you'll give her the gift of motherhood, to secure her place in your kingdom. In Jesus's name, we pray."

"Amen," we said together.

Lehi took my hand in his and planted an obligatory kiss on my skin. "It's time for bed. I have an early day tomorrow."

I nodded before climbing to my feet.

"You should wash that stuff off your face." His words were matter of fact, as if he was in denial that the "stuff" on my face was completely for him, for his desires and his needs.

Without complaint, I excused myself to the bathroom to scrub my face, and pushed down the irritation that bubbled beneath my skin. When I finished preparing myself for sleep, I returned to our bed. Lehi was facing the wall, his rib cage rising and falling as he breathed heavily.

I stared up at the ceiling, wondering how long I could keep my secret. How long it would be before I was found out—by Lehi or Leandra or the midwife who assisted in birthing all the Cluff children.

I knew that day would come. And I knew that God would punish me.

For preventing pregnancy and for keeping secrets.

For not loving my husband.

For not giving him all of myself, all of my heart, my body, and my soul.

Every day I merely went through the motions knowing that it was unacceptable, and that I would most certainly be punished. Perhaps not today or tomorrow, or even next year. But it would happen.

I knew that I should be determined to fix whatever it was that was broken inside me, to welcome a child into my womb, to accept my role as Lehi's seventh wife.

I simply didn't know how.

chapter 4

ANOTHER DAY GOING into town. I was elated. I'd been lucky that week and had been sent twice by Leandra. Today it was my responsibility to visit the local pharmacy for vitamins, batteries, and cosmetics. Leandra had obviously requested that I be discreet so as not to embarrass our husband and his desire for painted faces in the bedroom. Gladly, I accepted the chore.

As always, I grabbed my purse and reached in to check for the plastic disk in the hidden compartment. It was still there; no one had discovered my secret yet. I could only hope that by the time I was ready to stop taking them, the secret would remain mine.

When I stepped outside the confines of our home, I felt a prickle between my shoulder blades, as if someone's eyes were upon me. It was unsettling so I scanned the property, but couldn't see anyone following me. It had to be my imagination. When I approached the edge of the compound, my suspicions were validated.

"Pardon me," a gruff voice said behind me. A tall, handsome man with blond hair shot through with silver jogged to catch up to me.

I stiffened, knowing immediately who this man was.

Burt Jameson.

"I'm sorry to bother you," he said, running his fingers through his hair. His blue eyes were sunken and bloodshot, as if he hadn't slept well in weeks.

Just like Rebecca.

"Miss Brinley, right? You're my wi—I mean, you're Rebecca's sister wife?"

I nodded, trying to avoid direct eye contact. If I were seen talking to Burt, I could be in all sorts of trouble with Lehi, or even the prophet. It was best to be as dismissive as possible.

"I'm the project manager on the prophet's new home." He gestured a block away to the unfinished home behind us. "I saw you walk by and, well . . . I know I shouldn't be doing this, but I have to."

He extended his hand, a folded envelope clutched between his calloused fingers. "Would you please give this to Rebecca?"

"I don't think—" I shook my head and glanced around me, my heart racing in my chest.

"Please. I beg of you," he said, his voice cracking. He swallowed hard and his eyes glistened.

My heart broke for him. The love he felt for Rebecca radiated from every pore of his body. Quickly, I snatched the envelope from his hand and crammed it into my purse, then walked away as if nothing had happened.

"Thank you," he said in an anguished whimper from behind me. "Thank you."

I couldn't get Burt out of my head. So much so that I walked right past the store that Leandra had sent me to. I was in a daze; the anguish in his face haunted me. The obvious nights without sleep, the heartache that was plain in his eyes. I couldn't imagine how that felt, but I wanted to feel it. As strange as it might sound, even heartache sounded like a better alternative to the indifference I experienced each and every day.

So lost in my thoughts of Burt and Rebecca, I didn't notice the footsteps that dogged me, and probably had for several blocks. Unlike earlier, I didn't feel that sense of dread and self-preservation that one feels when they're being followed, when they're being stalked.

Until it was too late.

A man looped his arm through the strap of my purse and gave a hard yank, trying to pull it from me.

I was being robbed.

I'd heard of this, of people stealing from others in the outside world, but had never experienced it. We didn't steal. We shared, we gave, we accepted. But we never stole.

The placement of my hand inside the pocket of my dress was my saving grace. When the man pulled on my bag, he was unable to break free and run. Instead, the shock of the jarring pain to my wrist as he attempted to yank the purse from me was all it took to shock my system, making me fully aware of what was happening to me. So I dug in my feet and pulled back.

When the bag didn't give, the man turned back and glared. His blue eyes bored into me and I lost my breath. I knew those eyes. I hadn't seen them in so long, but I knew them.

"Porter?" My chin dropped as I said his name.

His eyes widened in shock, but his grip on the bag didn't lessen. Instead, he tugged harder and swept me off my feet. I landed hard on the warm sidewalk, still clenching the purse's strap in my hands.

"Let go," he hissed through his clenched teeth, his nostrils flaring. It was then that I noticed how different he looked. He was not the boy I remembered.

Porter Hammond had been one of the most handsome young men in the compound. He was several years older than me, and I wasn't supposed to admire him. After all, in our church, we were raised to view the opposite sex as villains, as snakes, as those we couldn't possibly trust.

Until we were assigned to marry them. Then we were magically expected to get over it.

But Porter—there was always something about him. Something that drew me to the light in his eyes, the dimple in his pale cheek, and the warmth in his smile.

That smile had been permanently etched in my brain since I was ten years old . . .

When I was ten, Porter was a teenager and was one of the most talented boys when it came to construction. From a very young age, the boys in our community were sent to work with their fathers at various sites—both on and off the compound. Porter was especially talented at driving the forklift. And he was on said forklift on the day his smile became permanently etched in my brain.

My sister Winnie and I were walking down a dirt road in the compound. In my dress pocket, I carried a small doll I'd made out of cloth, my hand clutching it tightly as we walked. One year prior, the prophet had ordered all our toys to be removed and destroyed, claiming that God had revealed toys to be destructive to our maturing brains. When my parents took my baby dolls away, I'd sobbed, ignoring my mother's stone-faced instructions to "keep sweet" and present a brave face despite my misery.

In perhaps my first act of defiance, I'd hidden remnants of fabric from my mother's sewing box. Each night, I twisted and cut and twirled the fabric to create a small doll. She was my new baby and I'd never let anyone hurt or destroy her.

On that day, Winnie and I were walking past a group of boys working hard to build an addition to one of the prophet's homes. Porter was driving the forklift while other boys walked, carrying two-by-fours on their shoulders.

"We should go the other way," Winnie said, pointing away from the boys. But I was curious and wanted to observe them, even if only for a minute or two as we walked past their work site.

The boy on the forklift called out, "Hey, girls."

"Don't say anything," Winnie whispered. "He's a snake."

Deep down I didn't believe her, or my parents, or the prophet. He was just a boy. A boy with a beautiful smile who was looking right at me. He didn't look like a snake or a predator, just a friendly boy. An innocent, friendly boy.

Without thinking, I released the doll inside my pocket and I waved. As I did, Porter's gaze darted to the ground and instinctively, I looked down too.

My doll.

Oh no.

He'd report me. I'd be in so much trouble.

Dread swept over me, causing my heart to pound, and Winnie gasped. But Porter was calm. Within seconds, he'd hopped off the forklift and had retrieved the small doll, then placed it in my hand. A sweet, nonthreatening smile wreathed his face.

He nodded his head toward me. "There you go."

Stunned at his kindness, I had looked up at him and breathed out, "Thanks."

"Brinley," Winnie had snapped, yanking me away by the elbow. "We need to go. Now!"

I'd never forgotten that day.

But this Porter was different. His skin tone was gray and sickly. The whites of his blue eyes were red, so bloodshot he looked as if he hadn't slept in weeks. His hair was tucked under a beanie cap despite the warm summer weather.

I said his name again. I had to. I needed him to know that despite his departure from our compound, from our world, I knew exactly who he was.

"Porter . . . Porter Hammond."

H closed his eyes, as if he were trying to block out any memory of that name or of someone who might remember him from his childhood in the compound. When he opened them again, the anger in his eyes was alarming. I didn't know those eyes. They looked possessed.

"Fucking drop it," he said through clenched teeth and I gasped, shocked by his choice of words.

What had happened to him? My grip loosened unintentionally and he managed to rip the bag from my hands.

And then he ran. Fast.

Suddenly, I remembered the two things in that bag that could not be lost.

I couldn't let Burt down . . . or Rebecca. And I needed those pills.

Within seconds, I had climbed to my feet and was chasing after the boy I had known for years, one who would never have stolen from others. A boy who was once kind and forgiving. I ran as fast I could, but the gap between us grew larger until the boy faded away.

I couldn't catch him.

He was gone.

chapter 5

"WHAT DO YOU MEAN? How did that happen?" Aspen stood with her hands hooked on her narrow hips, a look of disgust twisting her pale face.

"I was distracted and he snatched it away."

"Are you all right?" Rebecca asked, her fingers grazing my elbow.

I couldn't look her in the eye. She had no idea that I'd let her down, that I'd lost the note from Burt. Even though I was hesitant to help him, he'd trusted me the moment I put that envelope in my purse. If Rebecca didn't respond, he'd assume her silence was a message, a decision of some sort. He wouldn't know the truth.

I couldn't let that happen. They'd been through enough already.

"I think I bruised my bottom," I replied, "but I'll be fine. I'm just afraid of what Leandra will say."

"She won't be pleased, that's for sure," Aspen said, pursing her lips together. "How much money did you lose?"

"Twenty-five dollars."

Both women sighed. With eight wives and twenty-nine children to support now that Rebecca and her boys had joined our family, money was tight in our household. Lehi worked a minimum of fifty hours per week on construction projects both in and outside of the compound. I didn't want to add to his exhaustion or work load.

"She'll ground me, won't she?" I asked, starting to panic. If Leandra didn't allow me to leave the compound, I'd never get my purse from Porter, or be able to visit the clinic each month. I'd be pregnant by fall.

No, no, no, no, no!

It was happening again. My chest tightened, my cheeks turned hot, and the room spun in circles. Another panic attack.

"Brinley?"

I knew Rebecca was standing next to me, but her voice sounded as if she were whispering to me from the end of a long, narrow tunnel. I was slipping away.

"Come on," Aspen said, wrapping an arm around my waist. "Shh, breathe. You're safe. You're all right."

But I couldn't breathe. I couldn't settle down. I knew I wasn't all right.

"What's going on?" a shrill voice demanded.

Leandra walked in with Gloria in tow, the second wife. In my head, I referred to Gloria as "the shadow" because she was constantly in Leandra's wake. She didn't say much, but I knew not to cross her. Her loyalty to Leandra and Lehi was paramount to her, even above her own five children.

Aspen glanced up. "Something awful happened today. Brinley was robbed."

"Robbed? Oh sweet Lord above, are you all right, girl?" Leandra moved to my other side and slipped her arm around my waist to keep me upright.

I hated when she called me "girl." It was just another assertion of her superiority as the first wife. Aspen and I were both called "girl" on occasion, and I knew it grated on Aspen's nerves as much as it did on mine.

But that was the least of my worries. I was having a hard enough time focusing on the wallpaper of the kitchen, just trying to breathe, rather than worry about what Leandra had called me.

"She'll be all right," Aspen said. "It wasn't her fault. The man had a gun."

My heart twisted a little tighter inside my chest. Aspen had lied! She never lied.

And I was the cause of it.

I was affecting so many people—Rebecca, and now Aspen—with my irresponsibility.

Gloria gasped.

"A gun? Oh my word." Leandra clasped her hand to her mouth, tightening her grip on my arm. "How did you get away?"

Aspen paused. "She ran. I, myself, am amazed at her bravery. Don't you agree?"

"Yes, uh—of course," Leandra conceded, then turned her focus on me. "I'm so glad you're safe."

"Mon—mon . . ." I tried to speak, but couldn't enunciate the word.

"What is she saying?" Leandra turned toward me and pinned me with her eyes, making my heart race even faster.

"She's afraid," Aspen said. "That you'll be upset with her about losing the money."

"Oh."

"Even though it wasn't her fault," Aspen added.

Her words placed a protective cloak on the top of my scalp, one that slid down to cover my body all the way to my toes. She was protecting me from Leandra's anger, defending me in a way I'd never expected.

Gradually my pulse slowed and the harsh pain in my chest began to dissipate. The voices of my sister wives became louder and less muffled. The tunnel disappeared and the fuzzy objects in my line of vision sharpened. I could see the concern in Leandra's narrowed eyes, and feel her compassion as she stroked my shoulder.

"I'm not upset, of course not. The outside world is a dangerous place. That's what I've been telling you all for years. We're so lucky to be a part of the chosen."

"I agree," Aspen said, stroking my hair. "Will you tell Lehi?"

"Well, of course," Leandra said, taking a step away. "It would be dishonest not to. He deserves to know about the money and that one of his wives was in danger."

Still not trusting myself to speak, I shook my head back and forth violently, my silent way of begging Leandra to keep this to herself.

"I'm sorry, dear." She stroked my arm again. "I have to. Now, go lie down. We'll take care of supper while you rest."

Nodding through my tears, I reached for Aspen's hand and walked to my room. Without a word, I threw myself on the bed, knowing that Lehi would forbid me from my weekly errands. And then what would I have to look forward to?

Nothing.

Absolutely nothing.

"I'm sorry, Brinley." Aspen sat on the bed next to me and stroked my hair. "I tried."

"I know. Please, just—just give me a moment, all right?" I whimpered through my sobs.

"Of course."

The door closed with a soft click and my tears soaked the pillow. I dreaded the inevitable conversation I would have with my husband later that evening.

It didn't take long. The familiar knock on the door arrived sooner than expected. I'd finally wiped away my tears, changed my pillowcase, and splashed cold water on my face, desperately trying to figure out a plan to get my bag back from Porter.

"Brinley." Lehi ducked his head inside the room. His voice was flat, his posture rigid.

"Yes, come in." I sat on the edge of the bed, awaiting my punishment, staring at the beige carpeting below my feet.

"Leandra told me what happened." He cleared his throat and placed his hands in the pockets of his cardigan sweater.

"Yes, sir." I still couldn't look at him, terrified that another panic attack would swarm my body and mind.

"You must have been frightened."

I nodded, biting my lower lip to prevent tears.

"I'm so relieved you weren't hurt." He began to pace across my small room, back and forth, back and forth. "The outside world can be a terrible place. People will do anything to get what they want. I guess you learned that the hard way."

Again, I nodded as he cleared his throat once again. I knew what was coming, knew what my punishment would be. Devastated, I deflated before his eyes.

"From now on, you may not go into town unaccompanied."

There it was. My heart crashed into my belly. It was over. It was done. I would forever be trapped in this cage of a home. Tears stung at the corners of my eyes, demanding to be released.

"I'll speak to the prophet. Perhaps one of the guards will be able to escort you into town each week."

Amazed, I instantly perked up. I wasn't being punished. Lehi was still allowing me to go into town. I wanted to praise the Lord above right then and there, but knew better than to let my true feelings be known.

"Thank you," I said, tamping down my enthusiasm. The last thing I needed was Lehi questioning my motives for visiting town. Especially since I needed to go . . . and soon.

And then it hit me. Lehi said that one of the guards would escort me, and Samuel was one of those guards. He was Porter's best friend years ago before Porter left the community. Perhaps he knew where I could find him.

I smiled inside at the thought of retrieving my bag, my secret, and Rebecca's letter.

"I'm happy to see you smile. It's been a while," Lehi muttered, kissing the top of my head absentmindedly.

"Thank you, Lehi," I said. "And I'm so sorry about losing your money."

"Don't worry about that." He glanced back at the closed door before returning my gaze. In a half whisper, he said, "Here, take this." He placed a twenty dollar bill in the palm of my hand. "When you're ready, you can go to the pharmacy. I have something I'd like you to purchase."

Reaching into his pocket, he retrieved a folded piece of paper and handed it to me. His cheeks reddened slightly as I opened the folded advertisement. The model looking back at me had lips the color of a ripe plum, deep and dark. Her lashes were long and the color of night. I stared at the paper in my hand, its edge ragged, obviously torn from a magazine.

We weren't allowed to have magazines or books or television. Newspapers were forbidden to everyone but the prophet. My eyes widened and met Lehi's, silently asking where it came from. But the lack of connection between my husband and me prevented him from understanding my body language.

I paused a moment, then asked, "Um, where did—"

"On a job site. An obstetrician's office. We're remodeling the waiting area." He shrugged, apparently not embarrassed or upset with me for asking, which was a relief. I didn't want to anger him when he was being kind to me. "It made me think of you, and I'd like you to buy this."

"The lipstick?" I croaked, attempting not to shudder at the sultry nature of the shade.

"Yes. And anything else from Leandra's original list that you would like to wear."

I didn't *want* to wear any of it, but I nodded and hid my disgust. We'd only been married three years, and already I'd grown tired of his treating me like a doll. Maybe I could love him if he saw *me* . . . the real me. Not the painted face he insisted upon.

"I'll speak to the prophet this evening," he said. "Perhaps you can go into town tomorrow."

"But—" I interrupted, hoping he wouldn't become angry with me.

"Yes?"

"If you're sending someone with me, they'll know"—I gestured to the advertisement in my hand—"about this."

"Oh. Well, let me handle that. I'll specify that they should wait for you outside any store you visit."

"Yes, sir," I muttered, masking my elation at the possibility of tracking down Porter. I could only hope the prophet wouldn't assign someone to accompany me, that I'd be able to ask one of the guards myself.

And I would ask Samuel.

Perhaps there was hope for me yet.

chapter 6

SUNLIGHT STREAMED INSIDE my small bedroom, rousing me from sleep. I sat up and glanced out the window, struggling to focus my sleepy eyes on a tiny bird perched on the ten-foot wall that lined the Cluff property. Its beak pointed to the sun as if it were bathing in the glow of its warmth.

Propping myself up on one arm, I watched the bird, a desire building inside me to take on the day ahead. To bathe in the glow of the sun. To thank the Heavenly Father for my blessings. But something in the pit of my stomach wouldn't allow that.

The memory of my missing purse.

The loss of my pills, and the letter for Rebecca.

My cage.

My reality.

Wiping sleep from my eyes, I noticed the yellow sheet of notebook paper lying on the nightstand.

Brinley,

I have spoken with our prophet. He is unable to spare any of the guards from their posts at this time. The outsiders have been especially sneaky as of late. However, you have my permission to ask one of your sister wives to accompany you into town if you are comfortable.

Blessings,

Lehi

Rebecca. I would ask Rebecca.

She would keep my secret. She would be invested in finding Porter, if I was brave enough to tell her about the letter addressed to her inside the bag.

But what if we found Porter, the bag, and everything inside it . . . everything except for her letter?

She'd hate me, despise me. And I'd lose an ally in my family. No, I couldn't tell her. Not until I knew I could give her that letter. With new determination in having a plan, I walked to Rebecca's room and tapped on the door.

"Come in, please," she said.

The door creaked as I pushed it open. She looked up, her weary face brightening as I entered the room.

"Good morning, Brinley," she said, tying the laces of her youngest son's sneakers. His face was red, tears streamed down his cheeks. He'd been sleeping in bed with her the last few nights, missing his father like crazy, refusing to acknowledge Lehi. He missed Burt. They all did, including Rebecca.

But unlike her sons, Rebecca was obligated to hide her sadness, her mourning, her grief. She was required to obey the prophet's revelation and honor Lehi as her true husband—even when he slapped her oldest son across the face when he refused to call him Father like the rest of Lehi's brood. Even when he sent all four of her children to bed without supper because they wouldn't look him in the eye when he spoke.

They were unable to cope, but that didn't matter to Lehi. They were expected to fall into line and obey. Lehi had to demonstrate to the prophet that he was worthy of this choice, of this reassignment. If the boys acted out, his standing with the prophet would be lessened. And he simply couldn't have that.

Watching their struggle pulled at my heart, knowing that their father loved them—all of them—and wanted to be with them. I had to find that note. I just had to.

I knew it was wrong of me to have such thoughts, to want Rebecca and her boys to reunite with the man whom was deemed unfit to have them in his life. But there was this part of me, a tiny bit of resistance in my spirit that captured the portion of my brain that held my imagination. And I imagined. Oh, did I imagine.

I imagined Burt loading his belongings into his truck, waiting for Rebecca and the boys in the middle of the night. Rebecca would gather them, still sleepy in their pajamas, and I would help. I would hold their hands and whisper, "Don't worry, everything's going to be all right. You're going to be a family again."

We'd take them to where Burt was waiting. He'd hug me and thank me for giving her the note, for making this possible. I'd wave as they drove into the blackness of the night. And my heart would no longer mourn their loss. My heart, although committing a wicked sin, would delight in the love that would fill the cab of that truck.

I had to get that note.

I couldn't be the reason they weren't together. That sounded silly, of course. Rebecca had never admitted to me that she'd had contact with Burt, or that she wanted to leave the compound. But I knew he owned her heart. I knew she yearned for his touch, his attention, his affection. I knew Lehi would never even scratch the surface of the wall she had built around her heart.

She would lay with him; she would obey him. But she would never love him.

As I watched Rebecca soothe her son, the prophet's morning devotional boomed through the loudspeakers of the compound and streamed into her open window. His soft, monotone voice was meant to soothe, to seep into our self-conscious, but the words were filled with such heavy meaning, such responsibility and obligation.

In our home, we were required to stop our daily duties whenever the prophet gifted us with a devotional. Rebecca sat on the bed with her son, her arm wrapped around his shoulder. I stood with my hands linked in front of me, staring at the carpet.

"Good morning, sons and daughters of Zion," the prophet proclaimed. "Behold this beautiful day our Heavenly Father has given us. As you embark on your day, remember your duties. You are here to do the will of your prophet . . . and you will be happy. Sweet, willing obedience is the road to happiness. Keep sweet, do the will of your prophet, and find your happiness."

As the prophet's words continued, my gaze drifted from the carpet and landed back on Rebecca, back to the imaginings of my brain. And in my imaginations, she would no longer belong to Lehi Cluff, or to the prophet. She would be free. Like that bird sitting on the wall outside my bedroom window. She'd fly through her life with the man she loved, raising her boys in freedom.

And then she'd go to hell. She'd burn for all eternity. The fires of hell would swallow her whole, her *and* her children. She would damn them, she would destroy them, she would sentence them to an eternity of misery.

Wake up, Brinley. Your thoughts are sinful and Rebecca is where she belongs.

If the prophet knew of my vivid imagination, I would most certainly burn too.

Later I asked Rebecca agreed to accompany me into town, under the guise of visiting the pharmacy I was unable to visit the day before. I hadn't yet told her about the note, but knew that if Samuel was on duty I would have to tell her the truth, or at least a portion of it.

Against my better judgment, I asked Rebecca about her children as we walked, about how the boys were coping.

She looked away and muttered, "They're doing their best, I promise."

I sighed, realizing that Rebecca was merely following the mantra of our church, "keeping sweet." When faced with adversity, we were expected to push negative feelings down, to rise above and not let our emotions take control. Mind over heart. Every. Single. Day. It was exhausting, and I didn't want that with Rebecca. I wanted us to trust each other.

Abruptly I stopped on the dirt road and turned to face her head-on. When she looked at me questioningly, I met her gaze and said softly, "You don't have to do that with me."

She nodded. "It's hard. They miss him."

"And you?"

"Of course I do too. But he's no longer my husband. I have to move on with Lehi, with our new family. It's our Heavenly Father's will."

"I understand," I replied, taking her hand in mine. She squeezed it. And when we reached the clearing and I was able to see Samuel's full head of golden hair, I squeezed it back.

"Listen, Rebecca. You've trusted me with your true thoughts. Now I need to trust you with mine. Can I do that? Can I trust you?"

Rebecca's forehead wrinkled as she glanced around us, focusing finally on Samuel. Her eyes widened and her mouth dropped open as she put two and two together, coming up with the wrong answer.

I shook my head, denying the accusation in her eyes. "Please, I need to have a conversation with Samuel. Will you keep that conversation between the two of us? If not, I have to ask you to go back home and allow me to have it on my own."

"I can't let you do that. Lehi said you needed company--"

"I have to do this," I said with renewed strength. "Now, tell me the truth. Can I trust you?"

Rebecca swallowed hard. "You've been my only friend since I joined the Cluffs. And for that, I owe you so much. So, yes . . . yes, I will. You can trust me with your true thoughts, my sister."

Hearing Rebecca call me her sister was overwhelming in the best way possible. We'd connected just as much in her heart as we had in mine. I could only hope that by day's end, she'd still feel the same.

When we approached Samuel, he silently nodded as a simple greeting. Samuel was not yet married and still expected to see women as the enemy, as manipulative snakes who would attempt to claw at his regard for the prophet and for our Heavenly Father. His eyes were narrowed and cautious as he peered down at us.

"Hello, Samuel." I handed him a cookie, still warm from our kitchen.

A lopsided grin lit up his face when he saw my gift. "Good morning," he said after taking a bite of the cookie. Samuel was tall with skin tanned from months spent standing in the warm Utah sun. His eyes were deep brown, like a bar of chocolate my father had purchased for me once at the local candy store.

"Samuel, I-I have something I must ask, and I'm afraid I need your discretion."

Samuel paused, looked around him, and dug his teeth into his bottom lip, licking at the chocolate that was left behind. "What is it?" His tone was gruff with a hint of impatience.

"Years ago, you had a friend. I know that you two spent time together. He's gone now, and I hoped you might know where I could find him."

"I don't know who you're talking about."

"Porter . . . Porter Hammond."

"He's dead to me, and to all of us. You know that, Brinley. What do you want with him?"

"He took something from me," I said, and Samuel's eyes widened with curiosity. "And I need to get it back."

"I can't help you."

"Samuel, please."

He closed his eyes and sighed. "He lives with his cousin on Wilson Avenue. Some apartment building above a coffee shop."

"Thank you, oh, thank you, Samuel." I popped up on my toes, hopping up and down.

"Calm down. Act natural, would ya?"

"I'm sorry," I said, looking back down at the ground. "Do you know his cousin's name?"

"Travis. Charlie Travis, I think. He might go by Chuck now. He's like ten years older than me. He was kicked out a long time ago. That family's no good. Don't get involved with them, Brinley. The prophet would not be pleased."

Trepidation consumed me. Would Samuel tell the prophet about our conversation?

"I won't say anything," he whispered, "but this conversation never took place. Do you understand?"

"Yes, yes." I nodded my head, breaking eye contact. "We won't take up any more of your time. Thank you, Samuel."

"You're welcome."

I pulled Rebecca by the hand, and we walked out of the gates of the compound and toward town.

"Hey," Samuel called after us just as our sneakers hit the paved street of the outside world. "Tell him hi for me."

Shocked by his words, I turned to look Samuel in the eye, noting the sadness that had taken over his expression. And I knew, in that moment, that he missed his friend.

"Okay," I said. "I will."

Rebecca and I walked in silence toward Wilson Avenue. There was only one coffee shop on that street, the one that most outsiders seemed to be addicted to. Oddly enough, it had a green mermaid on the window, but the mermaid that didn't match the name. I didn't pretend to understand the people living in the outside world; they constantly surprised me.

But what I knew was this: they were not the chosen. They were bound to hell for not following the one true and righteous path of celestial love and plural marriage. They spent their days serving themselves rather than our Heavenly Father, and for that I had been taught to pity them, to feel superior in my righteousness. And as curious as they made me, that feeling of superiority was always with me.

It was with me when a car sped past us, its speakers loudly thumping the oddest of music—if you could call it that—through the open windows. It was with me when mothers used curse words in public and near the innocent ears of their children. And it was with me whenever I witnessed public displays of affection between a man and a woman. Once I even saw two men holding hands while walking down the street. After getting past my immediate shock, I had to take a moment to say a prayer for their souls, knowing it was pointless. I knew where they were headed, and there was nothing I could do to stop it.

Rebecca finally spoke when we reached the red door to the apartment above the coffee shop. I sighed at the significance of the color of the door. Somehow it seemed fitting that the lost boy who was now living a life of crime would live in a building with a red door—the one color that is forbidden in our community.

"I have to know what's happening before you ring that buzzer," she said, her breathing ragged and fast. "Who is Porter Hammond? Is he the one who took your purse?"

"Yes. He stole it from me on the street. But when I fought back, he yelled at me. And I recognized him. I have to get my bag back."

"But Lehi told you it was okay," she objected. "He even replaced the money. Do you have something special in the purse?"

"Yes."

"I don't understand. What could possibly be so important that you would risk seeing him again after what he did to you?" Rebecca blinked rapidly, her voice shrill and urgent. She was obviously terrified.

I was too, but I couldn't let her know that. I had to remain calm. I had to get my purse. For her, for me, and for Burt.

"Please, trust me. He won't hurt us, I promise. He's not a bad person. But this place," I said, gesturing to the buzzing of the town around us, "it's obviously hurting him, making him desperate."

Before Rebecca could object, I pressed my shaking finger to the gray button beside the name TRAVIS in white block letters.

No answer.

I pressed the button again.

"No one's home, Brinley. Let's go." Rebecca crossed her arms in front of her chest, hugging herself tightly, but she still trembled.

It was then that I heard his voice. "What?" he growled through the speaker.

"Um . . . delivery," I said, my voice cracking. If I revealed my true identity, he'd never let us upstairs. And I was not giving up. Not yet.

"Fine, whatever."

Buzzz.

Immediately I covered my ears at the dreadful sound. When it finally stopped, I waited for the door to swing open. When it didn't, I pressed the button again.

"Open the door while it's buzzing, would ya?"

The irritation in his voice pierced through me and I was mortified. I'd never visited an apartment building before. I had no idea that I was supposed to pull on the door while the intercom made that dreadful sound.

"I-I'm sorry," I said.

Buzzz.

This time I grabbed the door, finding it unlocked. I glanced back at Rebecca, whose expression remained apprehensive, her fingers still quivering as they rested on her arms.

We climbed the steps of the dingy building, the smell of coffee and pastries hovering in the air. I took a deep breath, enjoying the aroma, wondering what it must be like to enjoy that smell each day. It was a pleasant distraction from the fear that I'd suppressed in my belly.

I knew Porter Hammond wouldn't hurt me. I knew that in my gut.

But I didn't know what he'd say, or if he'd even talk to me once he recognized my familiar hairstyle, my old-fashioned garb, and my plain face. Once he knew who I was and that I'd returned to claim what was mine.

When we reached the third floor, his door was left open. My hands shook in trepidation as we approached. I inhaled deeply, attempting to rekindle the bravery I had felt when I pressed the button to his apartment outside the building.

"Leave it on the mat," he called from inside the apartment. "I'm a little busy."

"Let's go," whispered Rebecca.

"You can stay here if you like," I said, "but I must go in."

I stepped onto the welcome mat at the entrance to the apartment. I couldn't see Porter, but I had a decent view of the living area of the apartment. Sleeping bags were piled into the corner of the bleak room, and a tattered blue couch held several blankets and pillows. A large television set blasted from the living area.

Pots and pans banged in the kitchen, which was to my left. I couldn't see past the confines of the entranceway, but knew that was where Porter must be.

My lungs heaved as I rounded the corner. Porter was standing over the sink, his hands submerged in suds, a black-and-white apron tied around his waist. If I weren't so anxious, I would have giggled at his appearance. Men in our compound didn't assist in the kitchen, or wear aprons, or clean. To me, he looked silly working in the kitchen. That was a woman's place.

He must have caught me in his peripheral vision because he did a double take, his eyes as round as the pans in his hands. When he dropped them into the sink, soapy water splashed to the floor.

"Holy shit," he yelled, stepping back. "It's you."

I couldn't find words, so I nodded.

"Look, I don't have your money, all right?" He grabbed a towel and wiped his arms. "I spent it already."

He wiped his nose with the back of his hand and sniffed deeply, then reached up and rubbed his eyes, still as bloodshot as when I'd seen him before.

Still, I said nothing. From behind me, I could sense Rebecca inching her way toward the apartment. I imagined she wanted to hear our conversation, to know I was safe.

"So . . ." He tilted his head, narrowing his eyes. "Aren't you gonna say anything? I mean, you stalked me successfully, you might as well talk." He chuckled into the back of his hand.

This was not the boy I remembered. The outside world had changed him. And not in a good way.

"I need m—my purse," I said, stumbling over my words. In an attempt to appear strong, I crossed my arms in front of my chest, something Aspen did whenever going head-to-head with Leandra over child rearing or housekeeping.

"Oh, right," he said, dropping the dishcloth onto the bare counter. He stalked toward me in dramatic steps. "I should've known you'd show up here, considering what was in that bag."

Rebecca didn't know about my pills. I closed my eyes for a second and tipped my chin up to the ceiling, attempting to stay strong, knowing that one or both of my secrets would soon be spilled.

"You know you're not supposed to have those," Porter said. "What would your husband say?"

"How did you know I was married?"

"Oh, puh-lease." He squinted, tilting his head to the other side. "You're what—twenty-one, twenty-two? You're married."

I said nothing. He was right. In our community, women rarely married older than the age of twenty. And many were married much earlier than that.

His blue eyes were piercing and as many times as I broke our eye contact, whenever I glanced back at him, his stare was still fixed on me. I clutched the fabric of my pocket, twisting and turning the cotton between my fingers.

"Stop avoiding the question," he said with a sneer. "You're on the pill."

Rebecca gasped from the doorway. I snapped my eyes shut and clenched my teeth. I couldn't even imagine what she must be thinking of me.

A smug grin crossed Porter's face. "I'm kinda impressed, ya know?"

"What?" My voice cracked as I shook my head in disbelief. "Why?"

"I remember you, Brinley. You weren't exactly a rebel."

"Nobody is."

"Well, they made that next to impossible. Step outta line, look what happens—" He raised his arms and waved his hands, gesturing to the apartment that surrounded us. "So, be careful. It'd be a shame if anyone found out."

"You wouldn't—"

"Oh, wouldn't I? Maybe it's exactly what I need. I can show my loyalty to the prophet." He gritted his teeth and walked around me as he spoke. "I'd turn you in, they'd kick you out, and I'd be back at home in my nice warm bed."

Horrified, I clasped my hands over my ears and squeezed my eyes shut. "Stop, please!"

"Brinley!"

Rebecca stormed into the apartment, a mama bear ready to attack. I turned and waved her back, letting her know I was okay.

"Ah." Porter adopted a pondering pose, his hand clasping his chin. "So, *this* is Rebecca. How interesting."

"Please," I begged as my eyes stung, threatening tears. "Just give me the purse."

"Not yet. This is way too much fun." He waved his hand, dismissing me. "Re-bec-ca. It's such a pleasure to meet you."

"How?" Rebecca frowned and rubbed her bottom lip. "How do you know my name?"

"Ask your sister wife," Porter said, still smiling smugly.

"Brinley?" Rebecca was clearly petrified, and I was sure she must be mentally retracing her steps that morning to find how on earth she'd ended up at an apartment in town with a clearly possessed man . . . a man who knew her name.

"He has a demon inside him, don't listen." I turned my attention to Porter. "Please, I don't care about the money. Just let me have my bag."

"Fine, whatever."

He walked to the dining table and retrieved my purse. My stomach settled as he carried it back to me, holding it above his head, teasing me as though we were children. I stood on the tips of my toes, but couldn't reach it.

"Oh good God," he said. "You're not even trying."

Anger rose within me. I could handle his anger, his disdain for my presence in his home, but *that* I would not tolerate.

"No." I shook my head violently. "Do *not* take the Lord's name in vain."

"And what are you gonna do about it? This is my home, not yours, goddamn it." He slammed the purse on the counter.

Again I covered my ears, attempting to block out his sin. I now understood why people like Porter were exiled from our community. They deserved it. They were not part of the chosen; his actions confirmed that fact.

All the blood drained from my face, but I reached my hand out to take the purse. In that split second, Porter grasped my wrist and squeezed.

"Why are you on the pill?" he demanded. "Seriously, tell me why."

"Why? Why do you want to know?"

"Because, I remember you. You were the girl with the doll. All the toys were taken away, but you had a doll."

His eyes narrowed and I felt my defenses slide away and fall at my feet. My stomach flipped as he recalled my first act of defiance.

"It was just a doll," I said, attempting to downplay my actions.

"No, it was more than that." He lowered his voice and softly brushed at my wrist with his thumb.

My stomach flipped again in response to his touch. What was I feeling? Fear? Pleasure? I didn't understand it, but a strange part of my brain didn't want him to let go.

"And you know it," he insisted.

I opened my mouth to speak, but couldn't. He was right. There was a part of me that questioned my faith, questioned the prophet, my husband, all of it. It was as if he could see me, really see me in a way no one else could.

"Seriously, be careful. If they catch you, it won't end well."

Gone was his smug demeanor. In its place was a concerned expression, softer, gentler, much like the strokes that continued against the sensitive skin of my inner wrist.

Mesmerized, I nodded. "I will."

Our eyes were locked as we stood in silence. As he stroked my wrist, I did my best to control my breathing, to prevent him from knowing how fascinated I was by his touch. My cheeks burned, just as they did when Aspen embarrassed me in front of the other sister wives. These foreign sensations overwhelmed and confused me, yet I was consumed by them.

"We should go." Rebecca placed her hand on my shoulder, snapping Porter and me out of our daze. He blinked repeatedly and released my wrist.

He felt it too, didn't he?

"Thank you," I said. "For the purse."

He nodded, rubbing his red eyes. "Sorry about the money. Gotta eat, right?"

"Right." I shrugged and gave him one last glance before we walked out of the apartment.

When the door closed behind us, Rebecca turned on me, blocking my access to the stairwell.

"You have so much to explain," she said, narrowing her eyes. "How did that mongrel know my name?"

"He's not a mongrel," I said, surprising myself with my defensive tone and the bite of my words. "He's just . . . trying to live on his own. Out here, surrounded by evil."

"He's a lost soul, Brinley. Now, how does he know my name?"

Unzipping the tattered bag, I reached inside and felt the folded envelope. I pulled it from the bag and placed it in Rebecca's hands, which shook. Clasping the envelope with one hand, she covered her mouth with the other. The envelope had been opened. Obviously, Porter had been curious.

"What . . . when?" Rebecca's eyes grew wide and her mouth fell open.

"Yesterday, before it was stolen. I was going to give it to you, I promise. But I didn't get the chance. Please, please forgive me."

Rebecca didn't respond, she was too engrossed in the letter from Burt. Her hands trembled as she read it, one clutching the simple white paper, the other covering her quivering chin. When she finished, she handed the letter to me and dropped to her knees.

"Heavenly Father, please give me the strength to resist. Give me the strength to follow the revelation you have given, and to deny my earthly desires so that I may serve you in heaven."

I'd heard this prayer every night when Rebecca shared my room. It was her penance, her way of begging our Lord for forgiveness. She loved Burt, she missed him, and for that the guilt was eating her alive.

When she stood, I held out my hand. "May I?" I asked. She closed her eyes tightly and nodded.

My dearest Rebecca,

Every day since you were taken from me has been worse than the one before. Yesterday I was installing drywall at the diner I took you to years ago—when it was just you and me after our wedding ceremony, do you remember that? Anytime I visit that place, I think of my sweet Rebecca.

A song played while I was working, and I asked the owner what it was called. He said it was "I'd

Die Without You." I swear, my dearest, the words could have been taken directly from my heart, from my soul. I miss you and am not sure I can live without you as my wife. My only wife. Please meet me tomorrow night. Eight p.m. by our tree. There is so much to discuss.

With all the love in my heart,

Burt

"He wants to see you . . . tonight."

"I can't do that," Rebecca snapped. "He's not my husband anymore. My obedience and my love belong to Lehi now."

"But you don't love Lehi," I argued. "You love Burt."

"That doesn't matter." A tear rolled down her cheek. "None of it matters."

We walked in silence to the Cluff house. Rebecca never asked me about my pills, and I dared not say Burt's name again. With each step I took, I was desperate to know the rest of the words to the song Burt mentioned in his note.

And desperate, now more than ever, to feel the intense love that Burt felt for Rebecca. So much love that he felt he'd die without her. I was fascinated, captivated, and wanted their love story to succeed.

And in that desire, I realized one very important thing.

I wanted Rebecca, my sister wife and friend, to sin.

What was happening to me?

chapter 7

REBECCA WAS AVOIDING ME. Even though three weeks had passed since she'd read the letter from Burt, she wouldn't look me in the eye. She volunteered to assist Leandra in her sewing projects, even though she'd told me weeks ago that she despised sewing. Leandra was selective about who she'd ask to assist her, and I was one of the many who were banned from her tiny little sewing room in the garage.

When Lehi and I had first married, Leandra had attempted to take me under her wing, to teach me everything she knew about creating dresses, bedding, and curtains for the family. But after just one week with me as her apprentice, she was done.

"You're not ready, dear," is what Leandra had said to me. What I knew she *wanted to say* was this: "You can't sew a straight line, you've ruined a dress I've worked on for weeks, and you butcher the fabric when you cut it." And she would have been absolutely right in telling me those things, if she could have ignored the command to "keep sweet" and held back her emotions. Regardless, I knew I was no longer allowed in that room.

But Rebecca was another situation entirely. She hated sewing, since in Burt's household she had been in charge of mending any holes in the children's clothes and creating bedding for the newborn babies. She told me she had hoped for a fresh start in her duties when she joined our family. But Leandra was smart—she saw the talent that Rebecca possessed, and she noticed a break in the bond she and I had formed when Rebecca first joined the family. She took every advantage of our estrangement and kept Rebecca busy in the garage.

I missed her, and my heart broke for Burt as I wondered how long he had stood by that tree, hoping Rebecca would tiptoe toward him in the darkness. How long he stood there before he gave up, before he resigned himself to a life without her, the woman he felt he'd die without?

So I kept busy. Busy hands helped me avoid thoughts of Rebecca or Burt or Porter.

Porter.

That face. His face. It kept popping into my thoughts several times a day. When I was washing dishes, especially, remembering the suds splattering around him when I'd surprised him with my presence. Last night, I'd even dreamed about him.

When I woke from my dream, I sank to the floor, perching myself on my knees, praying to Heavenly Father to forgive me for my sins. To forgive my unclean thoughts about a man who wasn't kind to me. He took the Lord's name in vain and even yelled a few times. But his touch, the way it felt on the skin of my wrist . . . it was a mixture of fire and ice, both a push and a pull, simultaneously a scream and a whisper. His eyes, the way they softened and looked protective when he raised his concerns about my pills.

He intrigued me.

Enough to dream about. Bad thoughts. Good thoughts. Him touching me in other areas. Not just the soft inner skin of my wrist where he could feel my blood pulsing, flowing, my body trembling.

His hands were everywhere in my thoughts.

Everywhere.

When I woke, I was throbbing. My hand moved to that part of me only Lehi had touched.

What was that?

Young girls in our community weren't taught about sex, not even the least little bit. All we were told was that it must be reserved for our husband. That was all, and it wasn't nearly enough.

My wedding night was proof of that . . .

My first time with Lehi had been frightening, uncomfortable, and awkward. I was nineteen, and we'd just been married in the common area of the Cluff home. Our honeymoon was two nights away at a motel in Colorado City. Money was tight, but it was important to Lehi that all of his wives be given special alone time after their celestial vows.

The bedding of the motel room gave me hives. It was an odd tan color with swirls of chocolate and cream tones. The ivory-colored sheets smelled of mildew, and even now, three years later, I could smell it when I remembered that night.

"Would you like to watch television?" Lehi had asked when we'd settled into the drafty room.

"Um . . ." My mouth was agape, not knowing if my new husband was testing my loyalty to the laws of our church. Television was not allowed—was he tricking me?"

"Don't worry, it's okay. I watch when I travel for work. It's actually entertaining."

"Oh," I said, having never seen anything on a television screen before. "Whatever you like."

Lehi had stripped himself of his jacket, draping it on the armchair in the corner, and grabbed a small black device from the table. He pressed a button and the machine turned on! I'd never seen anything like it.

Lehi chuckled. "Have you never seen a television before, my dear?"

I shook my head. "No, sir."

"Your mother never took you to Walmart? Or Target?"

"Yes, sir, she did. But we weren't allowed in that section of the store. Sometimes when we were in the baby section, we could hear the televisions, but I never saw them. And I have no idea what that is," I said, gesturing to the small machine in his hand.

"It's a remote. Watch." He pressed a button on it that made the television pause and then change to another program. "You know," he said, "we can rent a movie."

"Rent?"

"Yes, they have movies. Special ones that might help."

"Help?" I didn't understand. "What could we possibly need help with?"

"Us." He walked to me and placed his hand on my shoulder, a half smile peeking out from behind his beard. "The movies will show you how to please me. You want to please me, don't you, Brinley?"

My nerves stood on end and my breathing quickened. I knew what response he expected, so I nodded.

"Good. A movie it is."

He walked to the television set, inspecting a cardboard advertisement of some type. Retrieving the small remote once again, he punched in several numbers and I gasped as three naked people appeared on the screen, two women and one man. I'd never seen a man's penis before, or other women's breasts or private areas.

My stomach churned and I looked to Lehi for answers when one woman climbed on top of the man and began rocking up and down on him. Was that what he wanted me to do? Rock on top of him? Was that what sex was?

The other woman stroked her hands over his back as she watched the two together, which disturbed me. All my life, I'd been told that sex was saved for your husband. Not your husband and another person. Who was this woman and why was she taking part in this intimate act between husband and wife?

"They're actors," Lehi said. "Just watch them and when you're turned on, tell me. Then we'll begin."

"Turned on?"

Lehi laughed again and crossed the room, running his hand over my French braid. "You're so young, aren't you? I have so much to teach you."

"I—"

I didn't have a chance to answer him because he thrust his mouth against my lips, and forced them apart with his tongue. His teeth crashed into mine as he thrust his tongue into my mouth. I gasped at the aggressive nature of his touch—Lehi had always been kind and gentle with me, but this was a new side of him that I hadn't seen. Fear built in my gut as I wondered how this would progress.

"I want you," he whispered when he finally removed his mouth from mine.

The sounds of moaning came from the television, and I could feel his penis growing hard next to my thigh. I wanted to scream, to run, to hide. But I knew I couldn't. This was the way to my salvation. To my Heavenly Father's kingdom.

I was put on this earth to marry and serve Lehi, to birth and raise his children, and to spend eternity with him in heaven. He said he'd teach me, and I had to be willing to learn.

Lehi unbuttoned the pearl buttons of my cotton wedding dress before lifting it above my head. He then removed my long underwear, and instinctively I covered my breasts and private area with my hands. The corners of Lehi's mouth raised in satisfaction as he took in the sight of me.

"You're so firm," he said, running his hand across my bottom. When I looked puzzled, he said, "Your muscles, your skin, it's firm. And it's turning me on."

That was the second time he'd referenced being "turned on." I still had no idea what he meant by it, other than he clearly was impressed with my body. I was slim with average-sized breasts, but I'd never compared myself to any of the other women in the compound. Yet as I glanced at the women on the television, I felt quite inadequate. Their breasts were large and round, and mine seemed to sag in comparison to theirs that stood at attention.

"Do you see what she's doing?" Lehi asked, pushing on my shoulders until I was kneeling in front of him. When I looked at the television, I was horrified to see that one of the women—the one who had been watching the couple earlier—had the man's penis in her mouth and was moving her mouth up and down it. I swallowed hard, hoping to suppress the hysteria that built within my chest.

"Yes, sir," I croaked.

Lehi unzipped his zipper, then pushed his pants down to his ankles. He reached for my hands and pulled me up as high as I would go without leaving my knees.

"Do it."

I shook my head. "But I don't know how."

"I'll teach you. You have to learn, Brinley. This is the only way. Watch her and then do it. Come on."

My fingers trembled as I pulled down his stark white boxer shorts, which dropped to his ankles along with his pants. He was still wearing his socks and shoes. My stomach twisted and turned as his penis, standing up straight against his midsection, seemed to be staring at me.

"Come on," Lehi ordered, his voice growing impatient.

I took one last glance at the woman on the television screen. She was making all sorts of noises as she moved up and down his most private part. The man leaned back, groaning. I could only imagine that she was pleasing him, and that Lehi expected me to make his face contort like the man on the screen.

Mimicking the movements of the woman on the screen, I wrapped my hand around the base of his penis, then moved it up and down.

"Your mouth, use your mouth," Lehi whispered, his voice raspy.

I couldn't avoid it any longer. My heart raced and my stomach churned as I placed my lips on the tip of his penis.

"Yeah, that's it," Lehi said, and placed his fingers in my hair, pushing my head farther down.

In shock, I snapped my eyes open. The taste of it, of him, was repulsive, and I fought the gag reflex that threatened to empty my stomach. I tried to pull away, but Lehi held my head steady.

"Keep going," he said. "You're doing fine."

Disgusted, I moved my head up and down again and again until Lehi tapped me on the shoulder.

"That's enough for now," he said. "Lay down on the bed."

"Okay."

"Okay, what?" Lehi narrowed his eyes at me.

I'd been calling him sir since meeting him the first time with our prophet. But I'd expected that eventually he would no longer expect that of me. Apparently, however, it was still very much expected.

"Okay, sir."

"That's a good girl," he said, tapping my bottom before ripping my underpants off and throwing them to the floor. "Lay down."

I did as I was told, despite feeling exposed and overwhelmed. The people on the screen were still grunting and groaning. Lehi took one last look at them before spitting into his hand and rubbing it on his penis.

"Wrap your legs around my back. Don't say a word. It will hurt at first, but do your best to relax."

Lehi spread my legs apart, then crawled over me and pushed his penis into my opening. The muscles of my private area fought against his entry, pushing him away. But he didn't care; he just pushed harder until his chest was flat against mine. Searing pain spread through the lower half of my body and I bit down so hard on my lip, I tasted the metallic taste of blood inside my mouth.

"You're so tight," he choked out as he grunted in my ear. "Oh, I've missed this."

Missed this? What did he miss?

I didn't understand, but had already been warned to keep silent. I'd have to ask him later. All I could do was pray to Heavenly Father to make the pain end. To make his hot breath on my shoulder go away, to make this agony stop.

The Lord answered my prayer. Lehi grunted, gritting his teeth as he made his final push into me. He twitched and sucked in a sharp breath through his teeth, then collapsed onto my chest and ran his hand down my neck.

"We are now forever linked. Husband and wife. Well done, Brinley."

I wasn't sure if I was allowed to speak or not, so I nodded behind tightly closed eyes. Relief came in the form of his penis growing soft and sliding out of me. Lehi moved to sit on the side of the bed, leaning his hands into the mattress.

"I'm going to take a shower, and then we'll sleep. You'll want to clean yourself up. Quite a bit of blood on the sheets."

Blood? I bled?

I managed to hold it together long enough for Lehi to walk into the small bathroom and close the door, then turn on the shower. But I couldn't contain the bile rising in my throat after seeing the small pool of blood on the ivory sheet. I hobbled to the sink, thanking God that it was outside the bathroom, then ran the water before heaving my dinner down the drain.

I knew that I had pleased Lehi, but my body felt like it had been robbed of something sacred, and I felt a tremendous sense of loss.

Once my heaving had stopped, I rinsed my mouth with water and wiped my private areas with a washcloth, then threw it in the garbage knowing that the blood had stained it permanently.

The man and women were still groaning in the background. I couldn't take it anymore. While the water still poured from Lehi's shower, I found the remote. I stared at it, wondering how I could turn off the sight of the sinful people on the screen. I fumbled with it again and again until finally I found the power button and it turned off.

The silence was freeing and peaceful. When his shower had ended, Lehi joined me in kneeling at the side of the bed and saying a prayer to our Lord, thanking him for our celestial union and for the consummation that had bound us together.

When he joined me in bed, I was surprised that Lehi welcomed me to sleep beside him so that his chest warmed my back. He stroked my back with his hands, easing my muscles and the racing thoughts of my brain.

"You're a lovely girl. Do you know that?"

Trying hard not to tremble, I mumbled, "Thank you," and stared at the wall.

"I'm going to take very good care of you." He kneaded my shoulder with his fingers, making me uncomfortable.

"I know."

"Do you have any questions, you know, about what we did?"

I hesitated, unsure if I should ask what was on my mind. But that tiny little brave voice in my mind took over. "You said you'd missed me being tight, but . . . we've never, um . . . we've never done that before, so—"

"Oh." He laughed. "All of my wives have birthed babies. They're not as tight as they once were. It's been a while since I've been intimate with a virgin. Almost three years, I think, with Aspen."

"Oh, I see."

"It'll get easier for you, don't worry."

"Okay."

"And next time, I'll have a surprise for you."

My heart raced, not sure I could handle any other surprises. Our entire encounter that evening had been shocking enough.

"Oh?" I asked, feigning interest.

"Have you ever worn makeup, Brinley?"

"You mean, on my face?"

I hadn't, although I'd always been fascinated by the women of the outside world. Their lips so pink, all kinds of colors on their eyelids, their rosy cheeks. It had never been allowed, but I'd always been slightly envious of those women.

"No."

"Well, I know you'll enjoy it. I'll buy you some when we go into town tomorrow. You can even pick your first colors."

"All right."

Lehi had yawned into my neck. "Time to rest. Good night."

But I hadn't sleep much that night. Like the movie on the screen, our encounter had played through my mind over and over again, making me wince and cry.

I was in no rush to do that again, but had somehow known it wouldn't be long before I'd be forced to relive it. At the time, I didn't know how many times I'd be expected to perform those acts during our stay at the motel, but I took solace from the fact that once home, he would have the opportunity to lay with the other wives, as well.

In the three years we'd been married, my private area had never throbbed at the thought of Lehi's touch, or in response to it while he was touching me. Never. Not once.

But my dreams of Porter had left a pulsing that was agonizing and enticing all at the same time. When thoughts of sex with Lehi forced the throbbing to disappear, I was disappointed and left wanting.

I wanted Porter to touch me again.

But for him to touch me would be the greatest sin imaginable.

I was Lehi's, bound to him for eternity. I could jeopardize everything I was raised to strive for—a place in the celestial kingdom with our Heavenly Father, with my husband, and with our children.

Porter Hammond knew better than anyone that the prophet could have you removed from our community in an instant. He was proof of that. I didn't want to end up like Porter. I had to be more careful, more in control of my thoughts and dreams. And I had to stay away from him, no matter how tempted I might become when waking from a dream where his lips caressed my thighs, where his fingertips lightly touched the swell of my breasts, and where my private area throbbed with my desire for him.

I had to clear Porter Hammond from my mind. No matter how good he tasted in my dreams.

chapter 8

"ARE YOU SURE you won't come with me?"

I stood at Rebecca's doorway, silently begging for her eyes to meet mine. Weeks of avoidance were making me paranoid. Rebecca spent more time with Leandra and less time with Aspen or me.

I was losing her.

"No, Leandra needs me. I'm sorry." Rebecca closed her dresser drawer and rose to her feet. Her gaze briefly darted to mine, then she looked back at the carpet.

"I hope you will forgive me, you know, for that day." My words hung in the air, so thick with tension in the silent room.

Rebecca sucked in a breath and closed her eyes, curling her fists in tight balls. Sister wives weren't encouraged to have one-on-one discussions when conflict arose. Instead, we were encouraged to keep sweet and share our concerns or complaints with Lehi, who would then mediate with the other wife. No arguments, no heart-to-hearts. The problem would be resolved and no one's feelings would be hurt.

But I'd held Rebecca as she sobbed just a few short months before. I thought our relationship was different.

"Are you going to see him? Is that what this is about?" She frowned, causing her forehead to crease, and her nostrils flared.

"No, I promise. I just—Lehi asked me to visit the drugstore. I thought you could join me."

"No, sorry." Her words were short, biting. Avoiding my eyes, she hurried from the room, her shoulder brushing against mine as she passed.

Dejected and feeling very alone, I walked to my closet, retrieved my purse, and walked into town.

I dreaded walking past Burt Jameson's construction project. Somehow I knew he could see me through the unfinished lumber that framed the house. I'd managed to dodge him for weeks, picking up my pace whenever I drew close to the site. Luckily, aside from the sound of a few hammers banging, the work site was quiet, as if most of the men had taken a break for lunch.

I sighed with relief that I was able to avoid him. For now, anyway.

When I reached the guard post, Samuel gave me a nod. He hadn't spoken to me in weeks, either. My world was getting smaller and smaller within the confines of the compound. I'd lost my only true friend in the Cluff household, and one of the few men I trusted in the compound wanted very little to do with me, not wanting to be dragged into anything involving Porter Hammond.

My stomach gave a little flip.

Just the thought of Porter caused a physical reaction. Thoughts of his fingers against my skin, his smirk when he hinted at my subversive nature, and the way his words made me think.

Could I ever leave this life?

I'd be lying to myself if I pretended the thought didn't cross my mind. But deep down, I knew the truth. I wasn't a brave girl. I was a dependent girl, a naive girl, a silly girl for giving in to notions of an outsider stealing me away to build a new life.

A silly girl to think that Porter Hammond had thought of me the way I'd thought of him.

Lost in thoughts of Porter, I didn't notice the footsteps behind me. When someone touched my shoulder, I spun around, my eyes widening in fear.

"I'm sorry to startle you."

Burt Jameson looked haggard. His face had not been groomed, his shirt was untucked, and he smelled of grain alcohol. His eyebrows resembled large caterpillars on his fair face. As unattractive as they were, all I could remember were Rebecca's words about how much she loved his eyebrows when he'd let them get a little too long.

How would she feel about those eyebrows now?

"Elder Jameson."

"I know I shouldn't be bothering you, Brinley, I know, but I've been watching you walk past for weeks and I just couldn't resist anymore." He paused, shaking his head and looking down at his hands. "I just have to know—"

"Know what?" Tears built in my eyes as I anticipated the question.

"My letter." He swallowed hard. "Did you give her my letter?"

I nodded as tears filled my eyes.

"Oh." Slowly, he licked his lips before gripping his bottom lip with his teeth. He turned away from me slightly and swiped at his cheek as he studied the ground at his feet. A moment passed before he raised his tortured eyes to me and asked, "Should—should I try again?"

I raised my shoulders in a helpless shrug as I shook my head and whispered, "I can't answer that."

"Of course not," Burt said, wringing his hands.

"I'm so sorry."

I wanted to yell at him, *Go see her, convince her, tell her you love her. Don't give up!* But I couldn't. There was nothing left for me to say to Burt Jameson.

When I turned to continue my walk into town, he startled me yet again. "Do you love your husband?" he called after me, his voice sounding desperate. But that didn't absolve his question of its obvious inappropriate nature.

I paused for a moment but didn't turn, just stared straight ahead, knowing that if I turned to look at him, he'd know the answer.

When I didn't answer, he choked out, "I hope not. So much easier that way."

Overcome with emotion, I ducked my head and hurried away. The man's obvious pain and distress at losing his family tore at me. His words played over and over in my head as I walked to the pharmacy.

So much easier that way.

So much easier that way.

Sure, maybe it was easy . . . but maybe I didn't want easy.

Maybe I wanted to be challenged, to be pushed, to be *seen.*

Burt Jameson saw Rebecca in a way that Lehi Cluff never would. How could she not see that? And if she did see it, how could she possibly abandon it?

Tiffany's face relaxed with relief when I walked through the door of the clinic.

"I was starting to worry," she said as I approached the desk. "You must be almost out."

"I am," I said in a low voice, then glanced around me.

"Be right back. There's something you need to know."

Oh no. Did Lehi know about my pills? Had Rebecca shared my secret?

Birth control was strictly forbidden and grounds for removal from the church. Children were a blessing, and a woman's reason for life. We were to conceive, birth, and raise our children in the service of our husbands and the prophet. Preventing pregnancy was unforgivable.

I knew that the day I accepted Tiffany's offer to get me a prescription. The day I placed that first pink pill in my mouth and washed it down with water, I knew I was sinning.

Maybe Porter was right about me after all. Maybe I was the type to resist. Maybe I wanted to be caught.

Maybe . . .

"Listen." Tiffany lowered her voice as she placed the small bag on the counter. "Do you remember a boy named Porter?"

Shocked to hear that name that ignited something deep within my belly, I bit back a gasp and nodded.

"You don't seem surprised to hear his name." Tiffany crossed her arms in front of her chest, a knowing smile on her face.

My face burned as I slipped the pills into my purse. "I ran into him about a month ago."

"Well, he came here, asking about you."

"What? Here?"

"He knew," she said, lowering a pointed glance at my bag. "About the pills. He knew where they came from."

"Oh." Terror swept over me, chilling me to the bone. "What did he say? Is he going to tell Lehi?"

She shook her head. "No, nothing like that. He wanted to know about you, like when you'd be here next. Stuff like that."

"I don't understand."

"I think he was hoping to run into you again." She raised her eyebrows and tilted her head meaningfully in my direction. I had no idea what she was trying to convey with that expression.

"Really?" The thought of seeing Porter again made my mouth dry and my palms sweat. A rush of moisture hit my private parts, and I clenched my thighs in response.

Tiffany's smile faded, and her eyes turned stern as she said, "Just be careful. He's a junkie."

"A junkie?" I didn't know that word or what it meant.

"He's a drug addict, Brinley."

"Oh." I covered my mouth with my hand as I attempted to hide my disappointment. "How can you tell?"

"He's been in here before, trying to get clean. But I could see it in his eyes. He's far from it."

Her words were boulders weighing on the dreams I'd had for weeks. I was such a silly girl. I'd been dreaming of a man who was possessed by the devil. Drugs were the gateway to possession; everyone in our church knew that. Only lost and weak souls would succumb to them, those who didn't deserve God's mercy. They were the damned, the forgotten.

But something told me I wouldn't be able to forget Porter Hammond. No matter how damned his soul might be.

"I know what you're thinking," Tiffany said, her voice stern. "It's not true. He's not damned."

Feeling angry and defensive that she'd read me so easily, I blurted out, "You only say that because you are too."

The words left my lips before I had the chance to stop them. Tiffany recoiled, her hand covering her gasp.

"I'm so sorry," I said, shaking my head as I reached my hand across the counter, hoping she'd accept it. And with it, my apology.

She didn't. A tear tracked down her cheek and she wiped it with the back of her sleeve.

"You should go," she said curtly, looking through me. "It's going to be crowded soon. I need to get back to work."

"Tiff—"

"Just go." She shook her head, turned on her heel, and walked through the swinging door to the back room.

I left the clinic not knowing if I could, or would, ever return.

When I stepped outside the clinic, I had a choice. I could do what was expected, keep sweet and return home, or I could let my anger be my guide. How dare Porter ruin my relationship with Tiffany, my one connection to the outside world, the one person I could count on outside of my confined existence within the compound. I had no idea if Tiffany would ever speak to me again after what I'd just said to her, and it was all his fault.

All of it.

I made my choice and walked the two blocks to his apartment over the coffeehouse. My chest heaved as I climbed the stairs, my anger growing inside me with each step. By the time I pounded my fist on his door, my face was hot, and I almost lost my nerve when a girl answered the door.

"Yes?" The girl stared at me with pity in her eyes. Her hair was short, almost like a boy's, but there was no doubt she was a girl. A tiny tank top exposed the cleavage of her breasts while her shirt crept up her midsection, revealing a ring through her belly button.

Ouch. Doesn't that hurt? Does she have no respect for the sanctity of her body?

"Um, I'm here to see—"

"Who is it?" a voice called from inside.

Porter.

Part of me wanted to run, but I was still angry so I stood my ground.

"I don't know, but she's not from around here," the girl said, stifling a laugh.

I resisted the urge to roll my eyes. I visited this town often enough to know when I was being mocked.

"Can we help you?" she asked.

"Porter Hammond, please." I crossed my arms in front of my chest, a stance I wasn't used to. I'd never been encouraged to be strong. Not once, not ever. But somehow I had it in me and I was ready to fight.

"Whatever you say," she said, laughing. "Porter, it's for you."

He groaned from the other room, and I could hear a rustling sound. When he rounded the corner and came into view, our eyes locked and his expression softened.

"Hey," he said, narrowing his eyes, taking in my aggressive stance. "Never thought I'd see you again."

"That's not what my cousin said," I snapped back.

"Who is that?" the girl asked. She hooked her hands on her hips, dividing her glare between Porter and me.

"A friend." Porter glared right back at her. "Don't worry about it."

She turned and narrowed her eyes at me, her upper lip curling as she spoke. "Seriously, who the hell is she?"

"She's no one, all right?" When the girl still didn't budge, he rolled his eyes. "Just go home. We're done here."

For a second or two, she glanced back at Porter with pain in her eyes, her lips pressed in a straight line.

"Whatever." She shook her head, grabbed her purse, and brushed past me hard, knocking me into the wall.

"Hey, watch it," Porter yelled at her.

"Again . . . whatever, asshole," she yelled as she clomped down the staircase.

Porter closed his eyes and shook his head, then turned his attention back to me.

"Who's your cousin?" he asked with a smirk. He knew exactly who I was talking about, which made me even angrier at him.

"Tiffany. She works at the clinic. Why did you bother her?"

"Bother her?" He enunciated each syllable, condescension hanging in his gravelly voice. "Um, she works there, Brinley. She was doing her job."

"Telling you when I'll be at the clinic is not her job."

"All right, so what?"

"So, I—she— Now she's not talking to me, and it's all your fault." My foot hit the tile as I stomped with anger.

Porter chuckled. He actually chuckled at me.

Never had anyone ever infuriated me this much—not Leandra, Aspen, or even Lehi. Porter Hammond was making me so angry I thought I might cry, or hit something, or both.

"Something to drink?" he asked, walking into the kitchen and pulling open his refrigerator, its door covered in magnets and smeared food.

Gross.

His casual attitude fueled my anger even more, and I said through gritted teeth, "No, thank you."

He shook his head, laughing again under his breath. "Even when you're pissed, you're still polite. How nice."

He placed two bottles of water on the counter, then opened one and took a large sip, gesturing for me to take the other.

"I already said no."

"Fine, whatever," he said, grabbing the other bottle. "Wanna sit?"

I froze, not knowing what to do. Porter invited me into his apartment, and I hadn't expected that. I thought I would release my anger while standing in his doorway and return home, but once I heard those words, I couldn't decline. I was drawn to him and didn't want to say no.

I glanced around, looking for other people in the apartment.

Porter noticed my discomfort and said, "It's just us. Amy's not coming back." He walked over and sat on a couch covered in blankets.

"Amy?"

"The uh—the girl you met a few minutes ago."

"Is she your wife?"

He exploded in laughter, tilting his head back as his hands dug into his knees. When his eyes met mine again, he took in my furious expression and became more serious.

"It's not like that out here, Brin. People don't just get married, ya know? You date, you sleep around, you meet people. I'm only twenty-six. I have plenty of time for that bullshit."

The idea of Porter laying with Amy or any other woman made my skin itch. Although I was certain he was far from a virgin, I didn't want to think about it. I didn't want to know.

"Please don't call me that," I said, sitting opposite him in a chair that smelled like dirty laundry.

"What, Brin?"

I nodded.

"Oh, sorry. Brinley just seems . . . young for you." He snickered, taking another swig of his water.

We sat in silence for several seconds. I smoothed the cotton of my pastel green dress, trying to ignore my leg as it bobbed up and down under my dress, something I always did when my nerves took over.

"So, *Brinley,* what brings you here? I mean, to what do I owe the honor of your presence?" He leaned his arms on his thighs, linking his hands together at his fingertips.

"I j-just saw Tiffany," I stammered, "and I . . . I—"

"You're cute when you stutter."

I hadn't stuttered since I was a young child. Anxiety rose in my chest. I had to go. I had to leave, to escape the confines of his apartment before a panic attack consumed me and I was unable to function. I rose to my feet and rushed toward the door.

"Wait." Porter hopped up from the couch and ran in front of me, closing the door. He turned, forcing me against the wall of the hallway. Then he placed his hands on the wall on either side of me, and stood much too close to me.

My heart thumped inside my chest and sweat formed on the back of my neck. He was trapping me. How could I have been so stupid? Why did I come here? What did I expect to happen?

Silly girl.

Foolish girl.

Stupid girl.

Porter tilted his head, narrowing his eyes as he asked, "Why are you really here?"

"I-I already t-told you." I clenched my eyes tightly, scolding myself for stumbling on my words.

"No, that's not why. Tell me the truth." He leaned in closer, whispering into my ear, "It's okay, you can say it."

Slowly, he inched closer. I felt like his prey as he backed me into the wall, one arm above each of my shoulders. With my back pressed against the wall and his breath on the sensitive skin of my neck, my anxiety ramped up and the area between my legs began to throb.

"Say what?" I whispered, finally allowing my gaze to meet his. His eyes had darkened, become intense, and focused on me as if everything else in the world had ceased to exist. No one had ever looked at me like that.

He sees me.

Really sees me.

What on earth have I gotten myself into?

"You've been thinking about me, haven't you?" he asked, his voice low. He lifted one hand from the wall and tucked a stray piece of hair behind my ear.

I shook my head.

"You're lying," he insisted. "I know it."

Again, I shook my head from side to side, closing my eyes tightly, resisting the urge to place my lips on his, just like I had in my dreams.

"I've been thinking about you," he said softly. "I don't want to, but I can't stop. Ever since you came here that day, I can't get you out of my fucking head."

I flinched. That awful word made my shoulders tense. But my heart fluttered at the idea of Porter thinking of me, wanting me, dreaming of me like I dreamed of him. I said nothing, but met his stare with my own.

"Tell me something," he whispered when I didn't respond to his confession. "Do you love him?"

Again, this wholly inappropriate question. Only this time, I wanted to answer. I wanted to scream it through the apartment. I wanted him to know that Lehi Cluff could never own my heart.

When I didn't answer, he moved in closer, so close I could feel the thumping of his heart against mine. I shook my head in answer to his question, and he sighed.

"I see." He nuzzled the hot skin of my neck with his nose, before he pulled back to look into my eyes. "Tell me something else."

I glanced away quickly, afraid to look back into his icy eyes.

"Does he make you come?"

I wanted to pretend that I knew what he meant. But I didn't. I had no idea. I glanced up, searching his eyes for an explanation.

"C-come where?" I asked finally.

He chuckled again under his breath. "*Come*," he said again as he ran his finger down the side of my neck, then skimmed it along the neckline of my dress.

"It's not a place, it's a feeling," he explained. "A feeling so intense you come apart."

Porter continued to drag his fingers gently across the delicate skin at the base of my neck. I held my breath, but the rise and fall of my chest didn't stop.

"It's what happens when a man knows how to touch a woman the right way. Make her feel things no one else can. Make her respond with the lightest touch, in just the right place."

His face was inches from mine. I could taste his breath. Feel the heat.

"Oh." I swallowed hard. My throat was dry, my breath harsh. He was talking about orgasms. Rebecca had explained them to me, about losing herself in Burt. I'd never lost myself, but something told me I could easily lose myself in Porter. Part of me was already lost in him, in his smoky voice, in the heat of his breath on my ear, in the tip of his finger against the fabric of my dress.

"I'd make you come . . . so hard." His voice was rough as his finger continued to dip down beneath the cotton.

The pulsing in my private area increased, so much that I had to press my thighs together to numb the sensation. He glanced down at my crossed feet and smiled.

"Come on, Brin. Admit it," he insisted softly. "You think about me, just as I think about you. I know you do."

Involuntarily, as if somehow detached from the reasonable side of my brain, my head nodded up and down. Slowly. So slowly.

"And that's why you came here . . ."

I nodded again, swallowing hard.

"But you're afraid. Afraid they'll catch you."

Again, I nodded, a barely perceptible movement.

He removed his finger from my neckline, smoothed my hair, and peered into my eyes with a gentleness he hadn't shown me since he grasped my wrist a month ago.

"I want to see you again." His blue eyes blinked rapidly as we stood in silence. Both of us waiting for me to summon a response.

My lips responded, turning up into a soft smile. Porter smiled in return. Something inside me shifted, and a boldness crept forward as my hand reached to grasp his. He released the wall and squeezed my fingers, sighing loudly.

"Tomorrow?"

"I don't know. I can't come into town every day."

"Try," he whispered, once again nuzzling his nose into my neck before placing a tiny kiss on my skin. When I sighed in response, craving more of his touch, he said, "Just try."

"I will," I answered. "I'll try."

Porter stepped back, rubbing his neck with one hand as he opened the door with the other.

I wiped my brow quickly with the tips of my fingers and walked to the doorway. When I stopped to catch one more glimpse of the man who made my heart pound and my skin sweat, he took my hand in his and kissed my fingertips.

"Try," he repeated with a nod before letting go and closing the door behind him.

chapter 9

REBECCA WAS SEETHING.

She'd started to feel guilty about avoiding Brinley. After all, Brinley was still a young girl. Rebecca was eight years older than her and had children; she was a role model for her sister wife and should act like it.

But it had been too painful. She'd blamed Brinley for bringing her that letter, as if Brinley wanted the conflict in her heart to rise to this unbearable state. As if Brinley and Burt were somehow plotting to make this life harder for her.

Lehi Cluff disgusted her. The first time they'd consummated their marriage, she excused herself to the bathroom where she purged into the toilet from sheer repugnance. His breath reeked of day-old food, and she knew he wasn't flossing.

Burt had always flossed. Every single day. She saw to that. Even when he stayed with one of the other sister wives, she had changed his habits. His teeth were impeccable for a man in the compound, and for that she was proud.

Lehi's teeth were pathetic. He didn't floss, and it was clear to Rebecca that he'd never used mouthwash either. His overall comportment in the bedroom was lazy and inconsiderate. It was clear to Rebecca that her comfort, her pleasure during their time together, was not anything Lehi worried about or cared for.

They were together to procreate. That was all.

And technically, that was how it was supposed to be. Perhaps Heavenly Father had removed her from Burt's arms for a reason. Perhaps she was where she needed to be.

That was what Leandra said, anyway, that the prophet was always right and that Rebecca had been given a second chance with the Lord. A second chance to truly live the principle of plural marriage and to sacrifice her own worldly pleasures, as was expected of her. In the sewing room, Leandra had her almost convinced . . . convinced that the reassignment was a gift, a fresh start, a second chance to join Heavenly Father in heaven.

Because of that, Lehi was her salvation.

And Burt was her demise.

But her heart . . . her heart hadn't caught up to her head. Her heart was angry at Burt for reaching out, for trying to convince her to turn her back against the Lord.

How could he do that?

Brinley had been kind to Rebecca when she first joined the Cluff household. She'd stroked Rebecca's hair when she cried, she'd listened to Rebecca's secrets and allowed her to vent her emotions. She was there for Rebecca in a way that no other wife had been, but perhaps there was a reason for that.

Perhaps Brinley was just as damned as Burt. Leandra seemed to think so.

"Something isn't right with that one," Leandra had said as she and Rebecca sewed curtains for the boys' new room.

"Why do you say that?" Rebecca had asked, still clutching that soft spot in her heart for Brinley.

"I can't put my finger on it. But trouble seems to follow her. And she's drawn to the outside world, like a moth to a flame."

Rebecca's stomach had churned. If Leandra only knew about their interaction with Porter Hammond or the letter Burt had written, she'd be horrified, absolutely horrified. And

Rebecca needed this friendship with Leandra. She was desperate for a new start and to cleanse Burt, and the past twelve years as his wife, from her mind.

"Just steer clear of her," Leandra had insisted. "She's a bad seed. I never wanted her in this family, but who am I to question the prophet?"

"I see," Rebecca had murmured, shocked at this revelation. Brinley was sweet, immature, and kind. But a bad seed? That label had never occurred to her in the months she'd been a part of this family.

"So, I pray for her every day that she'll mature and focus on what matters," Leandra had said, ending the conversation. But Rebecca couldn't forget those words.

She's a bad seed.

That day, Rebecca had made a decision to distance herself from Brinley, at least until Brinley focused on what was important: her husband, their family, and her devotion to the Lord.

But that morning, when Brinley had stood in her doorway, her eyes forlorn, hoping Rebecca would join her on a walk to the pharmacy, Rebecca's heart was tugged. She dismissed Brinley, but had second thoughts soon after Brinley left the house.

"Leandra, I'm going to supervise Brinley on her walk to the store. Just to keep her . . . focused." She tilted her head to Leandra, who raised her eyebrows with comprehension and nodded with a grateful smile.

Quickly, Rebecca grabbed her purse from her bedroom, then hurried out the door. Rebecca was never a runner, and she always felt silly running in her dress, so she walked as quickly as she could to catch up to Brinley.

When she reached the guard at the compound, she avoided his glance, not wanting to be connected to anything having to do with that boy, Porter. Luckily, Samuel wasn't looking her way; he was busy talking to another man, laughing at a joke.

When Rebecca rounded the corner, she gasped.

Brinley and Burt.

Talking.

On the street corner.

Burt's back was to her, but she could see Brinley's face . . . and she was crying.

Rebecca hid behind the wall of the compound, peeking around it, shocked at what she was observing. The anger she had pushed down for weeks built up once again, so much so that she struggled to compose herself, struggled just to breathe.

How dare Brinley speak to that man! How dare she continue to lure Rebecca away from the Cluff family and into a life of damnation! How dare she not respect Rebecca's wishes to keep sweet and accept the assignment of the prophet! Had they planned this? Was this why Brinley had asked her to come into town? To trick her into being in Burt's presence?

And then Rebecca had another thought. Perhaps Brinley wasn't crying for her. Perhaps she was crying for *herself*. Perhaps she and Burt had forged a friendship, a relationship, a bond. A completely inappropriate and unholy bond. Perhaps Brinley was nothing but a bad seed as Leandra had said, seeking comfort from the one man in the compound she should be avoiding.

Those thoughts burned through Rebecca's veins like venom.

Of course, she knew she had to let go of Burt and his love for her. She had to move on and embrace the love of Lehi and the plan the Lord had made for her on this earth.

But how could Brinley continue to speak to Burt? How could she meet up with him in broad daylight, against the wishes of the prophet and of the good Lord himself?

How.

Dare.

She.

So Rebecca seethed; her heart thumped wildly in her chest and her lungs expanded with every breath. Leandra was right. That Brinley was, indeed, the worst seed imaginable.

She took a breath from deep within her chest, turned, and walked with new purpose back to the Cluff household.

chapter 10

I'D TRIED TO SEE Porter the very next day, but Leandra had kept me busy with chores and child care. And then at dinnertime, I was reminded that it was my night with Lehi.

Thoughts of Porter had reigned the entire day. Somehow I knew those thoughts had no plans to retreat from my brain and I'd be unable to escape him while laying with my husband.

And I was right.

Lehi arrived at my bedroom shortly after dinner.

"Is now a good time?" Lehi asked after knocking on my door and peeking his head in.

"Yes." I gestured for him to enter the room. When he closed the door, he turned to me and frowned, so I asked, "Is everything all right?"

Lehi cleared his throat. "I'd expected you to be ready. That's all."

"Oh." I was confused. I'd worn my standard nightgown and my hair was pulled into its French braid.

Lehi rubbed his finger across his lips and it dawned on me. I'd forgotten to paint my face.

"Oh," I said. "I could—if you'll just give me a few minutes, I can—"

I'd been so wrapped up in thoughts of Porter that I'd forgotten to prepare for Lehi and his desires. As indifferent as I was to sex with my husband, I had no intention of raising any suspicions in his mind. He couldn't, and wouldn't, know about Porter as long as I played my expected part.

"No." He shook his head, arms crossed in front of his chest, pursing his lips with irritation. "I suppose this is fine."

He stood next to the bed, waiting for me to join him, asserting his control, reminding me that he'd *allowed* me to skip painting my face. It was not my decision.

"I'm sorry, Lehi. Honestly, I was just . . . I forgot."

"It's all right. It just makes me wonder if you don't look forward to our time together the way I do." His voice was calm, almost soothing. The wrinkles next to his eyes stretched as he spoke.

I was again confused by his words. Lehi looked forward to our time together? I was number seven of eight, and even though I was obedient in the bedroom, I was pretty certain that after three years of laying with my husband, I was still rather clueless when it came to intercourse.

"What is it?" he asked, running his fingers down my braid as he peered into my eyes.

"You look forward to . . . to me?"

"Of course, my beautiful girl."

I didn't like being called "girl." Not by Leandra and certainly not by Lehi. But I swallowed my irritation, forcing myself to replace the cringe that was begging to be released with an obedient smile.

Keep sweet. Keep sweet. Keep sweet.

"Tell me," he continued, moving his hand to the back of my neck. The rough calluses from his hand scraped my skin, and I forced myself not to pull away. "Do you think about me when I'm not here?"

Why all the questions?

Does he know something?

Did Rebecca tell him about the afternoon in Porter's apartment?

"Uh, yes," I said, my cheeks growing hot. "Of course, yes."

"Good. Lay down."

Following the instructions I'd been given, I pulled back the quilt of my bed before unbuttoning my nightgown, letting it fall to the floor in a puddle at my feet. Three years of intercourse with Lehi. Three years of letting him touch me and enter me and own me. Throughout all those years not once had I ever felt naked.

Until now.

Lehi waited for me to lie down on the bed before removing his clothing. He stared down at my bare breasts as he stripped himself of his shirt and pants.

I don't want this. I don't want this.

Just as every time before this, our intercourse followed the same pattern. He pushed into me and I struggled to relax my muscles, allowing him in. The whiskers of his beard scratched the surface of my skin like the needles of a porcupine, and I closed my eyes at the uncomfortable sensation. As he continued, my mind wandered and I pretended. Oh, did I pretend.

Instead of Lehi's rigid body, the heat of Porter was now above me, entering me again and again. The hot breath on my arm was Porter's, evidence of his desire for me. I imagined his blue eyes focused on mine as he ran his fingers through my hair, igniting something inside me I never thought possible.

The pulsing I'd awoken to several times in the past month returned, this time while laying with my husband. Lost in thoughts of Porter, I drove my hips forward, matching his momentum and his desire for me. Again and again, I thrust the lower half of my body, determined to show Porter exactly how he made me feel.

"That's it, that's my girl," a gruff voice said against my shoulder and I gasped. Lehi had pulled me from my fantasy and dropped me unhappily into reality. My eyes shot open and I stared up at the ceiling, horrified at the feel of his skin against mine, like sandpaper against the soft, delicate curves of a porcelain cup.

When Lehi groaned and collapsed on my chest, a tear slid from my eye. A tear of guilt.

I'd just cheated on my husband, which made me the lowest of the low. Even though he'd been the one to lay with me, I'd forgotten all about him and had given myself to another man in my mind.

When the tear rolled down my cheek and dropped to my bare shoulder, I knew. It was done.

I was damned.

Lehi pulled his boxer shorts on and turned to me. "I've never seen you like that. I could tell how turned on you were, the way you moved. It was sexy."

"Oh," I muttered, pulling myself to a seated position in the bed, pulling the covers to my breasts, noting the sensation against my taut nipple.

"You're coming into your own. That's a good thing."

"Thank you." I nodded.

"I hope you'll be like that from now on. It was enjoyable for me, that's for certain."

"Oh. Okay."

I gripped the sheet, realizing with dread that I'd changed everything between my husband and myself. I'd changed my role and altered his expectations. If he'd only known why I moved that way, why my hips thrust against his, and why my private parts throbbed with anticipation and lust.

I was so ashamed, utterly and completely ashamed. How could I have done this? How could I have let myself spin so out of control and deceive my husband?

And Heavenly Father. I had sinned against Heavenly Father in an unforgivable manner.

As desperately as I wanted to be forgiven, I wasn't sure that was even possible. In fact, I was pretty certain my fate had been sealed.

I was damned.

And it scared me to death.

chapter 11

REPENTANCE IS DIFFICULT when you resent it.

Two weeks ago, I'd cheated on my husband in my heart, and every day since then I'd been doing my best to repent. When I thought of Porter, I pinched the skin just above my wrist to snap myself out of it. When Leandra asked me to go into town today, I lied and told her that I was needed at my mother's house. My father was out of town and mother was suffering from a bad case of the flu. That *was* the truth. But Mother hadn't asked me to come by. I told myself that it was a lie with a purpose—it kept me from going into town. It kept me from allowing temptation to take over my body and lead me straight to the apartment above the coffeehouse.

But I resented it.

I wanted to walk to Porter's apartment. I wanted to be pushed up against his wall. I wanted the touch of his thumb against my wrist rather than the sharp pinch of my own fingernails.

"What are you doing?" Aspen asked, gesturing to my wrist, angry and blotchy from my own efforts. Quickly, I dropped my hands to my side and looked straight ahead.

"Nothing. I think I have a rash."

"Mm-hmm." The skepticism in Aspen's voice was apparent, but I ignored it. Aspen was walking to my mother's house with me. She'd offered to join me to get out of the house since she'd been left in charge of all the children the day before.

"It's a gorgeous day."

Aspen was overly chipper on that day. Not that she was a particularly somber person; she wasn't. But she was, in many ways, the yin to my yang when it came to personality. Devout plural wife and follower of Heavenly Father, she was proud of her role in the Cluff family. She was proud of her three children and hoped they'd marry in their teens, just like she had. She wanted their place in the celestial kingdom to be secured, just like her own.

She was sharp and opinionated, but she knew exactly when and where she could safely express those opinions without jeopardizing her relationship with Lehi, Leandra, or the prophet.

Aspen was also the most perceptive of the sister wives. I used to think she had some sort of mind-reading abilities, and it took me some time to feel comfortable with her for just that reason. When you were having doubts about your faith, your life, and your husband, the last thing you wanted was for someone to be listening in on your private thoughts.

"You're quiet today." She nudged me gently with her elbow. "Even more than usual."

I shook my head and shrugged, summoning all the energy I could to act natural. But since meeting Porter, acting natural had become increasingly difficult.

We passed by the open field where several children were playing some form of tag. They laughed as they ran, and I wondered how long it had been since I, myself, had laughed.

So long ago, I couldn't remember.

"They're having fun," Aspen said, watching the children.

"I miss fun."

"Kids are fun. You know you can play with mine whenever you like," she teased, and her elbow nudged mine again.

"I know." I stared at the ground as we walked.

"Is that why you're upset? I know you've been trying for a long time." Her voice softened.

I could feel Aspen studying my face, and I knew what I had to do. I had to lie.

"Yeah. Three years is a long time, right?"

She shrugged. "Everyone's different. Maybe it's the timing. You only see Lehi a few times a month."

"That hasn't stopped you from getting pregnant."

"True." Her brow knitted and she opened her mouth to speak, but said nothing.

We walked in silence. Guilt was the only emotion I could feel.

Yes, Aspen was not always the easiest to get along with, but she'd always been there for me when I truly needed her. And I was leading her to believe such lies.

I hardly recognized myself anymore.

When we entered my mother's home, I was disturbed by the eerie quiet of the house. Where were all the children? My brothers and sisters?

"Mother?" I called out.

She responded with a fit of coughing. Aspen narrowed her eyes and we jogged upstairs to the bedroom. My mother was on her knees, leaning on the mattress of her unmade bed.

"Mother." I knelt down next to her and placed my hand on the small of her back.

"I-I'm fine." She coughed again. "It's just the flu. You should go, I don't want you to get sick."

"Where is everyone?"

"I sent the kids next door with your Mother Peg."

"Oh, of course."

My mother was lucky enough to have her own small home in the compound, which she shared with the rest of my brothers and sisters. Jessa and Winnie were both married and lived with their husbands, but five children remained in the home.

"Come on, Mother, into bed with you."

Aspen and I supported my mother's frail body and eased her under the covers of her bed.

My mother winced, trying not to cough, then gave Aspen a wan smile. "Hello, Aspen dear."

"Hello." Aspen slid her hand on my mother's shoulder. "Tell us what we can do to make you more comfortable."

"A cup of tea would be nice."

"I'll take care of it," Aspen said, smiling down at my mother and leaving the room.

Mother turned her worried gaze to me. "You shouldn't be here, Brinley. You could catch this."

"I had no idea you were so sick." I placed the back of my hand on her blazing forehead. "I would've come here sooner. When does Father get back?"

"A few more days. The worst part is Jessa needs me. She needs me and I can't be with her."

An alarm bell went off in my mind. When Jessa and I had spoken last, she was elated to be pregnant with her first child. It was new, but she was excited to start her journey into motherhood.

"What's the matter with Jessa? Why would she need you?"

"Oh." Mother bit her bottom lip. "She hasn't told anyone yet, no one except me, that is."

I grasped Mother's hand and squeezed. "What is it?"

"She lost the baby."

"Oh no." My heart sank.

My mother nodded. Miscarriage happened often in our community, along with stillbirths and life-threatening birth defects. Family trees inevitably crossed and became muddled through marriage, and the babies we lost were reminders of that.

"She's devastated. Feels she's being punished."

"For what?"

Like Aspen, Jessa was a devout follower of the prophet and our faith. She'd been married for six months to a kind man named Curtis. She was the fourth of his wives and had been happy since committing her life to him and his family. When we were younger, Jessa was always rocking the little ones to sleep or volunteering to give them their bottles. She was a natural caregiver and mother. No one deserved to be a mother more than my sister Jessa.

"I'm not sure," Mother said. "Missing prayer sessions, raising her voice to Curtis, something minor. I told her to pray on it. She needs to find a way to move on."

"Maybe she's not ready. Losing someone can be difficult."

Mother narrowed her eyes. "Who have you lost?"

She knew the *correct* answer.

No one.

But she didn't know the real answer. The man I was forcing myself to lose.

I walked to the end of her bed and smoothed out the bedcovers, avoiding her eyes. "No one, of course. I just—I can imagine is all."

"Ah," she said, but I knew she wasn't convinced. Despite having eight children, my mother knew me all too well. Which was why I needed to leave her house as soon as I could.

"Here you are." Aspen rounded the corner and placed a bed tray over my mother's lap. Tea, butter cookies, and an apple sliced into wedges had been artfully arranged on it.

"Thank you, dear." Mother reached for the ancient teacup adorned with painted roses. "But I insist you two leave. You have responsibilities back at home. I'll be fine."

"Mother, I don't—"

"I insist."

Her tone was sharp and I dared not question her further. Disrespecting your parents was completely unacceptable, and that included questioning their judgment in any given situation.

As I stared down at my mother, so frail and small, her graying brown hair arranged into a loose bun, I realized the irony of the situation. No matter how tiny she was, no matter how weak, I had been taught that there was a line, a line that could not be crossed. And my tiny mother was, in all ways that mattered, ten feet tall rather than the five foot one she truly was. If she gave me an order, I was to follow it without question.

"All right," I said reluctantly. "But I'll return in a couple of days. How does that sound?"

"That will be fine." Satisfaction crossed her face as she sat back, sipping her tea.

I kissed the top of her head and walked to the door.

"Oh, and Brinley, dear."

"Yes?"

"Please don't say anything to Jessa. She'll tell you when she's ready."

"Yes, ma'am." I nodded.

Aspen glanced at me curiously, but said nothing. I waited until we left my mother's home before telling her about Jessa, and she let out a sad sigh.

"Poor thing."

"Have you ever . . . lost a baby?" I picked at the pocket of my dress, unsure how Aspen would respond. With anger? Embarrassment? Disgust? We weren't encouraged to discuss such things. It was hard to keep sweet when you were wallowing in past disappointments.

"Yes," she answered matter-of-factly. "Just before you married Lehi."

"Oh no." I froze, my hand raised to my mouth in shock. "I'm so sorry."

"It was sad, yes. But it happens." Her voice had softened, and I felt safe asking my next question.

"What was it like?"

She cleared her throat before answering. I knew I was making her ridiculously uncomfortable. But my heart was breaking for Jessa and I needed to know what she was going through.

"Scary, mostly. And painful."

"Did you—did you bleed?" I asked, feeling intensely uncomfortable with the conversation, but pushing ahead anyway.

"Yes, a lot."

"Did Lehi take care of you?"

Aspen pulled me to an abrupt stop and turned to me. "Brinley, you can't be serious?" Her words were sharp, cutting.

"What?"

Aspen crossed her arms in front of her and her nostrils flared. "Do you honestly think he would do that?"

I searched my heart for the answer. And it didn't take long.

"No."

"Exactly."

"Did anyone help you?" The thought of Aspen doubled over in pain, clutching her abdomen, broke my heart. The idea of her going through it alone brought tears to my eyes.

"Ruthie helped me."

Aspen's firstborn daughter, Ruthie, was only eight years old now. So at that point, she would have been only . . .

"But . . . she was barely five!"

Aspen shrugged, her eyes welling with tears. "She's all I had."

I bit my lip, willing my tears to stop, but they wouldn't. Several slid down my cheeks.

"Stop," Aspen said, closing her eyes and waving her hands wildly in the air. "It was a long time ago. I'm fine."

Despite Aspen's insistence, I knew my questions had caused her grief to resurface. Without thinking it through, I stepped forward and wrapped my arms around her. She stiffened at my embrace, but slowly she wrapped her arms around my lower back, allowing me to comfort her.

I pulled her closer and whispered in her ear, "I'm here for you."

"Thank you."

I rubbed my hands up and down Aspen's back, and soon felt her muscles relax at my touch. I couldn't make the past go away, but I could do my best to assure her that I would be there for her in the future.

"Now stop," Aspen said, pulling away and wiping the tears from her eyes. "Let's not make a spectacle of ourselves."

"Sorry," I muttered, and turned to resume our walk home.

"May I ask something else?"

"Oh goodness, Brinley. You are determined to have me sob, aren't you?"

"No, nothing sad. I promise."

"All right, then," she said with a reluctant chuckle.

"When you, when you have intercourse . . . do you enjoy it?"

Aspen kept her eyes focused on the dirt road ahead of us. We were still several blocks from home. She knew it was safe to answer, but that didn't convince me that she would.

"What do you mean?"

"With Lehi. Does it . . . Do you . . . I mean, do you have an org—"

"Brinley!" Aspen said, her eyes wide, her cheeks as red as plum tomatoes. "You've been talking to Rebecca, haven't you?"

"I just—"

"I lay with Lehi for procreation." Her voice raised. "I lay with him to make babies for Heavenly Father's celestial kingdom. That is all."

"But Lehi has them," I argued.

"Listen to me. Men have to have them. It won't work if they don't. Everyone knows that." She gritted her teeth. "Now, stop it."

"I just—"

"No! Ever since Rebecca came into our family, you've been odd and I don't like it, Brinley. I don't like it one bit."

"But I—"

"She loved her husband, and look where that got her. Don't let her lead you into false fantasies."

Her eyes were flinty in a way I'd never seen from her, fierce yet protective. Much like she'd look at her own children.

"Be smart," she told me. "Our duty is to produce children for our husband, for Heavenly Father. It is not to fornicate or indulge our desires." Aspen turned on her heel and quickened her pace, heading directly for our home.

"Yes, Aspen," I muttered, following several paces behind. And wishing I'd never opened my mouth.

I'd lost Rebecca. I couldn't be foolish enough to lose Aspen.

I had to be smart.

When we reached our block, something caught my attention from the corner of my eye. Samuel. He was waving at me, swinging his arms in a subtle attempt to grab my attention, and he succeeded. But acknowledging his gesture would be the most foolish thing I could possibly do. There was only one reason Samuel would want to speak with me.

Porter.

I couldn't handle that. Not at that moment. Possibly not ever.

So I ignored him and obediently followed my sister wife to our home, all the while pinching the skin of my wrist until it bled.

chapter 12

I COULDN'T AVOID it any longer. It was time to go to town.

Luckily, Leandra was more than pleased to give me a rather long list of errands. None of the other sister wives had volunteered when I'd declined the week before to visit my mother. Leandra had asked Lehi, but conveniently he'd forgotten. When she pressed him about it, he reminded of her of the giant responsibilities on his shoulders.

"There are eight of you," he'd told her. "You cannot expect me to run errands. Get it done."

As much as I disliked Leandra, I knew it was time for me to volunteer. Time to face my fears. So I offered to run Leandra's errands, and she shoved the envelope with the money and the list with a grateful sigh.

It didn't rain often in our little corner of Utah, but on this day the skies were overcast, the clouds ominous. When a cool breeze brushed past me, goose bumps ran up my arms, stinging the open wound on my wrist. I pulled my sleeve down to cover it, but wished I'd remembered to cover it with a bandage.

When I approached Samuel's post, he crossed his arms in front of his chest and hardened his expression. I wanted to run back to my house and hide, but I couldn't. It was time to face my first obstacle of the day.

"Well, look who it is."

"Hello, Samuel." He'd always been kind to me, but not today. Today, he was hostile, angry. I glanced briefly in his direction before looking down at my shoes.

"Stay right there," he said, then walked to rummage inside a backpack behind the fence. When he returned, he placed a folded piece of paper in my hand. "I told you to keep me out of it."

"What?"

"Don't play dumb." He gestured to the paper in my hand. "He told me to give that to you. Threatened to kick the snot out of me if I didn't."

"Is that what he said?"

Samuel grimaced. "Well, those aren't the words he used, but yes."

"I'm sorry. I had no idea." I clutched my stomach as it churned, upset that Samuel was angry with me. The list of those who were currently displeased with me seemed to be ever growing.

"That's fine. But tell him to keep me out of it. You hear me?" Samuel's eyes grew wide, and a large vein in his neck pulsed as he spoke.

"Y-yes, I understand." I nodded quickly, then cleared my throat and walked away as quickly as possible. When I reached the corner of the next block, I opened the note. My fingers trembled as I unfolded the paper.

Where ARE you?

Those simple words were scribbled in the center of the paper. I flipped it over once, and then again, looking for more but there was nothing. Despite its brevity, his message was clear. He'd asked to see me again and I'd gone against my promise to try. Instead, I'd hidden from him, from us.

It seemed that no matter what I did, I'd be haunted by guilt. I could abandon my family, my belief system, and my God, or I could walk away from Porter, the one man who had ever stirred my heart. But the guilt would follow me nevertheless. I wouldn't escape it, I couldn't.

No matter what.

When I reached the door of the clinic, I told myself to stand up straight, to walk tall, to be strong. But I felt my body betray me as my shoulders dropped and drew in from shame.

Tiffany stood behind the front desk, speaking to a mother who was cradling her screeching child. Tiffany's compassion was generous, evident in her expression, her soft eyes, her sympathetic nod as she listened to the woman list her child's maladies.

When the woman and her daughter retreated to the waiting area, Tiffany stiffened, then inhaled deeply and closed her eyes as she exhaled, pulling herself back together as she filed their registration forms. When she closed their manila folder, our eyes met and she flinched.

Her reaction made me tremble. My cruelty, my feelings of superiority had hurt her, that was obvious. Slowly, I managed to walk to the counter, trying to ignore the burning behind my eyes.

"What are you doing here?"

"I-I came to apologize."

"You're out of pills, huh?" She crossed her arms and frowned at me.

I hung my head in shame. "Yes. Almost."

"I figured." She shook her head with a sigh, then began to reorganize stacks of paper behind the counter.

"Please, Tiffany, I don't know what to do, where to turn. You're the only one who knows."

“About what?” She slammed her hands down on the counter. “The pills? Porter Hammond?” She glared at me. “It feels like all I do is carry around your dirty secrets.”

“I know, but I—”

“If you’re so unhappy, just leave. I did it, Porter did it. You can do it too, Brinley.”

I pressed my lips together, fighting tears. “It’s not that easy.”

“No, it’s not. It’s hard, really hard. But it’s *worth* it.” She looked up at the ceiling, a small smile peeking through her anger. “Geez, Brinley, you have no idea what freedom really is, what it feels like. There’s nothing better. Nothing.”

I had no reply. She was right; I had no idea what freedom was. Not one single, solitary clue.

“Can you tell me?” I asked through my tears.

She paused and took a deep breath before saying, “It’s like flying. So scary, so unsettling, but when you get your bearings, you just . . .” She shrugged. “You glide. And you forget what it was like to walk instead of using your wings.”

“Wow.” I stared at the beige counter, letting her words wash over me again and again. I wanted to fly, wanted to be free, but my fear wouldn’t let me leave the ground.

“I’ll keep hope for you.”

She placed a box of tissues in front of me. I nodded, closing my eyes and wiping the fresh tears from my skin. When I opened my eyes, she was gone. I looked around the waiting area, wondering where Tiffany had disappeared to.

Seconds later she returned through the door to the back room, holding the familiar bag containing my birth control pills. “Until then, here you go.”

A sigh of relief left my lungs. "Thank you," I said, tears spilling anew. "And I'm sorry, so very sorry for what I said to you. I didn't mean it."

"Yes, you did," she said with a shrug. "But it's not your fault. It's all you know, and it's been drilled into your head for twenty-two years. But there's more to this world than life in a compound, Brinley. I swear to you, there's so much more. More than you ever imagined."

I picked up the bag and tucked it inside my purse. Unable to look up, I whispered, "I want to be brave, but I'm not. I'm just not."

"I didn't think I was either." Tiffany reached across the counter of the desk and rubbed my shoulder. "It's in you, you just have to find it."

Not sure what else to say, I simply said, "Thank you." I didn't believe her. I knew I wasn't brave or strong. I knew my feet would never allow me to grow wings. They'd never allow me to fly.

"I have to get back to work," she said kindly. "Take care of yourself now."

I nodded, turning to walk to the door, and as I did, Tiffany said, "He misses you."

"What?"

"You know who I'm talking about. Go see him, Brinley. He cares about you."

Her words stopped me in my tracks.

"Why do you say that? How can you tell?"

First a note given to Samuel, and now I knew he had visited Tiffany again. My desire for Porter was creeping back into my subconscious. As if under a trance, I reached for my wrist and pinched the skin, wincing from the pain of the open flesh.

"Yesterday he sat over there," she gestured to the chairs to my left, "for three hours straight. He'd just come from work and was sweaty and gross. I told him to go home and take a shower, that you weren't coming and that I wasn't sure if you ever would."

"And?" I asked, my heart racing.

"He just shrugged his shoulders again and again and said, 'I'm fine here, thanks.' It was sweet in a weird, stalkerish way."

"Stalkerish?" I asked, having no idea what she meant.

Tiffany shook her head and laughed. "Don't worry about it. I was just kidding. Go see him."

I nodded, knowing there was no way I could go back home after this conversation.

I had to see Porter.

The short walk to Porter's building seemed to take hours instead of minutes. The sun was setting behind the buildings, and I knew I should be on my way home, but I didn't have a choice. I had to see him again.

A man wearing a baseball cap was entering the building and, without even thinking, I grabbed the door handle before it shut behind him and locked, and followed him up the staircase. The anticipation built with each step I made toward Porter's apartment.

When I reached the door, I heard the thumping of loud music. I sighed with relief, knowing he was home.

I knocked.

No answer.

I knocked again.

This time, a slightly familiar face answered the door. It must have been his cousin, Charlie. He took in the sight of me—my pastel blue dress, my 1980s bangs and long braid, my unpainted face. He knew exactly where I was from.

He groaned and rolled his eyes. "Porter!" he shouted over his shoulder.

"What?" Porter yelled back from deep within the apartment. "I'm busy!"

"Whatever," Charlie grumbled, gesturing for me to enter. "He's in his room."

I walked into the apartment and stopped in the living area where several men in their twenties were playing some sort of game on the television. Each of them was holding a small rectangular gadget in their hands with a cord that dangled toward a machine on the coffee table. None of them glanced up at me, their eyes fixed on the bright screen where soldiers were running, shooting, and jumping.

Odd.

I turned to Charlie, not knowing which bedroom belonged to Porter. He rolled his eyes again.

"Second one on the right."

"Thank you," I muttered, but he had already focused his attention on the television with the rest of the men in the living room.

The music coming from Porter's room scared me. It was angry, as if someone was screaming at the top of his lungs. Was this music? It certainly didn't sound at all like the church hymns we'd sung while growing up. I'd heard music in shops and in Tiffany's clinic, but nothing like this. It was nauseating.

Despite my extreme distaste for his music, I knocked on the door, knowing I had to see him. I heard him curse, and something heavy seemed to hit the door on the other side of the room. I jumped.

"Charlie, leave me the fuck alone!" Porter yelled from inside.

"It's not me, asshole!" Charlie shouted back from the living room. "Open the door!"

A second later, the door swung open and Porter's gaze landed on me.

"Holy shit." Porter ran his hands through his mussed-up hair, his eyes alight with surprise, and the muscles of his chest flexed in response—his shirt nowhere to be seen. "It's *you*."

Aside from his chest, which was quite attractive, he looked awful. His eyes were red, swollen, and looked as painful as the wound on my wrist. Was he having trouble sleeping? He was so pale, his skin as ashen as the day he stole my bag on the street. His eyes were open wide, revealing the whites of his eyes both above and below the irises, and his pupils were dilated, so much so that there wasn't much left of his normal beautiful blue color. When he crossed his hands over his chest, they shook, and he scratched at them absently.

What was the matter with him?

"I can't believe you're here." He crossed the room and turned off the music, then pulled me into the room and closed the door behind me with a thud.

"I'm sorry it took so long. I couldn't get away," I lied.

"I see," he muttered, narrowing his eyes and scratching his cheeks, which were covered with acne.

"Are y-you all right?" I asked, reaching to touch his elbow. His muscles tensed slightly at my touch.

"Why?" he bellowed. "Why wouldn't I be?" He began to pace the small room. "I mean, you show up after, like, two fucking weeks. I thought you were gonna try!"

His eyes were wild and he pulled at the roots of his hair. And then I remembered Tiffany's words. *Be careful. He's a junkie.*

Porter had drugs in his system.

"I was scared." I closed my eyes, unable to lie to him again. I could lie to Leandra, to Lehi, to Aspen. But for some reason I didn't understand, lying to him was painful.

"Of what? Of me?" He glowered at me, his hands still shaking as he moved them to his hips. "What the fuck?"

"Not you, but you and me. Us."

He was silent, taking in my words, then he nodded. "Look, I get it. Leaving that place isn't something I wanted. Hell, I would've fought it tooth and nail if I could have."

"You didn't want to leave?"

"No. But I don't want to talk about it, all right? I don't want to tell you my fucking sob stories. I don't want you feeling sorry for me."

"I don't. I promise." Again, I reached out to touch his elbow. This time he placed his hand on top of mine, releasing a deep sigh from his chest. "What's the matter with you, Porter? You don't look well."

"It's nothing." He shook his head. "I've been pissed off, and I needed to let off some steam. I needed to forget about things."

"Oh. I understand." I dropped my hand back to my side. When he looked down at his elbow, his lips pursing into an angry scowl, I asked, "Should I leave?"

"Do you think I *want* you to go?" he snapped, raising his voice to a yell. The deep pitch of his anger reverberated through the tiny room.

"I don't know." I shook my head, fighting tears. This wasn't the reunion I'd hoped for. I turned to grab the doorknob. "But maybe I should—"

"What is that?" Porter demanded, storming toward me.

"I don't know—"

"On your wrist. Did he do that to you?" He ripped my hand from the doorknob and inspected my arm, his eyes growing even wider when he saw the damage I'd done to myself.

"No, of course not."

"Tell me the truth, Brin. Did that sick fuck do this to you?" His eyes were wild, flaring with anger.

"No! I told you no!" I yelled.

I never yelled. Not since I was a child playing games with my siblings, had I shouted at another human being.

What is this man doing to me?

"Fine," he conceded. "Then what the hell is this?"

He obviously wouldn't stop until he got an answer, so I whispered, "I did it." I stared into his eyes, feeling disgusted at myself and my reasons for doing what I did.

"Why?"

I couldn't answer. I turned my gaze to focus on the window, wishing I were a bird, wishing I could fly away from the truth. Every last bit of it.

"Why, Brin? Why did you hurt yourself like this?"

I closed my eyes as tears streamed down my hot cheeks. "You," I whispered. "When I think of you, I pinch myself. So I'll stop."

He dropped my hand, his mouth agape. He took my cheeks in his hands as tears formed in his eyes. Then Porter lunged at me, claiming my mouth with his own, his body a live wire wanting to feed upon me. He pressed his body against me, pushing me against the door, and the sharp edges of the lock dug into the small of my back.

I yelped in pain. My cry didn't faze Porter, still aggressively pressing his lips against mine. Fear built within me and I shoved at his chest, pushing him away from me.

"Stop!" I yelled when he wouldn't pull away. When I turned my face, denying him access to my mouth, he pressed forward anyway, inadvertently ramming his forehead into the door. I gasped in surprise and Porter pulled away, his eyes crazed from the drugs in his system.

When he took in the fear evident in my face, in my body language, he trembled and turned away, then paced to the other side of the room. Suddenly he pulled back his fist and punched the gray wall, leaving a dent in the smooth surface. He grunted in pain and clasped his knuckles close to his chest.

I wanted to run to him, to comfort him and kiss his hand. But I was too afraid.

Porter slumped onto the edge of his bed and dropped his head into his hands. His breathing was ragged, his chest and back heaving. I reached back to the doorknob, not sure of what I should do. I wanted to run, to go back home where I knew I was safe.

But I couldn't leave him. Not like this.

And so I stood there mutely, watching him breathe deeply and calm himself. I was too afraid to go to him, but leaving the apartment wasn't an option I could accept. I had to know he'd be all right.

"Brin, I—" He lifted his head and searched my eyes with his. "I'm so, so sorry. I know I'm fucked up right now. I *know* that. When I'm like this, I just . . . I can't kiss you. Because I want more. Too much more."

"You scared me."

"I know, and I'm so sorry. Please don't go. I won't kiss you, I promise. Just—please, stay."

He patted the bed next to him and I hesitated, not knowing if I could trust him while he was clearly on some sort of drug. I swallowed hard, not breaking eye contact.

"Hold on a second. I'll be right back." Porter leaped from the bed and walked past me, opening the door and closing it behind him.

Willing my body to calm, I distracted myself by inspecting his room. I wanted to understand Porter, to feel connected to him again.

His bedroom looked nothing like the rooms I was used to. Ours were clean at all times, yet his was a disaster. Clothes were flung across the floor. The walls of my bedroom were covered in photos of the Cluff family, as well as pictures of my parents, sisters, and brothers. Porter's walls held no pictures. None. Porter had no memories to cling to, nothing to keep him going. He only had the present, and the possibility of a future.

The door opened, jolting me back to our reality. A wicked smile lifted the corners of Porter's mouth as he revealed his hands to me, both covered in dark blue oven mitts. There he stood, wearing nothing but a pair of faded jeans and two ridiculous oven mitts.

I burst out laughing. "What on earth?"

"I told you, I won't touch you. I promise. Here, I brought tape," he said, awkwardly lifting one of the mitts to reveal a large roll of packing tape. "You know, in case you wanted to tape them to my arms."

"I don't want to hurt you."

"You won't."

"Don't be silly." I took the tape from his mitt-covered hand. "That tape will rip your skin off."

"I don't care." He shrugged, placing his hands on his hips. He was obviously being sincere, but I couldn't help but laugh again.

"I can't take you seriously when you're wearing those things."

"Okay, fine." He chuckled. "Will you stay? We can just talk."

"I'd like that."

He walked to the bed and I followed. We crawled over the rumpled blanket and sat next to each other, leaning our backs against the painted wall. Porter rested his mitt-covered hands on his thighs. True to his word, he didn't try to touch me. Not once.

I slid him a sideways glance. "Why do you do this to yourself? The drugs, I mean."

He shrugged. "I don't know. I mean, the first time was just sheer curiosity. I wanted to know how it felt. Charlie and I had a shit day at work, and one of our buddies offered to share."

"What is it, exactly?"

"Meth."

"That's a weird name." The only drug I'd ever heard of was marijuana or "pot." A few of the boys had been caught smoking pot in the woods, and were removed from our community that very night. "What do you do with it?"

"Smoke it, usually."

"And what does it do?"

The concept of anyone using drugs was so foreign to me; I couldn't help but be curious. I wanted to understand Porter, to know why he felt the need to alter himself to such a degree. Didn't he see how appealing he was all on his own?

"It takes the pain away," he said simply. "Until it doesn't."

"Oh." I wasn't sure what to say. I didn't want him in pain.

"I feel strong," he said. "I feel all this energy swoop into my body. I don't think about my family or where I came from. I feel powerful and important. Like the best version of myself."

"Until . . ."

"Until the comedown. Then it's like all that power, all that energy and life, is being drained from every cell of my body."

"Is that what's happening right now?"

He nodded. "Bad timing, I guess. I'm sorry."

"Have I seen you . . . you know, while you were on a high?" I hoped the answer would be no. I didn't want to question the sincerity of our interactions in the past.

"No," he said. "Honestly, I've been trying to get clean. Today I'm coming down, and I was coming down that day in the street. I was out of money and really wanted another hit. That's why I was desperate enough to take your purse. I hit bottom that day."

"Why?"

"I'd never stolen before. The people of our community don't steal. You know that."

I nodded.

"But this shit's strong. When you come down, you don't just want more, you need more, you crave more. You have to have more. It's fucked up."

"Can you stop?" I felt nervous for him, and selfishly for myself. I didn't know what the next comedown would bring.

"I've tried . . . a couple times. But being here, living with these guys, it's never lasted long. Someone's always got some, and I get wrapped up in it again and again." He paused, turning so he could look into my eyes. "Can we talk about something else?"

"Sure."

"What do you want to talk about?" Porter asked, his eyebrows raised.

Lehi had never asked me what topics I'd want to discuss. In fact, I was pretty certain that no one in the Cluff household had asked me that question. And for that reason, I was stumped. I opened my mouth to answer, but then had no words. I could only shrug and give him a sheepish grin.

"Do you like music?" Porter asked. He jumped up from the bed and crossed the room to a large black box sitting on his desk.

"I don't know. I only know the songs the prophet plays in the mornings."

"I want to play something for you. It's a bunch of songs that make me think of you. I burned it on my computer."

How he could "burn" something into the shape of a flat metal doughnut, I had no idea, but his eyes were calm, his voice serene and genuine. And my curiosity was piqued.

"I'd love to hear it."

"This is called a CD." He placed the disk into the machine and within moments, the soft sound of a guitar filled the small room. Then a gentle voice began to sing.

Porter crossed the room and sat next to me. "I know I said I wouldn't touch you, but would you like to lie down with me, just lie down and listen?"

I smiled and scooted my bottom down so that I was lying flat on Porter's bed, my head resting on his fluffy pillow. Porter hopped into bed next to me. We stared up at the ceiling as I listened to the man sing. The song soothed my nerves and spoke to my heart. When the last notes played, I turned my head to Porter as a new song began.

"That was beautiful. What was it?"

"It's called 'Such Great Heights' by Iron and Wine. I listen to it . . . a lot."

"And this?" I heard the melodic sound of a piano and another man's voice. This song was less muted, more intense. I was drawn to it, to the words, and to the tone of the singer's voice. He sounded desperate, needy, and so very much in love.

"It's called 'Without You.' It's a really old song by Harry Nilsson. But it speaks to me. Ever since you came back here that day and demanded your bag, I can't get you out of my head. And I'm sorry if that scares you." He paused. "Does it . . . scare you?"

It probably should have. The intensity of the song made my heart thump within my chest, at the idea of Porter feeling this way about me. It should have made me run, to claim sanctuary in the house of Lehi Cluff. But it didn't. It only made me want to kiss Porter gently on his lips.

And so I did. I leaned forward slowly and caressed his lips with a feathery kiss, then smiled as I inched away from him.

"I guess that's a no." Porter chuckled.

"You can take the oven mitts off," I whispered.

His eyebrows drew together in a cautious scowl. "Are you sure?"

"Yes. I trust you."

Slowly, he slid the bulky mitts from his hands, then interlocked his fingers and placed them on his chest. Despite my little kiss, Porter didn't break his promise. We stared at the ceiling, listening to every song on that CD. When each song ended, I asked him to tell me about it—why he loved it, why he chose it. Porter didn't hesitate, telling me all about the lyrics and what they meant to him, to us.

And as I lay there with him, staring at the stark white ceiling above us, I knew there was so much more to my feelings for this man than the electricity of his kiss, his touch, his passion. I was drawn to the softness of his voice when he was confessing his deepest feelings, the complexity in his expression when he was trying to explain a concept that he knew would be foreign to me, and to his vulnerability . . . the way he was able to admit his struggles, his failures, the most shameful parts of himself. Men in our community didn't do that. Porter was showing me every part of himself; I just had to pay attention. I had to accept the good with the bad.

And before that CD came to an end, I knew that I could.

I was tired of fighting this.

I didn't just want to *kiss* Porter Hammond.

I wanted to *be* with Porter Hammond.

chapter 13

RESISTANCE WAS GETTING EASIER.

"C'mon, I'll walk you home," Porter said. He reached out to smooth down the wrinkled sleeve of my dress, attempting to make my appearance less rumpled after several hours of lying in his bed.

"I'm not sure that's a good idea. Someone could see you."

"We'll be careful, I promise. But I won't take no for an answer, Brin. You shouldn't be out on your own this late. Something could happen to you."

"Oh," I muttered under my breath. "Thank you."

And then it hit me. The list in my pocket. Leandra would have my head.

"Oh no." The happiness I'd felt just moments before was instantly replaced with dread. I slid down to the floor. "She'll know. Oh no, oh no, oh no."

"Whoa, slow down. What are you talking about?"

Withdrawing the paper from my pocket, I placed the list beside me with shaking hands. I'd been gone for hours. If I returned with absolutely nothing on Leandra's list, she would know I'd been dishonest. She'd be certain that her misgivings about me were correct—that I couldn't be trusted.

"This is a list . . . of stuff."

"I was supposed to buy all of those things. Hours ago."

Porter crouched down and lifted my chin with his fingertips. "Listen to me, okay? We've got this. C'mon, I go shopping all the time. I'll help you."

"You do?"

The idea of a man shopping seemed so silly to me, but then I remembered that Porter lived here in the outside world, where no one was going to take care of him but himself.

He nodded and reached for my hands, pulling me from the floor.

"C'mon. I told you, we got this."

Our shopping trip was brief, but somehow Porter made it fun by cracking jokes about the different products lining the shelves. For just a moment, I allowed myself to imagine that we were a married couple running a simple errand together on a Wednesday evening.

That thought warmed me. It warmed me like no other thought had before it.

"What's that for?" Porter asked when, without even thinking about it, I reached for Lehi's favorite shade of crimson lipstick and placed it into our basket. "You can't wear that."

I didn't reply but simply scratched it from the list, moving on to the mascara and eyeliner.

"What the fuck, Brin?"

Porter's voice was low but intense. He didn't understand, and I didn't have the heart to tell him what Lehi required in the bedroom. When I turned to face him, I begged him with my eyes. Begged him not to push me.

"Oh wow." Porter raised both his arms above his head, locking them behind his neck as he walked several paces away from me. I could hear him inhale and exhale loudly as he walked. He turned and stormed back to stand just inches from me, his teeth clenched. He grabbed the lipstick and held it in front of him like it was somehow toxic. "Are you kidding me right now?"

I shook my head and stared at the floor. He gripped my chin and raised it so I was forced to look at him.

"Do you like wearing this stuff? For him?"

"No!" I yelled, then covered my mouth in shame. Several customers glanced our way and Porter took a few steps back, his hands held up in front of him in that universal gesture that said *I'm not a threat.*

An older woman with flaming red hair and brown tortoise-shell glasses narrowed her eyes at Porter, then focused her attention on me. "Are you okay, honey?"

I knew what she was thinking. Occasionally women of our faith were taunted by men when we came into town, which was why I'd avoided ever being out this late.

"I'm fine, yes. He's my friend."

"Are you sure?" She took a few steps toward me, eyeing Porter with suspicion.

"Y-yes, thank you." I turned my attention to Porter and grabbed his hand. "We should be going."

Porter was silent at the register until the cashier gave me the total, then he retrieved his wallet and paid the bill. When I opened my mouth to protest, he simply said, "Keep it. Don't tell them. Just keep it. Besides, I owe you, don't I?" He winked, referring to the twenty-five dollars that had been in my purse the day it was stolen.

I thanked him and nodded, appreciating the gesture. I'd never had my own money before. And now I had twenty-eight dollars. Money of my own opened up thoughts that had never occurred to me, ultimately leading to independence and a life outside the compound. With that simple gesture, Porter had shown me that it was, indeed possible. My stomach filled with excitement and butterflies.

Oh yes. Resistance was becoming much easier.

As promised, Porter and I parted ways a block from the compound. He pulled me behind a massive tree to say our good-byes, and apologized for assuming that I enjoyed wearing makeup for Lehi.

"It kills me, Brin. I can't stand the thought of him dressing you up like some sort of doll."

"I know," I whispered.

"I would never do that to you. Ever."

"I know."

"I mean it. When you're with me, I want you—no one else. Just you."

"You barely know me," I whispered without thinking it through.

I was finding my voice. Instead of questioning every little statement to leave my lips the way I was forced to in the Cluff household, Porter made me comfortable enough to speak from the heart. With him, I didn't feel the need to wrap my words in pretense or correctness. I was just . . . me.

"But I want to. I want to know everything there is to know about you, the real you. Not the fake mold they've placed you in. The real Brinley. The one who matters."

He pressed his forehead to mine and wrapped his hands around the back of my neck, pulling me as close as possible. My lips curled into the most satisfied smile of my life as I replayed his words in my head again and again.

Unable to deny my own desire, I allowed him in, loving the feel of him, realizing how much I'd missed and craved his touch. I ran my fingers through Porter's sandy-colored hair as he ran his hands down my back, then squeezed my bottom, making me gasp.

"God, I've missed you," he said between kisses.

"Me too," I whispered, knowing I could no longer deny the attraction I felt for this complicated man. A man who scared me and excited me. A man who could render me speechless one moment and cause me to yell the next.

"Stop fighting this. Stop hurting yourself. Promise me." He kissed my chin, my cheeks, my neck.

"I want to, but I don't know how," I whispered, soothed by the feel of his lips against my skin. "I don't know how."

"Let me teach you," he murmured between kisses. "Please, please let me."

When the sun had set completely, I forced myself to pull my lips from Porter's. With gentle fingers, he smoothed down my disheveled hair, tucking unruly strands back into my braid. When he finished, his face softened and he reached down to touch my wrist with his fingertips. He lifted my hand to his lips and kissed my injured wrist.

Since his eyes were no longer crazed, his lips gentle and compassionate, I knew the drugs were leaving his system. The real Porter was showing through the harsh exterior I'd encountered earlier.

The scary thing was, I was drawn to both sides of this man.

When he was gentle, I was overwhelmed with amazement and wonder. He soothed me, and when I was with him, hope expanded within me. But his forceful nature, his passionate exasperation aroused something inside me, something intoxicating. Something that drew out the resistance in me. And I craved the fire that he created between us, the fire he lit inside me.

I closed my eyes and nodded. I couldn't lie to him, and didn't want to avoid him any longer.

With one last kiss and promises to see each other again, I was on my way back home. Feeling hopeful rather than afraid. Feeling resistant rather than complacent. Feeling empowered rather than imprisoned.

When I got home, the family was gathering in the kitchen and dining areas for dinner. My sister wives were fussing over their children, spoon-feeding their babies and doling out responsibilities to the older children. Lehi was, as usual, reading the church bulletin rather than paying attention to his family.

The only eyes that focused on me when I entered the room and dropped the plastic bags on the counter were Rebecca's. They were narrowed and angry. I had to look away; her stare made me uncomfortable. Quickly, I scurried to my bedroom.

I was placing my purse in the shoebox in my closet when my door opened.

"Where have you been?" Rebecca asked. Her voice was loud and I cringed, not wanting her to draw attention from Lehi or the other wives.

I stood to face her and squared my shoulders. "I was running errands. Leandra gave me a rather long list. Everything's in the kitchen."

"You went to see him, didn't you?"

Oh no. Oh no. Oh no.

Rebecca's lips pressed together in a tight line as she awaited my answer.

"I . . . we . . . he . . ." My voice trailed off.

Deep down, I knew I couldn't trust Rebecca to keep my secret if she knew I'd gone to see Porter. She studied my face with narrowed eyes as if she were holding an invisible magnifying glass. Would she notice my lips, still swollen from stolen kisses? Would she see the redness in my eyes?

"Why can't you just leave it alone? What's done is done." Rebecca's voice was demanding, but her words confused me.

What is she talking about?

She stepped toward me, her jaw tight, her eyes flashing with anger.

"I don't know what you're talking ab—"

"Enough," she shrieked, throwing her arms into the air. "Do you think I'm stupid? I saw you two together with my own two eyes, Brinley!"

Of course she did. She was with me when I first visited Porter's apartment. She wasn't making any sense at all.

"Yes . . ." I said slowly, hoping she'd explain herself further.

"Oh, I see." She let out a little huff and crossed her arms. "Leandra *was* right about you."

My heart squeezed at those words. "What do you mean?"

"You're a bad seed. I didn't want to believe her, but it's true."

I shook my head violently. "*No*, you're wrong. Dead wrong."

"I don't think so." Rebecca walked to the door and wrapped her fingers around the knob. "Stop seeing him."

"You don't know what you're talking about." The lie left my lips so easily.

"I'm smarter than you think I am." And with that parting shot she left my room, closing the door behind her.

Devastated, I collapsed onto the bed and wept into my pillow, muffling my howls by cramming the fabric into my mouth. But despite the sadness I felt at the loss of Rebecca's friendship, anger and resentment brewed within me.

I was changing.

My thoughts, my desires, my ideals—all were altered by each contact I had with Porter. I was tired of resisting the effect he was having on me. I was tired of resisting feeling like an actual person, rather than just a cog in a wheel.

Rebecca was satisfied with being a cog.

But I wasn't. Not anymore.

chapter 14

"BRINLEY." ASPEN POPPED her head into my room. "Family meeting in ten minutes. Get yourself together."

"All right."

Forcing myself out of my warm bed, I wiped the sleep from my eyes, dreading our weekly Saturday morning check-in with Lehi and all the sister wives. Leandra didn't hesitate to monopolize each meeting with complaints, demands disguised as requests, and demonstrations of her control over the household. The rest of us spent the hour keeping sweet, nodding along and accepting any requests made of us.

All seven of the other wives were seated at the table with Lehi when I joined them. Leandra scowled at me, her arms crossed in front of her. Rebecca's words from a few nights ago echoed through my mind.

Leandra was right about you. You're a bad seed.

Deliberately I averted my gaze, unable to look Leandra in the eye knowing she thought so little of me. I'd never done anything to intentionally cause problems for her or any of my sister wives, and I resented her animosity toward me.

"Now that we're *all* here," she began, shooting a nasty look in my direction, "Brenda has some unfortunate news."

Brenda was Lehi's third wife, and the most private of the wives. She didn't socialize with many of us, preferring to keep her interaction to a minimum. She was, however, an extraordinary mother who treated her four daughters with love and kindness.

"My mother passed away last night," Brenda said softly. "My daughters and I will be with my family for the remainder of the weekend. If someone would please—" She choked on her words as her emotions overcame her, then sat up a little straighter. "I'd appreciate it if someone would complete my daily tasks today."

I spoke up. "I'll help you, Brenda. What can I do?"

Relief eased the wrinkles on her pained face. "Thank you. I, um, I have a list." She reached across the table and slid a small tablet of paper my way. When I read the list, my stomach dropped in disappointment. With her chores on top of mine, there was no way I'd be able to sneak away to see Porter.

"I'm so sorry for your loss," I said. The other wives nodded, but none of them expressed their condolences to Brenda. A chill ran down my spine. She was our sister wife; weren't we supposed to support her in times like this? And what about her husband? Shouldn't Lehi join her this weekend, to support her through this difficult time?

My thoughts focused on Brenda as the meeting continued. Leandra recited a list of complaints she'd compiled throughout the week. Gloria's children had been too loud. Aspen's sons had broken a vase that belonged to her mother. The carpet in the common area was in need of deep cleaning, etc.

Finally Leandra was ready to wrap things up. "Lehi would like to conclude our meeting this week. Dear?"

"Yes." He cleared his throat. "Thank you. There are a few things I need to cover and then I'll let you go about your day. First, a great honor has been bestowed upon our family. Brinley?"

I lifted my gaze quickly to meet his. An honor? What was he talking about?

"The prophet's mother is ill, and she's in need of a caregiver. The prophet has asked for you, specifically, to care for his mother."

Caregiver? For the prophet's mother? What did I know about caregiving?

My mind raced as I stammered, "Well, I—um—"

Lehi cut me off with a dismissive wave of his hand. "She is aging rapidly and is becoming quite senile. She'll need you to assist her with basic tasks. She sleeps quite a bit, so you can spend time cleaning or running errands for her."

"Errands?" I asked, seeing the possible silver lining of the situation.

"Yes. The prophet keeps her home well stocked, of course. But occasionally she may run out of toiletries or milk, and you can make a quick trip. Do you feel you can accept this honor?"

"I'm sorry to interject," Ida interrupted. "But may I ask why Brinley has been chosen for this honor? She has no children, or any background in caregiving—"

Ida was the fourth wife of Lehi. She was in her early thirties and had given up a job in caring for elderly adults in the community when she gave birth to her third child, and Leandra informed her that she was needed at home. The other wives were not willing to care for her children while she worked outside the home. According to Aspen, she'd been bitter ever since.

Ida and Aspen were not at all fond of each other. Their personalities were similar: strong, opinionated, and devout. Ida, like Gloria, was devoted to her quest to please Leandra and Lehi at all times, which Aspen despised. Aspen was devoted to Heavenly Father, but she would not compromise herself for anyone. She refused to brownnose anyone in our household.

"We are not to question the prophet's will," Lehi snapped, his eyes boring into Ida's. "He knows best. He specifically requested Brinley."

Ida quickly dropped her gaze as her cheeks reddened. Aspen snickered quietly under her breath, and both Ida and Gloria whipped their heads up, glowering at Aspen.

"Besides," Lehi said, "Brinley does not have children . . . yet. So this makes the most sense for our family."

"It would be an honor, Lehi," I said, attempting to calm the energy at the table.

Although I wanted to snicker right along with Aspen, it wouldn't be smart to ruffle any feathers. Rebecca was already angry with me, and I couldn't afford to earn any more enemies in the household. Ida and I had always managed to stay friendly despite our separate allegiances in the house.

"Very good," Lehi said. "The prophet expects you to begin on Wednesday. I'll have the address for you and will walk you there that morning."

"Thank you."

He nodded, and I knew he was relieved that the tension was abating. "Next order of business. Rebecca, dear?"

Rebecca responded with a soft smile aimed at our husband. My stomach climbed into my throat. Would she tell my secrets? Embarrass me in front of Lehi and the sister wives?

"Would you like to tell them, or should I?" Lehi continued. Rebecca shook her head, her smile transforming into a look of discomfort.

What on earth?

"Very well, then." Lehi sat up straight in his seat. "Rebecca is expecting. We're having our first child together."

All of my sister wives, Leandra included, proceeded to celebrate this news. Congratulations were given. Her due date was discussed, and offers of assistance with chores and her children were offered by several of the sister wives.

But me? I cried.

My tears were silent as they slid down my cheeks. As the rest of the family marveled at this news, I was crushed. And I knew Burt would be too. Rebecca had officially moved on, given up on the love she'd shared with her first husband. I wiped the tears from my cheeks and watched her as she gracefully accepted the well wishes and hugs from our sister wives. I wanted to stand up, pound my fist on the table, and shout, "No!" But I couldn't. Instead, I remained silent, watching . . . just watching.

Aspen glanced my way, giving me a look of pity. She must have assumed my tears were for myself, for my supposed infertility. I glanced away quickly, playing the part, feeling terrible for lying without saying anything at all.

When I turned, Rebecca's eyes met mine and her smile disappeared, her lips pressing together so tightly the skin above them turned white. The warmth in her eyes froze to form daggers meant only for me.

The woman who had sobbed in my arms was no longer my sister, no longer my friend.

She was my enemy.

And it broke my heart.

After hours of completing my own chores around the house—laundry, yard work, and assisting Clea, Lehi's fifth wife, in the kitchen for lunch—I was ready to retire to my room to rest when I remembered the list from Brenda. Taking a deep breath, I mentally prepared for a few more chores.

I swept the garage, organized the toys in the common area, and ironed her daughters' cotton dresses. When I brought them to the girls' rooms, I sighed. Their normally tidy rooms were destroyed, whether by their own doing or by the hyper boys who were playing hide-and-seek earlier in the house. Whatever the reason, I didn't want Brenda to come home to this mess. I rolled up my sleeves and made their beds, straightened their desks, and emptied their garbage cans.

Before finishing, I returned to the garage, retrieved a simple glass vase from the shelf, and walked to our backyard where a small patch of flowers grew. I picked several flowers, added water to the vase, and took them to Brenda's room. The bright flowers brightened the somber air of her bedroom, and I knew they would make her smile. I contemplated leaving a note, but decided against it. It wasn't important for her to know who left the flowers, only that someone had remembered her.

Grateful that this evening was not to be shared with Lehi, I retreated to my room and flopped on my bed, staring out at the sun as it slowly disappeared behind the mountains in the distance.

My eyelids were fluttering, my body exhausted from the day, when I heard my name. Rising up on my elbow, I stared out my open window, wondering if my brain was playing tricks on me.

"Brin," came the voice again, this time slightly louder and higher in pitch.

Porter.

As I hopped up from the bed, adrenaline coursed through my veins. Porter, a sly grin on his face, was standing beneath my window, a baseball cap on his head, hiding his face. But I'd know that smile anywhere. His blond hair poked out from beneath the cap.

“What are you doing here?” I whispered down to him, fighting the smile that crept across my face.

“I had to see you. Can I come up?”

“No!” I screeched, then lowered my voice. “Of course not!”

“C’mon, Brin. Relax, I can do it. It’s easy.”

Paranoia took my brain hostage and I glanced left and right, looking for anyone who might see us. But Porter was hidden behind the large wall of our property. Lehi was spending the evening with Leandra, and I was certain she was keeping him busy with her complaints.

I had missed Porter. Terribly. Not just his touch but his humor, his kindness, the way he understood everything I was going through.

“Okay, fine,” I called out softly. “But be careful.”

Porter rolled up his sleeves and climbed the tree that grew just a few feet from the side of the house. I watched him in awe, wondering where he’d learned to climb like that; he made it look easy.

“Move out of the way, I have to jump the rest of the way,” he said, clutching the branch that reached as close to the house as he was going to get. Within seconds, Porter leaped from the branch and landed with a grunt on the windowsill. I reached out to grab his hand and pulled him into my room. We sat on the floor, beneath the window, and he placed his hand in mine.

“So, this is where you sleep?” He waggled his eyebrows at me.

All at once, I felt naked, as exposed as the day I was born. If I had known he’d see my room, I would have cleaned it until it was spotless. As it was, my closet door stood open and two pairs of sneakers sat on my carpet.

"Yeah," I replied with a shrug.

"It's nice." He stood and walked around the room, perusing the pictures on the walls and the trinkets on my desk that had been made by Aspen's children.

"You shouldn't be here."

"I know, but I couldn't wait."

He walked back to me and smoothed down the hair of my braid before planting a gentle kiss on my lips.

"You're terribly impatient, aren't you?" I narrowed my eyes as he pulled me in for a tight hug.

So this was what flirting was like. It was fun, and I liked it. It was easy to flirt, I realized, when I felt comfortable and didn't need to censor myself.

"Guilty," he said, raising his arms in surrender. "I can't help it. I miss your face, your smile, your voice. God, I love your voice."

"You do?"

"Mm-hmm." He nodded, kissing me gently on the neck. "It's gentle and melodic, like you."

"You think I'm melodic?"

"Yep." He removed his baseball cap and ran his fingers through his hair. "I hate not knowing when I'll see you again, it's torture. Pure torture."

"I don't think there's anything we can do about that. I mean . . ." I paused when Porter's smile turned into a devilish smirk. "What? Why are you looking at me like that?"

"I think I have a solution. I have something for you." He reached into his back pocket and removed a small phone.

Lehi didn't allow phones in his household, but some husbands did, so I'd grown up used to seeing women walking along our dirt roads, talking on their phones.

"We can text each other," he went on, "figure out when to meet, stuff like that. I already programmed my number in."

"But I-I've never used a phone before."

"It's easy, I'll show you."

A creaking sound came from the hallway and I froze, paralyzed with fear that someone may have heard us.

I pushed Porter down to the floor behind the bed while I crossed the room to check. As I stood with my ear pressed against the door, I could hear nothing but the pounding of my heart. Porter had to go. He was risking too much by being there with me.

A moment passed and no other sounds came from the hall. I tiptoed back around the bed, only to find the room empty. Porter was gone. I sighed and plopped dejectedly on my bed, wishing I had been able to say good-bye.

My heart nearly leaped into my mouth when a hand grasped one of my hanging ankles. In a split second, I was on my knees, staring at Porter who was laughing under the bed, covering his mouth to muffle the noise. I swatted him on the chest as he scooted out from underneath my bed.

"Sorry," he whispered, holding back laughter. "But that was hilarious."

I couldn't help but chuckle. "Fine, I guess it was."

Porter pushed my boundaries, and I loved that. I loved the way he viewed the world. He was playful, yet smart. He had a rough exterior, yet a considerate heart.

"Come here." He stroked the collar of my dress, tugging at it slightly, pulling me down so that my chest was pressed to his. He nipped gently at my bottom lip, then took it into his mouth, and my eyes widened at the unfamiliar, but enticing, sensation. He released his hold on my lip, allowing himself to smile in satisfaction. His hand traveled down my back and landed on my bottom, where he squeezed, and I wriggled with pleasure.

A familiar pulsing in my private area returned and I knew that if he didn't leave soon, our clothing could soon be shed, and we'd be committing adultery in the house of Lehi Cluff.

I couldn't do that. Not there, not in Lehi's home. I just couldn't.

"But you have to go, Porter. We can't—we can't do this here. Someone could catch us. And I can't risk that."

"All right." He groaned. "Fine. I'll go. But first, let me show you, okay?" He reached into his other pocket and retrieved another phone, dialing a number. The phone in my hand buzzed and I flipped it open.

"What do I do?"

"See that? It says *new text.* Just press this button." He pointed at a small button that was labeled ENTER. When I pressed it, a message popped up on the screen.

P: Cool, huh?

I giggled behind my hand. "Yes, very cool."

"That's all you have to do." He wrapped his arm around me and pulled me closer. "And if you want to text me, you press ENTER on the last text I sent, then just type with the keyboard."

"The letters are so tiny."

"You'll get used to it." He laughed. "I don't have a charger for you. But I will. And you should be good for a while. I charged it before I came here."

"Thank you." Delighted at his gift, I gathered my courage and lifted my hand, allowing my fingers to trail down the side of his face. His skin was so warm, and a little thrill shot through me.

He took my hand in his and kissed it. "I should go." He reached for the phone and pointed to a red button and then a green. "This button turns it off, this one turns it back on. Simple enough, right?"

"All right."

"I'll miss you." He placed a chaste kiss on my lips and squeezed my hand.

"I'll miss you too."

"Hide that." He pointed at the phone. "Right away, okay?"

"I will, I promise."

Porter sat on the edge of my windowsill, placed his baseball cap back on his head, and hoisted himself onto the nearest branch. His body hung for a moment before he gained the momentum to fling himself onto the tree.

Relieved that he would make it down without injury, I closed my window and scurried to my closet. I flung open the shoe box and retrieved my purse. My heart racing, I tucked the phone in its secret compartment, right next to my birth control pills.

My secrets were mounting. And as nervous as I was, I didn't care. Not enough to stop.

He'd given me a way to contact him whenever I wanted to, whenever I needed to.

That little phone gave me a feeling of control that I hadn't had in twenty-two long years.

The thought of it made my nerves calm, made my mind wander, and made my heart dance.

chapter 15

EVERY SPARE MINUTE I had was spent pushing the little plastic keys of the phone Porter gave me. Porter called it texting, but I called it freedom. Even if it was only the tiniest of slivers, it felt glorious. Each morning when I awoke, I ran to my closet, turned on the phone, and read the latest message from Porter.

This morning, however, I couldn't enjoy my new morning ritual.

Lehi was in my bed, fast asleep and snoring, his nose whistling with each exhale.

The defiant part of me wanted to tiptoe across my small room, open the closet door, and crouch down to read my latest text. But smart and cautious Brinley won that fight. I had to be patient. Soon Lehi's alarm clock would chime and rattle him awake. He'd be out the door without even saying good morning.

Despite the fact that Lehi slept in each of the wives' bedrooms, all his personal belongings were kept in Leandra's large walk-in closet. Since we shared one large residence, there was no need for him to leave fresh clothing or toiletries in each wife's bedroom—all he had to do was walk down the hall and Leandra would provide him with whatever he needed to start his day.

Aspen was convinced it was Leandra's determination to maintain control that kept Lehi in this routine. Her cryptic words alluded to some great secret kept between Lehi and his first wife. When I became curious, when I pressed her for more information, a wicked curl of a smile appeared on

Aspen's lips and she'd simply said, "Don't worry about it. But I'm on to him."

On to him? She had me intrigued. Did Lehi have secrets? Of course he did; didn't we all?

I, myself, was relieved that he didn't take up any sort of residence in my space. It kept my secrets where they belonged—hidden from his domineering eyes.

Ding dong. Ding dong.

Lehi groaned, then swung his arm like a pendulum to slap the sound from the clock. I stayed quiet as he sat up.

"Wake up." He yawned. "Today's the day. Jorjina is expecting you, as is the prophet."

Jorjina Black was the mother of our prophet. Before that day, I knew next to nothing about her. When I was younger, she would parade through our compound, her nose pushed up toward the clouds. She was our royalty, the queen who bore the prophet, blessing us with his guidance and wisdom in our time on this earth.

But as she aged, we saw less of Jorjina—and most of us forgot about her. I, however, was about to become more than reacquainted with the woman. I was chosen to care for her and would do so to the best of my ability.

"We'll leave in one hour. Can you be ready by then?" Lehi ran his fingers through his disheveled morning hair, turning to look me in the eye. I could smell the foul odor of his breath when he turned my way to speak. Desperately trying to be inconspicuous, I held my breath and nodded, biting my bottom lip.

"All right then." He stood, stretched his arms toward the ceiling, and left the room.

Exhaling a large blast of air, I ran to my closet and turned on the phone, thrilled to see a couple of texts from Porter.

P: I hope today goes okay. Be strong, they can smell fear. ;) I miss you like crazy.

P: Oh, and flip off the prophet for me. I hate that asshole.

A giggle left my mouth as I texted back.

B: What does flip off mean?

I rose to my feet and stood with my back to the wall as I stared down at the small screen, hoping I'd get a response. I didn't have much time to wait as I needed to bathe and prepare myself for Jorjina Black's company.

P: I have so much to teach you, Brin.

I rolled my eyes, but a smile bloomed on my face. He was right; he had a lot to teach me. And the more we talked, texted, and saw each other, the more willing I became. With each passing day, it was getting easier to imagine myself in the outside world . . . no long hair, no braid, no long dresses with long underwear beneath.

Freedom.

Could I do it? I wasn't sure.

But I was warming up to the idea. The voice in my head had started out as disjointed whispers, so unconnected that they didn't make any sense. But those whispers were coming together, becoming more cohesive, clearer and louder in my head than ever before.

From a whisper to a scream.

I was waiting for the scream.

Dust collected on my already dirty sneakers as Lehi and I walked to the new home that had been constructed for Jorjina Black.

"Remember what an honor this is," he told me.

"I will."

"At *all times*," he said pointedly.

I nodded my head in submission, focusing on the dust covering my shoes.

"The prophet will give you specific instructions. You must obey them, no matter what."

I frowned in confusion. Of all of Lehi's wives, I knew I was one of the more submissive women in our home. What would make him think I would disobey any directions given to me by Jorjina or the prophet?

As I pondered the meaning behind Lehi's words, I almost missed the eyes on me.

Almost.

Burt Jameson stood on the porch of the house he and his crew were constructing. He clutched the railing, his knuckles white as he stared in our direction, a pained expression on his unshaven face. New creases in his forehead and bracketing his mouth telegraphed his sorrow and despair. He wasn't far away but I couldn't acknowledge him, no matter how much I wanted to ease his pain, to beg him to move on as Rebecca clearly had with her new husband.

But I couldn't.

When we approached his building site, Lehi pushed his shoulders back and stiffened. From the corner of my eye, I could see Lehi deliberately lift his chin. And for the first time in three years, he took my hand in his, and turned his head toward Burt. Burt's mouth opened in response, then he turned away, walking back to his crew and his work.

My throat turned dry as I stared at Lehi's clammy hand clutching my fingers, and I wondered what he knew. Was he simply reminding Burt of his control over his wives? Or was there more to that display of possession?

Lehi maintained his grasp on my hand even as we approached Jorjina's grandiose home in the center of the compound. The prophet had spared no expense on the residence of his mother. Lush gardens surrounded the thin brick walkway that led to the elegant French doors on the front porch. I'd never seen a home with such a fancy entryway. Apparently, when your son was the prophet, you could have whatever you liked.

A young man scrubbed at the beveled glass of the doors, making them shine. I couldn't help but wonder how he had come to deserve the honor of scrubbing Jorjina's windows. Cynical thoughts such as these were popping up more and more.

The whispers were growing louder.

"Good morning, Elder Cluff," he said, bowing his head slightly and stepping back to give us access to the doorbell. Lehi didn't respond to the boy, he simply cleared his throat and pressed his finger to the button.

The prophet opened the door and met us with an expressionless face. He looked older since I had seen him last—wrinkles had formed at the creases of his dark eyes, and his hair seemed thinner. He was not a tall man; in fact, Lehi towered over him in height.

Yet the prophet's willowy frame belied the power he carried in our community. The irony of his appearance was not lost on me.

Since marrying Lehi, my interactions with the prophet had been limited. I was accustomed to hearing his sermons each morning over the loudspeakers, but it had been quite some time since he'd visited the Cluff household. And I suspected Lehi preferred it that way. Visits from the prophet usually meant trouble for a man or his wives.

Like Burt and Rebecca.

The prophet didn't smile, but greeted us from the door. His voice was a soft monotone, lacking emotion. "Welcome. Mother has been expecting you."

"Thank you for this honor," Lehi said, tipping his head slowly to the prophet in deference.

The prophet watched as Lehi finished the gesture. The way he stared at Lehi made me shift with discomfort; it was a look of entitlement, of expectation, and it made goose bumps rise beneath the fabric of my sleeves. Yes, I knew that our prophet was God placed on earth. I knew he owned our people, that he was our direct link to Heavenly Father and to heaven, but still something stirred in my belly that unsettled me.

The prophet took Lehi's outstretched hand and silently studied his eyes. When the prophet shook a person's hand, he could see their spirit. He knew if they'd sinned. He knew if there was light, or darkness, in their eyes. That was what my mother had always told me, anyway, and I'd believed.

I clasped my hands together in dread. Secretly, I hoped he wouldn't touch my hand. If the prophet knew my sins—what I'd done, the thoughts I'd had about our faith, our community, our way of life—I'd most certainly become an apostate. My disobedience against the prophet and his teachings would give me the title worse than death. I'd be sent away, like Porter, never to return. I'd never see my mother or my sisters, Jessa and Winnie.

"Brinley, you look well." The prophet's eyes devoured me, starting at the top of my coifed hair and skimming across the subtle rise of my breasts beneath my dress, inspecting me all the way down to my sneaker-covered feet. The goosebumps on my skin remained raised at attention.

Keep sweet, keep sweet, keep sweet.

Knowing I needed to respond, I murmured, "Thank you."

His hand reached for mine and my breath caught. I forced a smile for him and my hand went limp, squeezed between the fingers of the prophet. He paused, hesitating, his hand still gripping mine as he peered into my eyes, tilting his head to the side ever so slightly.

What does he see?

"As I'm sure you know," he murmured as he dropped my hand, turning to walk down a long hallway filled with photos of himself, "my mother is ill. She's having trouble knowing what is real and what is not. My father passed away years ago, and she's remained faithful to his memory. But this means she is alone, and I cannot be here with her. The people need me."

"Yes, of course," Lehi replied. The prophet shot a glance at Lehi, then brought his attention back to me.

"I will need you to care for her each day, and make sure she doesn't wander into the outside world. Last week she was discovered in town sitting beneath a tree, singing to herself. We'd searched the compound for hours, but were unable to find her. She gave me quite the fright." Despite the emotion laden in his words, the prophet's expression remained blank as he spoke of his mother going missing.

"She sleeps quite a bit, but will need reminders to eat and to use the bathroom. I'll need you to cook her breakfast and dinner. She sleeps through lunchtime. I'll provide groceries and necessities for her and will have them delivered every week."

I nodded as he listed several other chores needed in the household, then he paused when we heard the creaking of the stairs. A tiny woman, no taller than five feet, appeared at the bottom of the stairs. Her eyes were heavy from sleep, her gray hair tousled but still styled in the expected braid. She walked slowly to the kitchen where we stood.

"Get out," she snapped, glowering at me. I flinched, not expecting that reaction from her.

"Mother, enough." The prophet's voice raised slightly, but I assumed it was only to assist her in hearing him.

"I'm fully capable of taking care of myself, Clarence," she snapped, and the prophet seemed to cringe at hearing his name.

I'd never known the prophet's first name. To me, he'd only been known as "the prophet."

"I raised nine boys, I don't need a nursemaid." She brushed past me and retrieved a glass from the cabinet. Her fingers barely reached the cabinet's knob when she raised onto the tips of her toes to choose a glass. She filled it with water at the tap and stood, staring out the window above her sink. "Besides, the last one you brought here was deplorable. Absolutely deplorable. Head completely in the clouds. And she burned my eggs. What proper wife doesn't know how to fry a simple egg?"

There had been others?

Quickly, I glanced at Lehi, wondering why that hadn't been mentioned. I was under the impression that Jorjina Black's need for a caregiver was a new one. I hadn't realized this was a merry-go-round that she and her son were starting and stopping, each time opening a spot for a new rider. I envisioned the prophet welcoming the rider as Jorjina attempted to push them off the ride once it began. Could I withstand her push? Was I being tested?

When I heard my name leave the prophet's lips, I snapped back to attention.

"She'll be here with you each day. She'll cook and clean and help you with anything you may need."

"Yes, I know how this goes, son." His mother didn't bother to turn her body or her eyes to the prophet. She sipped her water and stared out the window.

The prophet looked to me, his eyebrows raised with expectation.

Nervously I cleared my throat, then said, "Mrs. Black, I'm happy to be here," to which she merely grunted in response.

The brave part of me made the decision to join her at the sink. Without a word I helped myself to a glass, filled it with water, and stood next to the frail woman. She recoiled slightly when my arm brushed hers, and I took a small step away to give her the space she required.

But then I took a sip of my water and looked out the window to see two small birds sitting on a branch just outside the kitchen. I smiled when I realized that Jorjina was simply studying them, watching them as they chirped and took tiny hops across the branch. Perhaps I wasn't the only one so fascinated by these creatures. Creatures who, to me, represented freedom in all its glory.

Perhaps we both yearned to fly free.

After a moment watching the birds, her face softened. Mrs. Black turned to me and her lips pulled into a half smile.

"You can stay."

Those three words gave me the acceptance I craved in that moment. I'd been given this honor, and intended to fulfill all the expectations that were placed on me.

"Can you cook eggs?"

I scanned her face, noting she looked tired. The woman had to be at least eighty-five years old. She seemed frail and shrunken, with liver spots prominent on the pale skin of her hands. My heart reached out to her as I wondered what lay beneath that question, so I spoke with confidence, willing Jorjina Black to give me a chance.

"Yes, ma'am. They're one of my specialties."

"Good." She took another sip of water. "I miss eggs."

Her tone made me smile. The frankness in this woman's speech made her different from the other women in our community. I sensed resistance from her in complete opposition to the submission that was expected from women of our faith. But she was the prophet's mother, and with that came privileges the rest of us couldn't even begin to comprehend. Jorjina Black didn't need to keep sweet. She didn't need to keep herself composed or well-mannered. And there was a freedom to that.

She'd lived her life. She'd raised her sons. She'd raised our prophet. She had no need to seek anyone's approval or opinion.

I wasn't looking for a new mother figure or even a friend. I just wanted to do my job, and do it well. Little did I know that this tiny woman would quickly become one of the most important people in my life.

chapter 16

JORJINA BLACK WAS not what I had expected. I'd spent two weeks assisting her in her home, and each day she managed to surprise me in some way. Her favorite food was chocolate cake. On my first day, after Lehi and the prophet had left us alone, she told me that she expected to have chocolate cake in the house at all times.

"Deep, dark chocolate," she said with a sparkle in her eye. "Don't skimp."

I'd never heard that term before, and had to ask her to explain it to me. She shook her head, then looked at the kitchen floor and back at me before explaining the term.

She believed in the power of exercise, insisting that we take walks each day to "cleanse our minds." So each morning, after I fixed her breakfast—which usually consisted of eggs and/or chocolate cake and a large glass of milk—we walked several blocks to the open field where children came together to play. We'd take a short rest on the green park bench, and she'd pontificate on the importance of family, the blessings of Heavenly Father, and the relevance of polygamy in the modern world.

I'd nod along, listening intently, hoping for some sort of light bulb to glow above my head, and pull me away from the rising voice that echoed inside: *Porter, Porter, Porter.*

But that didn't happen.

And after several trips to the park, I started to notice that the Jorjina who spoke in the light of day was a different woman from the Jorjina within the confines of her home. In her house, she was a different woman; she didn't discuss polygamy, our community, or even Heavenly Father. Instead, our discussions focused on the home. She enjoyed sharing her secret family potluck recipes: casseroles, Hawaiian haystacks, and frog-eye salad. She relished telling me about unexpected ingredients that made her dishes tastier than the standard recipes found in our community.

"You serve it like this, and that husband of yours will be wrapped around your pinkie," she joked while placing her latest casserole in the oven. When I didn't reply, she looked up at me sharply.

"Interesting," she said with one eyebrow raised, her lips pressed together tightly.

"I . . . I . . ." I stammered as I cast about, trying to figure out what to say.

"Anyway . . ." She enunciated each syllable dramatically, then tossed the oven mitts on the counter before straightening her collar and giving me a wink. "Let's get started on another cake."

Jorjina was on to me.

She knew I wasn't in love with Lehi. But then again, there were dozens of wives in our community who weren't truly in love with their husbands. We all had our own reasons for wanting to please our spouse. For women like Leandra, it was power and control. For me, it was maintaining harmony and avoiding confrontation.

It was no great effort for me to shrug that off.

But the hints continued, the heavy-handed statements about love, marriage, and happiness. And I found myself questioning her motives. I wasn't sure if I could trust Jorjina. As much as I was enjoying her company, I had to remember that she was the mother of the prophet, and my secrets could not be trusted with her.

"I miss my husband every single minute," Jorjina said sadly. "He was a good man. There aren't many quite like him."

Her husband was the prophet when I was born. I was nine when the role of prophet had been passed on to his son after Jorjina's husband suffered a massive heart attack.

"Even after all these years?" I asked. I didn't doubt her love for the man she lost, but was surprised that she spoke of him as often as she did. He'd been gone for more than a decade.

"That's how you know it's true. When you think of him all the time, whether he's with you or he's not."

When Lehi wasn't with me, I wasn't affected. Before becoming involved with Porter, I'd craved my time with Lehi, but I didn't know why. Was I lonely? Confused?

With Porter in my life, I could never be lonely. When we couldn't be together, he found ways to communicate with me, to show me how much he thought of me. The way he treated me, felt for me, showed me his emotions was such a drastic shift from my experiences with my husband.

If I never saw Lehi again, I wouldn't be sad. In fact, I'd be relieved.

"You seem lost in thought," she said as she set the timer for the cake.

"A little bit."

"Sharing is hard. I speak from experience."

"It is." I nodded, but I was lying. I was never jealous of my sister wives. I didn't care enough to be bothered.

"Cherish that alone time, dear. It can be so special, and quite enjoyable, I might add."

Did she . . . did Jorjina Black just hint about the pleasures of intercourse?

My mouth fell open as I stared at her. Her gray hair threatened to pull from her braid as she pushed it from her forehead again and again, wiping the sweat from her skin. I had no idea how to respond, so I stood there gaping at her until she chuckled.

"When you're with the right man, it does wonders." She winked. "Oh, come on, dear, I may be old, but I'm certainly not dead. My husband was . . . *generous*, and we enjoyed our time together very much."

She giggled under her breath as she leaned against the counter, studying me. But I couldn't say a word. Lehi had never been "generous" with me, nor had I ever enjoyed my time with him.

But Porter was another story.

His kisses swept me away to another place, another time. I felt alive, revived from my complacent life. If his kisses did that to me, I could only imagine what laying with him would be like. My cheeks reddened at the thought. The temperature of the room rose in seconds, and I found myself wiping the sweat from my brow just as my employer had moments before.

Sex with Porter. Sex with Porter. Sex with Porter.

I couldn't shake the thought from my head.

I was ready, ready to explore the intensity that being truly intimate with another human being would bring. Like a fool I craved his touch, standing there in Jorjina's kitchen and wishing I could see him, touch him, and understand what both Rebecca and Jorjina had experienced with the men they loved.

When the cake was cooled, frosted, and placed under the glass dome of the cake stand on her counter, Jorjina turned to me and yawned.

"I'm going to lie down."

"Okay," I said, wiping the remaining crumbs from the counter into my hand. When I dropped the crumbs into the sink, I realized Jorjina hadn't moved, and turned to find her staring at me.

"Ma'am?"

"Would you stop calling me that? I told you to call me Jorjina."

"Sorry." I hung my head. "Is there something else I can do for you?"

"Go. Take a break. Leave me be."

"I can't do that, ma—Jorjina," I said and shook my head slowly.

"You're a young girl, go outside. Spend time with your friends."

"I don't have any friends."

"Well, perhaps it's time to fix that. Go." She crossed her arms in front of her chest.

Stunned, I opened my mouth but had no idea what to say. I felt like I was being tested, as if this were some sort of trick.

"I ca—"

"Don't tell me you can't. I'm giving you permission. Let me rest. I'm an old woman, I need my privacy whenever I can get it. Please, Brinley." Her eyes softened, and her eyebrows drew together in a plea.

"All right. I-I'll go home and come back in a little while?" Uncertain if I should leave, my suggestion came out as a question.

"Yes, I'll let you make me dinner." Her chin lifted upward in pride. "Now, go. Leave me be. I'm tired."

"Are you sure?" Leaving Jorjina alone like this was risky for me, so I couldn't help but fret, yet in the next second I wondered if Porter was on a job site.

Jorjina linked her arm through mine and ushered me to the front door. "Yes, now scoot."

When my shoes hit the heat of the pavement, my mind was already racing a mile per minute. I wanted to see Porter, but couldn't go home to retrieve my phone. If Leandra, or any of the wives, caught a glimpse of me, I could be in major trouble with Lehi and the prophet. No, if I was going to do this, if I was going to take advantage of the freedom Jorjina had afforded me, I had to be smart.

I would risk it. I'd go into town and attempt to see Porter.

My heart raced as I walked faster and faster to Porter's building. I climbed the steps two at a time to reach his door, then pounded on it with my fists as adrenaline made its way throughout my body.

I hadn't seen him since he'd climbed through my window, and I'd missed him terribly. I'd missed his voice, his lips, the feel of his skin against mine. Jorjina's words had reverberated inside my brain, permeating my thoughts and desires.

I wanted the moments she cherished in her memories.

I wanted to act on my lust, my passion, and feel it reciprocated.

I needed to be desired.

I needed Porter.

Not Lehi, Porter.

I hoped so badly that he'd be home. On most work days, he woke before the sun and was home shortly after lunch. I just hoped I'd catch him at his apartment.

Porter's eyes grew wide when he opened the door. Before he had a chance to greet me, I pounced, crushing my lips against his with urgency and need. He responded by wrapping his hand around my braid and pulling me close to him, then deepened the kiss immediately, his tongue stroking mine in delicious movements. My body was on fire as he tugged at my braid, forcing my head back so he could pepper my neck with kisses. I wrapped my arms around his back, clawing at his shirt, wishing I could remove it right there in the entryway of his apartment.

He pulled away long enough to say one word. "Bedroom."

Porter pulled me into the apartment, slamming and locking the door behind us before dragging me behind him to his room. We passed Charlie and a few other guys who sat on the couch, staring off into space, and for a moment I hesitated, worried that Porter might be high. But I didn't care. I wanted him, I needed him, and that was all that mattered. I wanted his skin on mine, his gravelly voice whispering into my ear, and the throbbing in my private area reminded me of my desire.

When he'd closed his door behind us, again locking the lock, he closed the space between us and ran a fingertip down my cheek. The sensation sent shivers up my spine—the kind of shivers you crave, that stir desire within you.

"Brin," he whispered. "I want you."

"Me too," I replied, my heart pounding.

I was no virgin, this was true. But with Porter, everything was different than with Lehi. With Lehi, our time in the marital bed was a duty to be fulfilled, a purposeful union between a man seeking to impregnate his obedient wife. But with Porter it was lust, pure desire that demanded to be released.

And I was ready to release it.

"I want to make you come." His fingers popped open the top buttons of my dress. "Will you let me?"

I had no words, but I wanted to know what he was talking about. I wanted to lose myself, to trust Porter with my body, with my soul.

The pressure of his lips scorched my neck as his fingers attacked the fastened buttons of my dress. Panting with anticipation, I could feel my panties growing damp. I didn't understand the sensation or meaning of moisture there; it had never happened before. But as the swelling of my private area escalated, I began to understand his words. That demand of release.

I wanted to come. And I wanted Porter to do it to me.

"Yes." My voice cracked and I looked up at the ceiling, lost in Porter's touch. "Please, make me forget him and his touch. I want to feel you, just you."

Porter cracked a satisfied smile as he walked me backward to his bed. "Lay down, Brin."

"Here?" I asked, confused. Lehi had always preferred the other side of the bed. The covers would form a cocoon over us as he attempted to impregnate me each week.

Porter nodded, placing one finger on my lips, urging me to stop speaking.

"Do you trust me?" he asked, his eyes narrowed as if he wasn't sure he knew the answer.

But I didn't hesitate. "I trust you more than anyone else. Anyone at all."

"Good." He smoothed down my hair before unfastening the remaining buttons of my dress. It fell to the floor, but the mandatory long underwear remained, covering my body completely.

Porter shook his head. "Such beauty, covered like this. It's a sacrilege."

Within seconds, the long underwear fell in a heap beside my cotton dress, and Porter urged me to lie flat on the bed. I reached for him, expecting him to lie above me. But he shook his head, instead kneeling on the floor, and wrapped his hands around my thighs. He tugged my body gently, pulled me closer to the edge of the bed, then removed my underpants.

My heart raced and I started to panic. I had no idea what he was doing. Or what he planned to do to me. "Porter, wha—"

"Shh," he said. "Just lie back. I told you I was going to make you come, Brin. Just relax and trust me, all right?"

I swallowed hard, lowering myself to lie flat on the bed, once again looking up at the ceiling of Porter's bedroom. His lips touched the inner skin of my thighs and I jumped slightly. The sensation tickled.

"Try to relax, Brin." His whisper was so soft, I almost didn't hear him.

I exhaled loudly, trying desperately to follow his directions. I didn't want to disappoint him, to make him think I didn't trust him.

What he did next was almost indescribable. He placed feathery kisses from my thighs all the way to my private area, where his tongue pressed into me, into the ache that had been building since he first touched me. Again and again he pressed his lips, his tongue, his mouth over me, and I writhed beneath him. My hands balled into fists, grasping the cotton sheets tightly as the ache continued to grow and build and expand. My body climbed higher and higher until the desire to burst became painful. My entire mind focused on the ache and his tongue and the burning desire—no, *need*—for him to go deeper.

"Don't stop. Please, Porter. Don't stop."

"Tell me," he murmured. "Tell me what you want, Brin."

"I-I can't . . ."

"Yes, you can. What do you want me to do?"

"Make . . ." I paused, embarrassed by the words. "Make me come, Porter. Please."

Porter matched my moans with his own, the pressure and intensity of his mouth on me increasing with my pleas. I wanted to see him, to see what he was doing. I lifted up on my elbows only to fall back to the bed, writhing with another surge of bliss. Until the climbing was no longer possible, until my body seemed to open, to explode over the precipice of absolute ecstasy. Porter continued to lick and stroke my sex as I thrashed beneath him, his hands holding my hips in place as I cried out in pleasure.

Oh. My. Word.

Porter's grip on me loosened and he returned his lips to the sensitive skin of my thighs. His kisses were gentle and his hands rubbed my scorching skin, urging me to return back to earth.

"What *was* that?"

"You came." He smiled. "You had an orgasm."

My breath was ragged and tears formed in my eyes. "I-I have no words. I . . . didn't know that was possible . . . to feel like that."

Porter rose to his feet and lay down beside me, stroking the stray hair from my eyes. "I know."

"How did you do that?" I asked, so curious, wanting to understand what he had done to me.

He threw his head back in laughter, returning his gaze to mine with a proud grin. "That was only the beginning, Brin. I want to make you feel everything. I want to worship you, your body, your heart."

A tear slipped down my cheek as my heart filled with his words.

"Will you let me?" he asked, his expression so earnest as his eyes glistened.

"Yes." I nodded. "I want you, Porter. More than you can imagine."

"Good." He glanced at his watch. "You never told me how you got here. Shouldn't you be taking care of Jorjina?"

"She asked me to leave her be for a while. I have a few hours to myself. I came as quickly as I could."

"Wow." He rolled over to look up at the ceiling.

I leaned up on my elbow and ran my fingers up and down his chest, exploring his muscles beneath the soft cotton of his T-shirt.

"Do you . . . want to lay with me now?"

I couldn't imagine that Porter wouldn't want a release similar to what I had experienced. Now I understood why Lehi had always collapsed onto my chest, groaning into my shoulder. But unlike Porter, Lehi had no intention of ever sharing that sensation. It was a secret he kept all to himself.

Porter stretched out his arm to stroke the bare skin of my back. "Not today. Today was about you."

"Are you sure?"

"You don't owe me anything, Brin. You know that, right? I'm not like him."

"I know."

"Do you?" His voice was sharp, doubtful.

"Yes. You're nothing like my husband."

Porter flinched at the word *husband.* I didn't say it to hurt him, but it was the reality. Lehi was my husband in the eyes of our Heavenly Father.

"Tell me something. Something about you. About why you left."

"Ugh." He groaned. "Now?"

"Please." I begged him with my eyes to humor me.

He rolled to his side, rising on his elbow, mirroring my position on the bed. "Okay, well . . . it was years ago. I'd gotten in trouble a few times. A few buddies and I were meeting up in the woods to drink beer, smoke weed. Shit like that. My parents found out, and so did the prophet."

"Oh."

"Yeah." He stared off into space. "Within a day, we were gone. All of us. My mom dropped me on the street downstairs with a hundred dollars and a suitcase filled with clothes."

"That must have been awful."

"Worst day of my life."

We lay in silence. Porter stared at the wall, gritting his teeth while I gazed into his icy blue eyes. Eyes that were moistening with each second. He blinked twice and returned his gaze to mine.

"That suitcase . . . I can't bring myself to use it. The second my mother pulled it from the bed of my father's truck, I recognized it. My father had used it for business, but I always think of this one day . . ."

"Tell me," I urged him.

"One morning, two of my little sisters had decided to run away from home after receiving spankings from our mother. They packed some dresses, their long underwear, and toothbrushes into the case and had walked to the end of the block. They were like six and seven, ya know? Just little girls. So I ran to catch up with them. I convinced them to come back home with me, that they were just being silly, that they needed to keep sweet, to follow the rules and return home. And they did."

"Wow."

"I can't explain it, ya know? But that memory haunts me."

"Maybe you miss your sisters?"

"Maybe, but I think it's more than that. Like no good deed goes unpunished or something. I tried to be a good kid and I don't know why that went unnoticed." Porter appeared to shake those thoughts from his head. "Anyway, I can't stand to use it, but I can't throw it away either. It just sits in my closet. I borrow duffel bags from Charlie when I'm away on a job site or whatever."

"I'm sorry."

"Don't be," Porter said, his words insistent. "I have choices now that I never thought I'd have. I'm in control of my life. There's nothing better."

"Tell me more. Please." I reached out and linked my fingers through his, wanting to be close to him, curious about his life in the outside world. "What were your first days like? You know, here in this apartment."

"Charlie was awesome. He was happy to have me here. Hooked me up with a job, eventually. But I swear I played video games for like two days straight. I'd never seen anything like it. And the movies. Oh my God. The first time Charlie and I went to the theater, I was dying. Seriously. I had this big tub of popcorn, a giant Coke, all this candy. Shit cost me a huge chunk of the money from my parents, but I didn't care. I saw this awesome movie with all these special effects and shit. It was incredible."

"I'll bet." I smiled. I had almost no idea what he was talking about, but his excitement, his passion about life outside the compound was intoxicating.

He stared off into space again, but this time with a contented smile on his face. It was infectious. I found my lips turning up as I watched him reminisce.

"I want to feel what you're feeling," I said without thinking.

"Don't say that, Brin. Not until you're sure." He looked back at me, his expression hard. "Are you sure?"

I shook my head, compelled to be honest. I wanted to feel the elation that clearly came with experiencing life outside the compound, but I wasn't brave enough to take that leap.

Not yet.

We sat in silence before I braved the question I had wanted to ask him for days.

"Our compound . . . it's so painful for you, but you came to see me anyway. Why did you do that?"

He paused, looking at me with surprise on his handsome face. "Don't you already know the answer to that?"

Again, I shook my head.

Porter cleared his throat, taking a deep breath. "That place . . . it's my hell. But I'd go into hell for you, Brin, no questions asked. I'd do it again and again to make you mine."

"But I am," I insisted, tracing his chin with my fingertips. "I'm already yours."

Porter sighed and positioned himself above me, rolling me to my back once again. His lips pressed to mine, then moved to my chin, my neck, my collarbone. The sensations made me tremble, and the throbbing of my private area resumed.

Again? So soon? How is that possible?

"I want you," I whispered. "So badly."

"No," Porter insisted, pulling away.

"Why?"

He pulled his bottom lip between his teeth and stared into my eyes. "I have to say something . . . and it might seem weird."

"Okay," I replied, confused.

"I can't sleep with you, knowing that in a few days you'll be sleeping with him. I can't share you. I won't."

"Porter, I ca—"

"Do you enjoy fucking him?" he spat out.

"Fucking?" I'd heard Porter use the curse word before, but never as a verb. Honestly, sometimes talking with him was like having a conversation with someone from a foreign country.

He rolled his eyes. "Sex. Do you like having sex with him?"

"You know the answer to that," I said with a frown.

How could he possibly think I enjoyed my time with Lehi? It was my duty, my obligation. It was never for my enjoyment.

"Okay, so—?"

Unsure of his meaning, I shrugged.

"Stop sleeping with him," he said flatly.

"I have no choice." I sat straight up in Porter's bed, scooting down to the edge to retrieve my dress.

"Yes, you do. There's always a way. We just have to find it."

"It's my job, Porter. I'm supposed to produce a baby for him. It's my entire reason for being."

"That's what they want you to think, Brin, but it's not true. You're here on this earth to be you. That's all."

"I wish it were that simple. Lehi expects . . . no, he *demands* a baby."

The long underwear felt like a straitjacket against my skin. But I ignored the suffocation of the garment, buttoning it all the way to the top.

"So, give him one," Porter said, his eyes widening as if he was finally making sense of the universe.

But I was still clueless. I didn't want a baby with Lehi.

"No!" I shouted. "I'm on the pill, Porter. I don't want—"

"That's not what I meant. I wasn't being literal."

"I'm confused." I gritted my teeth as I fastened the buttons of my dress.

"Lie."

"What?" I gasped. How could Porter ask me to lie?

"Make it up. Tell him you're pregnant."

"But I—"

"No, listen, it's all making sense to me now." Porter stood and paced the room as he spoke. "Lehi follows the doctrine, right? He doesn't sleep with his pregnant wives, right?"

I nodded. When any sister wife of mine had been pregnant, Lehi did not lay with her. In fact, he didn't even share her bed. He'd check in with her from time to time, but would spend his nights with the wives who could give him the release he sought in the bedroom.

"So, tell him you're pregnant and he won't touch you. It's perfect." Porter grinned from ear to ear, as if he were a detective who'd just solved a mystery.

"I don't know . . ."

He walked to me, taking my hands in his. "Please, Brin. I'm begging you. I can't share you, I won't."

"He'll expect me to show." I frowned and reached down to cup my belly.

"You'll tell him you lost it."

"What?" I screeched. "No, I could never do that. That's . . . that's an abomination. To fake the death of a child, I can't."

"Brinley, you're on the fucking pill! What's the difference? Every single month, you trick your body into not getting pregnant. Every goddamn month! Seriously, what's the difference?"

I had no answer. I was speechless.

"It's no different." He pulled me closer to him. "I know this is insane. I know I'm asking you to do something totally crazy, but I can't be with you knowing you're sleeping with him. I just can't."

"I . . ." I had no idea what to say.

"Please," he whispered, pressing his forehead to mine. "You possess my soul. So much it hurts, Brin."

Tears welled in my eyes.

"I need you to be mine."

"I *am*," I insisted.

"Mine alone, Brin. Not shared with some fuckhead who has no idea how special you are, how absolutely remarkable you are. Please, please do this. For us."

We stood in silence for several minutes as I processed his request. I knew my answer, but was terrified to say the words. I knew what I wanted; that much was clear. But my fear was nothing to ignore. It was a beast inside me, dominating my every breath.

I swallowed hard, pushing the beast down.

"I'll do it."

chapter 17

Several years ago . . .

ALICE HAMMOND KNEW.

She knew the prophet was not pleased with her husband.

And she knew why.

Her eldest son, Porter.

Alice was the second wife of Ron Hammond, and her firstborn son had always stood out in their family. Her two sister wives had no trouble reminding her each time he spoke his mind, broke a rule despite being punished many times before, or was caught speaking to a girl in the compound.

He was trouble. Always had been.

And now his behavior was threatening her husband's place in the priesthood. And not just from one transgression. Everyone knew that God's revelations weren't solely based on single incidents, but on the ramifications of repeated behavior. And Porter's behavior had been insubordinate for years. But he'd crossed the line when they found him in the woods engaging in completely outlandish behavior, drinking alcohol and smoking marijuana.

Ron had returned home after a lengthy meeting with the prophet. Exhaustion filled his expression when he asked Alice to join him for prayer. Together, they prayed to Heavenly Father, pledging their devotion to the prophet and to the Lord above. It was during this prayer that Ron shared the prophet's revelation with Alice.

"Porter must leave our home. Our community. The prophet received a revelation from our Lord." His face was stern, and the harsh tone of his voice told Alice this was not up for discussion.

Rather than argue with her husband, she simply said, "Please tell me more, husband."

He nodded, accepting her compliance. "If Porter does not leave, you and the children will be reassigned to a community in Texas. We will never see one another again. Not only would I lose you, but I would never be able to take on another. I would have two wives . . . for the rest of my days. And I will no longer, and may never, have a secure place in the celestial kingdom.

Alice gasped; this was her greatest nightmare. Ron was an exemplary member of their community, an elder of the church and a respected member of the priesthood. She couldn't allow this to happen.

Texas? She'd never been outside Colorado City, and the idea of being relocated to a different state, to a different home with a different man, terrified her.

No, the answer was simple. Ron was right. They had to listen to the prophet, for his message was straight from the Heavenly Father himself.

"When?" Her question was simple, but her husband understood her perfectly.

"Tonight."

She gasped and pinched her eyes shut as the realization slammed into her. Tomorrow morning, Porter wouldn't be present at the breakfast table. He wouldn't join his father at the construction site in town. He'd be gone, and she'd be forced to remove his pictures from their home. Group photos would be altered, ink scribbled across his face to erase his presence in the family.

It was required of her, and she knew it.

She had to be brave and listen to the prophet, and to her husband to whom she had devoted her life.

"May I go with you?"

Ron nodded. "The prophet revealed that you should be the one."

"I don't understand." Alice shook her head as tears pricked at her eyes.

"Porter and I have a history of arguments; he won't listen to me. But you, he is loyal to you and will go with you. It's easier this way, my dear."

Of everything her husband had shared with her on this cold winter's evening, the realization that she was to be the one to send her firstborn child into exile was almost more than she could handle. But handle it she would. It was her obligation, her duty, her role in securing her husband's place in the celestial kingdom.

This moment would define her—the moment she was tested by the Heavenly Father. And the day she succeeded by doing exactly what was expected of her.

When Ron dismissed her from the conversation, placing a hundred dollar bill and a folded piece of notebook paper in the palm of her hand, she made her way to the hallway closet. Standing on her tiptoes, she reached for a simple suitcase Ron had used for the occasional business trip for his construction business. Without a word, she entered Porter's bedroom and gathered several outfits from his closet, two pairs of shoes, and his toiletries, enough to last him through the end of the week.

It was then that she summoned him from the common area where he was cleaning the tables with his younger brothers. Her eyes welled up with tears when she saw him, knowing that this would be the last time he saw his siblings.

"Porter."

He placed the sponge on the table in front of him and stood tall. "Yes, Mother."

"I need your assistance with something. Please drive me to town."

"Tonight?"

"Yes. Your father has requested that I visit the pharmacy. But I need you to drive me. It's too cold to walk this evening."

She knew he'd be more than pleased to drive her into town. It beat washing tables splashed with applesauce and milk from his twenty-two siblings, many of them under the age of five. Besides, he hadn't driven his father's truck at all that week, and she knew he welcomed any chance he had to leave the compound.

Porter had always been curious about the outside world. Perhaps, Alice thought, that was the reason for his troublesome personality. When his cousin Charlie had left the compound two years prior, Porter had asked about him incessantly. Alice had repeatedly tried to explain that Charlie was dead to the church and to his family. He would burn in hell for choosing to join the outside world filled with demons, temptations, and countless people devoured by sin.

Alice told herself that Porter would want this, that she was delivering him to where he was meant to be. But her heart warred with her brain.

Despite his persistence regarding the fate of his cousin, and the trouble he caused his father, perhaps he would be eager to repent if given the chance. But that was not to be, and she needed to accept the will of the prophet and Heavenly Father.

They knew best. She was just a woman overcome with her emotions, emotions she needed to learn to control.

"Turn here," Alice said, two blocks before the pharmacy. "Stop at this coffee shop."

"Mother, you don't drink—"

"Do as you're told," she snapped, clenching her teeth.

"Yes, ma'am."

Porter placed the gearshift into park and sat back in his seat, looking to Alice for direction. The coffee shop was still open, but Alice imagined it would be closing soon. When her fingers gripped the door handle, Porter's expression changed and he swallowed hard. She knew he'd figured it out. He knew that she had no intention of buying anything from the shop.

"Mother?" he whispered, and his voice cracked.

She turned her gaze to meet his, tears streaming down her cheeks. Her hands trembling, she placed two items in the palm of his hand. His chest heaved as he opened the envelope filled with cash. Alice knew it was more money than Porter had ever seen in his life. She only hoped he'd find a way to make it last.

"Your cousin lives above this shop. Your father is certain he will allow you to stay with him until you find a place of your own. You'll be seventeen next month—it's time for you to be an adult."

"Father never said good-bye," Porter croaked. "And I'm not going to see him again, am I?"

She shook her head, again closing her eyes.

"And this?" he asked, opening the notebook paper.

"The address of a construction company just outside of Colorado City. You can apply for a job. Your father said they'll be expecting you."

"So this is it?" Porter asked, turning to stare out the front windshield of the truck.

Alice knew it was time for him to go, to leave the only life he'd ever known. To say good-bye to her for the last time. And it broke her heart.

Pulling herself together, she steeled her spine and said calmly, "I placed a suitcase in the bed of the truck. It has everything you need for the next few weeks, until you're able to begin working and earning money of your own."

"I see," Porter said, his hands gripping the steering wheel so hard his knuckles turned white.

For a moment, Alice worried that he might strike her in anger, take the truck, and leave her by the side of the road. But she pushed her nerves aside and delivered the words of the prophet.

"This is how it must be. It was a revelation from the Lord himself. Our way is not meant for you, Porter. You're meant to be . . . well, you're meant to be here."

"I'm meant to be damned?" Porter asked, glaring at her.

She bit her bottom lip and nodded. Porter's nostrils flared as he ripped off his seat belt and flung open the driver's side door.

In her side mirror, Alice watched as Porter reached for the suitcase, pulling it from the bed of the truck. She followed his movements as he walked to the sidewalk, looking back at the truck with such a helpless expression that her heart lurched painfully.

Alice couldn't take the emotions building inside her. She had to leave before she changed her mind. She slid across from the passenger side to the driver's side, then buckled her seat belt and adjusted the mirror. Without a glance in her son's direction, she put the truck into gear and drove away.

She prayed as she drove back to her home, knowing that she had secured her husband's place in heaven.

chapter 18

SEVEN PAIRS OF EYES fixed on me as Lehi delivered the news. Despite the storm developing inside me—the guilt that threatened to demolish any hope or happiness I had for a future with Porter—I did my very best to appear happy to my sister wives. If I didn't seem elated about the blessing that was to be my first child with our husband, the other wives would know it was all a lie, the most foul form of deception.

And so my lips curled up, and with every ounce of strength within me, I forced "happy" tears to build in my eyes.

"This is new," Lehi boomed, his voice bursting with pride at his ability to impregnate the one wife who had always been a challenge in that regard. "So we must be cautious. But it is also worthy of much celebration. Please join me in prayer."

The wives joined hands, Aspen's squeezing mine tightly, and we bowed our heads as Lehi led our prayer.

"Heavenly Father, we thank you for the continued blessings of this household. We are especially grateful for the new life inside Brinley. May you keep her well so that she may produce a healthy child for our family."

When I heard the words "new life," my gut clenched in disgust. At myself.

Lies.

So many lies were mounting. Higher and higher they climbed.

How would I ever keep up with all them?

When our meeting came to a close, Aspen followed me to my bedroom. It was a Saturday morning, and I was hoping to sneak away to the free clinic and to Porter's apartment. He'd greeted me this morning with an invitation.

P: Please come by. I'll wait all day. But hurry. I miss you.

Despite the anger I felt toward myself for my lies, my feelings had not changed for Porter. I understood his reasons—he couldn't share me, wouldn't share me because of the intensity of his feelings. It was flattering and wonderful and scary. I knew that I was falling in love with Porter, stolen moment by stolen moment, text message by text message. I knew that if I were brave enough to leave Lehi's home, Porter would welcome and support me, no questions asked, no hesitation whatsoever.

I was the problem . . . the roadblock . . . the bump in the road.

Because I wasn't brave enough to go.

And so the lie I told my husband was mine alone. I owned it, claimed it as my own deception. Porter might have thought of the lie, but I was the sole reason it had to be announced.

So his text messages gave me just as many butterflies in my belly as they did before I informed Lehi of my pretend pregnancy. And I hoped that Aspen wouldn't prevent me from seeing him that day.

"I'm so happy for you, Brinley," Aspen said, picking up pieces of laundry from the wicker basket on my floor, and laying them flat on my bed. "I'll do your ironing today."

"Really?" I asked, surprised. "That's so nice."

"You'll need to rest as much as possible. Have you had any morning sickness yet? Lehi said it's early . . . how early?"

My pulse quickened. I took a breath before continuing my lie, making sure that my story remained consistent.

"Just a few weeks. My period was due two weeks ago."

"Did you take a test?"

I nodded.

"I always keep mine, you know, as a memento or something," she said, tilting her head to the side. "Did you?"

"Um, no," I replied, avoiding her curious eyes. "I didn't think of it."

"Oh well." Aspen shrugged, forcing a smile. She was keeping sweet, which was odd for Aspen. When we were separated from the rest of the household, she usually ignored that mantra, instead sharing her honest thoughts and opinions. She'd always been what Leandra called an "open book" when it was just the two of us.

So, what was different now?

"You rest, I'll take care of this." Aspen scooped the basket into her arms and walked to the door. "If you need anything, just let me know, all right? Pregnancy can be scary."

"Scary?"

She nodded. "It's a whirlwind of emotions. Excitement, curiosity, with a lot of fear mixed in."

"Why fear?"

"Remember Jessa? What she went through?"

"Yes."

"And what I told you about myself?" Her voice cracked, and the memory of her little daughter Ruthie playing nursemaid as Aspen lost her baby came rushing back to me.

This time, the tears that left my eyes weren't forced. They poured freely, filled with guilt and sadness for the only sister wife who seemed to actually care about me. The rest of them just looked through me.

"I'm so sorry, I—"

"Brinley, I have four healthy children. I'm not reminding you of this to make you feel bad. You asked why there's fear, and so I answered. That's all."

I used my sleeve as I attempted to brush the tears, and guilt, from my face as Aspen walked out my door. But when the door clicked shut, I couldn't contain the remorse that consumed me. I slid to the floor, leaning my back against the side of my mattress, and hung my head in my hands, tears dripping past my palms and landing on my dress.

How could I ever look Aspen in the eye again? Or Jessa?

I was taking their pain, taking their horrific experiences and, what? Trivializing them? Using them to my own advantage? Using them to indulge in my own need to lay with a man who was not my husband.

I was the type of person the prophet preached about. The kind that could "infect" an entire family.

And if Lehi or Leandra discovered the truth about this fictitious pregnancy, my existence would be altered forever.

Tiffany was slumped over the counter at the free clinic, filling out paperwork for a patient with an injured arm. When I approached, we exchanged our usual verbal volley, a conversational dance that had become familiar. She always pleaded with me to ask for help, but this time I shocked her by taking her up on her offer.

"Actually, I-I could use some help."

Her eyes snapped open wide. "Brinley! Are you leaving? Do you need a place to stay? A job?"

"No . . . no. I, uh, I need to know some things . . . about pregnancy and stuff."

Her expectant smile fell into a frown. "I don't understand. Those pills are keeping you from getting pregnant. What exactly do you want to know?"

"What is it like? When do women start to show? What is morning sickness like? Stuff like that. It's no big deal, I can ask someone else."

"No." She raised her hand to stop my dismissive response. "We're slow today. I'll get you an examination room and we'll talk. I've never been pregnant, but I can certainly do a Google search."

"A what?"

Tiffany rolled her eyes. "I'll show you." She leaned down and retrieved several pamphlets, then placed them in my hand.

YOUR PREGNANCY: HOW TO PLAN

SO, YOU'RE GOING TO BE A PARENT

and:

MORNING SICKNESS, THE FIRST TRIMESTER

"This is a good start. But I'll answer everything I can. Come on back." She grabbed a small device from the edge of the counter and led me to a cramped exam room.

I perched atop the paper-covered table, my heart going a mile a minute. I knew I could trust Tiffany, but that didn't stop the dread from building. What would she think of this decision I'd made? What would she think of me and my desire to have a sexual relationship with Porter?

Should I tell her?

Could I?

"Okay," she began. "Start from the beginning. Why do you need to know anything about pregnancy? Clearly, you have no intention of having Lehi's babies anytime soon. So, fill me in. Because I'm kinda confused."

"I'm not sure how to say this." I rubbed at the crispy paper beneath me again and again until the sweat from my hands ripped it to soggy shreds. I was tentative in my words, my movements, afraid of losing an ally that I so desperately needed.

"Brinley, you don't have to hesitate with me. Seriously. I'm not one of them. I'm on my own, remember?" Her sincerity soothed me, creating a cocoon of safety in the room.

Taking a chance, I inhaled deeply and closed my eyes, embraced the security of her promised trust.

"Lehi thinks I'm pregnant."

"Okaaay," Tiffany replied. My eyes still shut, I had no idea if hers were filled with judgment, confusion, or even empathy. "Why does he think that?"

"Because . . . because . . ." Tears streamed down my cheeks.

"Brinley, c'mon. Just tell me."

"Because I lied. I made it up. I made up a pregnancy so I wouldn't have to sleep with him."

I brought up my hands to cover my face, and hung my head in my hands. I expected Tiffany's disapproval, her scorn.

But instead, she laughed.

"Are you kidding me? That may be the smartest thing you've ever done!" I could hear her rise from her seat and walk to me. Her hand rubbed my back in a soothing motion.

Stunned, I lifted my face and my eyes met hers.

"What?" I couldn't even begin to comprehend her reaction to my twisted, deplorable behavior.

"I mean it, cousin. That dirty old man doesn't deserve to touch you, to have his hands on you. I'm proud of you for making this decision. Now you won't need your pills."

"Well . . ." Averting my eyes, I bit on my bottom lip and flinched from the pain.

"Oh my God. Are you . . ."

As her voice trailed off, I focused my attention on the wall, too ashamed to meet her eyes. But I nodded my head.

"Porter?" she pressed.

I nodded again.

"Holy shit."

"Tiffany!"

"Sorry, sorry." She shook her head. "But this is a big freaking deal. I mean, you're sleeping with him? How long has this been going on?"

"It hasn't yet, but I want to. So badly, I can think of almost nothing else."

"Wow." Tiffany returned to her seat, then picked up the small gadget and slid her finger on the screen. "Make sure he wears a condom, okay?"

"Why? What is that?"

She rolled her eyes.

"Please don't do that," I begged her. "I feel silly enough as it is."

I surprised myself with my demand. It wasn't like me to stick up for myself in any given situation—let alone one like this where I felt so vulnerable, so foolish for not understanding the outside world, and things with such silly names as "con-dum."

"It's important," Tiffany said absently as she focused on the tiny screen. "You need it to keep yourself safe from diseases. I can give you some pamphlets on that too."

I was confused, but I trusted Tiffany and didn't want to stray too far from the topic at hand . . . my fake baby.

"What's that?" I gestured to the small device in her hand.

"It's an iPad."

"What does it *do*?" I peered at the flat device, wondering how this could possibly help me in any way.

"It's like a mini computer. I'm going to do a Google search for you, and I'll print off a bunch of information."

I nodded, watching her tap her fingers on the small machine.

"Do you know your due date?" she asked.

I shook my head. "No."

"All right, let's calculate one for you. What did you tell him? About how far along you are."

"He thinks my period was due two weeks ago."

"Perfect, I can figure it out for you."

Her fingers continued to tap and slide from side to side with abrupt movements as she stared at the screen.

"May first."

"Wow. It all feels so real now, even though it isn't."

"I just realized," she said, looking up from the "pad."

"What?"

"This pregnancy has to end at some point. We'll have to figure out when that would most likely happen. Are you going to fake a miscarriage?"

I bit into my lip once again, and cringed at the harsh taste of my own blood. Tears flooded my eyes.

"Stop," Tiffany insisted. "There's no shame here. Not with me."

"Do you mean that? I mean, really mean it?"

"Absolutely. I'll help you in any way I can. Always. You don't belong there, Brinley. I feel it in my gut."

"I wish I did too. But I'm too afraid."

I wanted to run my fingers through my hair, knowing it would calm me, but was hindered by the bulky braid. That braid represented years of repression, years of being stifled by my upbringing, by my beliefs and community.

"Do you think I wasn't?" Tiffany's hands pressed into her hips as she glowered at me. "I was ridiculously afraid, Brinley. But I knew I didn't belong there. And you don't either. I promise that when you make the decision to leave—"

"*If*," I said, correcting her.

"*When*," she repeated, "it'll be hard. I won't sugarcoat it. It will be the most difficult, grueling thing you'll ever experience. But you'll fly, remember? Your wings won't be clipped anymore. You'll soar through the air, answering to no one but yourself."

"Really?"

"Yes." She smiled at me and patted my shoulder. "You just have to take a leap of faith. One so giant it's frightening. But you have to do it or you'll never be free. You'll remain chained to Lehi Cluff for years, decades, and eventually, fake pregnancies won't be an option. You'll find yourself pregnant with his babies. Again and again you'll bear his children, and your chains will grow tighter and tighter. You need to jump off that cliff now, Brinley, before you no longer have a choice. *Trust me.*"

I found myself tongue-tied, with no response to her plea. Everything she said made sense, *everything*. So, why was I fighting this? Why was I clinging to a life I resented? To a life that brought me nothing but frustration, secrets, and shame?

Maybe Tiffany was right. Maybe it was time to go.

Or at least consider the idea.

The whisper was not quite a scream yet, but it was growing louder.

I just had to listen.

"I thought you'd never get here," Porter murmured into my ear, pressing his hand into the small of my back and pulling me close. So close, I could feel the pounding of his heart through my thick cotton dress.

"I got here as soon as I could." I relaxed fully, snuggling closer as I submerged myself in the touch of Porter. I hadn't seen him in days, not since he'd given me my first orgasm.

Since then I'd craved more, so much more. I wanted to feel that way again. And this time, I wanted Porter to feel it right along with me.

With nimble fingers, I unbuttoned the buttons of my dress . . . one by one.

Porter pulled away and stared at my hands, then cleared his throat. "What are you doing?"

"I'm ready."

"But—"

I pressed my finger to his lips. "We announced my pregnancy this morning. Lehi won't touch me."

"Oh." His eyes brightened with those words, and the restraint in his expression disappeared. The hunger he'd repressed for months broke free as his hands joined mine in unbuttoning my dress.

"This body," I continued, feeling bolder, more feminine and seductive, "is for you . . . and you alone."

Porter whipped the dress over my head, then focused on removing the long underwear that covered my skin. Soon that dropped to my ankles along with my dress. I resisted the urge to cover my naked body once he'd removed my bra and panties. The ravenous look in his eyes made adrenaline shoot through my veins, and the throbbing of my private area returned. He gripped the hair at the base of my scalp, inhaling deeply as his eyes met mine. His nostrils flared, and his eyes darkened.

"I've waited so long, Brin . . . so long to have you like this. I'm going to savor it, make you scream my name. Make you mine."

"Yes." An intense sigh left my lips as rolled my head back, losing myself in the passion of his kisses against the hot skin of my neck. "Yes, please."

"Lay on the bed."

"Yes, si—"

I pressed my hand to my mouth in shock. How could I have said that?

Porter lifted my chin with his hand and stared deeply into my eyes. "No. Don't you ever call me that. This is about us. Not me . . . us. I'm *not* him."

"I-I know, I'm so sorry. I just—"

"Shh." He closed his eyes and shook his head. "Don't apologize. But that's the last time either of us thinks about that shithead in this room. All right?"

I nodded, holding back tears, terrified that I had quite possibly spoiled my first time with Porter by falling into old habits I shared with Lehi.

Crawling onto Porter's bed, I turned my body to rest on my back, propped up by my elbows, waiting for Porter. He opened his nightstand drawer and retrieved a small square packet.

"What's that?" I stared down at the packet as he ripped it open and removed a rubbery-looking sleeve from the packaging.

"A condom," he said softly, stripping himself of his jeans and underpants. He slid the condom onto his hard penis. The throbbing of my private area returned as I stared at the length of him.

"You . . . um . . ."

"What?" he asked with a laugh.

"You're so . . . big."

His laughter grew, turning into a hearty chuckle as he shook his head. "I'll be gentle, I promise. Now come here."

He pressed his lips to mine and immediately opened his mouth, inviting me in. Embracing the bold nature within me, I touched my tongue to his, exploring the taste of him. My skin tingled at his touch as his fingertips exploring each curve of my body. He pressed me against the mattress, planting kisses on my naked breasts. My nipples rose to meet his lips and tongue. Within seconds, he'd pulled one nipple completely into this mouth, sucking hard, causing me to gasp at the intensity of his need for me. His teeth grazed against the taut tip, then he teased it gently with his tongue.

"Mmm," I murmured.

"You like that?"

"Oh yes."

"Good." He lightly touched the skin of my private area, and I jumped slightly at the sensation of his touch. "Relax, baby."

My nipples ached, missing the teasing of his lips as he moved down my torso, skimming my skin with his tongue. Within seconds, my legs were draped over his shoulders and he was kissing me passionately in my most sensitive spot.

I arched my back in ecstasy as his movements reminded me of our encounter the other day.

My first orgasm.

Oh, how I wanted another.

Again and again, Porter brought me to the brink. Pleasure mounted and climbed within me, then I'd groan with frustration as he'd pull his mouth away and give me a wicked grin just before I reached a release. With each round of intimate kisses and strokes of his tongue, the pleasure grew stronger, until I felt like I might break apart if he continued, and die if he didn't.

"Please, Porter . . . Please."

"Tell me what you want." He growled playfully, then kissed my inner thighs.

"I want to come. Please, let me come," I begged, my hands clutching the sheets. He tipped his head back to my private area, and I squealed. "No. Not like that."

"What do you want, Brin?" he asked again, then licked me again.

"Inside me," I cried out. "I want you inside me."

Without another word, Porter hoisted himself on his knees and pulled my legs apart, then sank himself deep within me. Unlike my experience with Lehi, my muscles didn't clench, they didn't resist—they opened for him, welcomed him. A smile crossed my face at the realization.

Porter slowly began to pump inside me, and my hips lifted against his in response. Within seconds, I felt the buildup once again and dug my fingers into his shoulders as I arched my back and screamed his name. The orgasm shot through me with an intensity I never could have hoped to experience. It felt as if every cell of my body had broken apart during that moment. Porter continued to thrust as I bucked beneath him, my arms flailing against the mattress.

"Oh God, Brin . . . I'm so close."

Porter's brow was knitted and sweat dripped from his forehead as he pressed it to mine. He groaned as he found his own release, taking my mouth once again in a passionate kiss as he rocked against me again and again before collapsing on my chest.

He rolled to his side but draped his arm over my belly, running his fingertips gently against my ribs. It tickled slightly. My entire body hummed in the afterglow of our lovemaking.

"How was it? I mean . . . it sounded good, but—" Porter's cheeks were flushed. He shrugged after asking the question that I felt he should already know the answer to.

"It was the most amazing experience of my life."

I stared up at the ceiling, still trying to process the emotions that were filling me from head to toe.

Elation?

Satisfaction?

Joy?

Love?

Porter shifted to perch on his open palm, his elbow digging into the mattress. Out of the corner of my eye, I could see a smile growing on his handsome face.

"And you?" I asked, nervous that I might not have given him the pleasure that he'd clearly given me.

"I've had sex," he admitted. "I can't lie to you. I mean, it's physically impossible for me to lie to you." He chuckled uncomfortably, scratching the five o'clock shadow that was forming on his chin. "But that . . . that was different from anything in my past. It was like . . . I don't know. Anything I compare it to will make me sound lame."

"I don't care." I turned to him, reaching out to touch the prickly stubble on his face, urging him to tell me the truth. "You can say anything to me."

"I've never been in it emotionally, ya know? I mean, it was always just sex. Just physical. But with you, it was so much more. You make me feel alive . . . like anything is possible." He shook his head. "God. I'm an idiot."

Quickly, I raised up on my elbow and my gaze met his. "No, you're not. You're saying everything that I feel. It's scary, right?"

"Yeah." His eyes began to glisten with that simple word. "But I don't care. Bring the fear, bring the pain. You're worth it."

"I agree."

"No regrets?" he asked, his eyes concerned.

I smiled and ran my fingers through his hair. "Never."

"Good." He sighed and brushed at the stray hairs that hung over my forehead. "That makes me happy."

"*You* make me happy," I whispered.

Porter scooted himself off the bed, tossed the condom into a garbage pail, and walked to a bookshelf on the wall, retrieving a small notebook.

"So . . . that thing . . . the condom. What is it, um, *for* exactly?"

"It's protection . . . for you."

His words confused me. I tried to remember what Tiffany had said, but my brain felt like mush after our lovemaking.

"I've been with other women, and I know I've been fucked up some of the time and skipped using one of these." He gestured to the packet in his hand. "I can't risk giving you anything."

"Giving me anything? What do you mean?"

"Look, I think I'm clean. I don't think I have any STDs, but I won't gamble with your health. No way."

"STD? What is that?"

His expression softened and he sat next to me on the bed. He rubbed my back slowly, his fingers tickled the skin of my shoulder. "Sexually transmitted diseases."

Goose bumps rose on my arms. Porter could have a disease? The pamphlets. I never looked at the pamphlets.

"Are you . . . sick?"

"No, no. It's just something you're supposed to do to be safe. I promise I'll get myself tested. I'll do anything you want."

His eyes were sincere and I trusted his intentions. "Thank you."

Porter glanced at the notebook in his hands. His Adam's apple bobbed as he swallowed hard, his fingers lightly tapping at the plastic of the cover.

"I want to show you something," he said. "But I don't want to scare you away."

"You won't," I insisted. "I promise."

"Sometimes when I can't see you for a while, my mind wanders, ya know? And I have to get it out. I have to find some way to have you with me, even if you're only in my imagination."

"Oh."

He placed the notebook beside me. I sat up, not bothering to cover myself with a sheet, and opened the first page of the notebook. His handwriting was difficult to decipher, but I could see that a short poem was scrawled on the page. I turned the pages again and again, finding poem after poem scrawled there. Some words were scribbled out, others written in such horrible writing, I couldn't understand them. But they were love letters—about me.

My heart felt as if it might burst.

Skipping back to the front page, I read the first poem that Porter had written for me.

"That Fucking Purse"

She doesn't know what she does to me

the way her hair tickles her forehead,

the innocence of her eyes.

She brings me back to darkness,
yet heals my broken heart.
She tempts me with her curves,
yet I'm afraid I'll break her.
I'm too brash, too honest, too scarred.
Could she ever want me?
The skin of her wrist—
the softest I've ever felt—
the pleading of her eyes.
She reminds me of my home,
my hell,
my darkest hours.
And yet I can't break free.

"This is beautiful." My voice shook; I was overwhelmed at the depth of his feelings. That anyone could love me like this, even when I wasn't yet his? It soothed my soul and satisfied my heart.

"The title could use some help." Porter chuckled self-consciously.

"No," I said, pressing the notebook to my chest. "It's honest. And it's perfect just the way it is."

Porter gave me a half smile before pressing his lips to mine. "How did I get so lucky?" he asked, his expression so sincere.

"You're just . . . you make everything all right, Brin. Everything."

My cheeks grew hot; I'd rarely received compliments. But I didn't allow myself to clam up, to grow embarrassed, or hide my scarlet cheeks. Instead, I pressed my forehead to his and simply said, "Thank you."

chapter 19

I'D READ THE PAMPHLETS from Tiffany at least seven times each. I knew my due date by heart, and the day my period was "due" but according to my lies, never arrived. Each morning I skipped breakfast, instead opting for crackers and water, clutching my belly as I nibbled on the bland, salty excuse for a meal, wishing I were eating with the family. Brenda would cook her famous French toast and my stomach would growl in defiance, demanding the feast the rest of the family was enjoying.

"You need to keep up your strength, girl," Leandra would say each morning with a slight roll of her eyes. Rather than argue with her, I kept sweet, nodding and gesturing to the crackers on my plate.

Brenda and Aspen helped me with my morning chores each weekday before I pretended to muster the energy to walk to Jorjina's house several blocks from our home. I pushed the guilt down, knowing how horrified my sister wives would be at my betrayal, knowing that this was a means to an end. These lies released me from my obligations to Lehi; they allowed me to lay with Porter, to experience bliss that was unimaginable to me just months earlier.

I was falling in love. And I'd do almost anything to keep that love intact. If necessary, lying would just be the tip of the iceberg.

Porter was quickly becoming the most important person in my existence. And the idea of losing him made me physically sick. I couldn't let that happen.

As long as he wanted me, I would be his.

"Take an umbrella today," Aspen said from across the expanse of the dining room table. "It's misty this morning."

"Thank you," I replied. "I will." I rose to my feet and carried my uneaten crackers to the sink. Joseph, one of Leandra's older boys, took the plate from my hands and patted me on the shoulder. I thanked him and retreated to my bedroom before leaving for Jorjina's home.

Aspen followed me, but I pretended not to notice. She'd been more protective than usual since I'd revealed my pregnancy to the family. And as deceptive and deplorable as it was, I knew what I had to do. Acting as though I was oblivious to the footsteps behind me, I walked to my bedroom, closed the door behind me, then entered my private bathroom and closed that door.

I leaned over the toilet as tears built in my eyes, knowing what I needed to do. Without thinking, knowing that if I dwelled on my actions, I might avoid them, I forced my index finger to the back of my throat. My paltry breakfast made its way into the toilet as I retched while clutching the plastic seat. When the heaving ceased, tears of humiliation and shame streamed down my cheeks.

As she always did, Aspen knocked softly on the door. "Can I get you anything? Are you okay?"

"No." I cleared my throat and flushed the toilet, moving to the sink to splash cold water on my face. "I'll be all right. Just need to brush my teeth."

I'd hoped that Aspen would be gone by the time I stepped into my bedroom, but she was seated at my vanity, her hands placed neatly in her lap, her auburn braid hanging in front of her chest. "It's a good sign, you know."

"I know," I said, acknowledging my supposed morning sickness.

"The sicker you are, the healthier the pregnancy. You should feel better when you get to twelve weeks. That's how I was with every one of my children. It's like clockwork."

I knew what that meant—two more months of this routine. Two months of deception, forcing myself to skip the food I enjoyed, to vomit the food that I hated, and to lie to my husband and sister wives.

But that didn't change a thing. Two months, two years . . . it didn't matter. It was a means to an end. And I was determined to see it through.

"Your eyes look awful. Maybe I should go to Mrs. Black's home today instead of you."

"No, no." I reached out to pat her shoulder. "I'll be all right. It doesn't last long."

A weak smile crossed my lips as Aspen's hand covered mine, squeezing gently. "I'm here for you. You know that, right?"

To say that I was struggling to understand Aspen's behavior since announcing my pregnancy would be a gigantic understatement. She'd always been protective of me; this was nothing new. But now I felt as if I'd reached some new level of sisterhood with Lehi's sixth wife. I felt like she'd developed claws and wasn't afraid to use them if anyone were to put me in harm's way. It was as if she'd adopted me as one of her own. A mama bear and her very own grown-up cub.

It was strange, but it felt nice. And awful, because it was based on a lie.

"Thank you, though, Aspen. I do appreciate all of your help."

"I know you do." She stood, smoothed the wrinkles from her dress, and retrieved my wicker basket from the corner. "I'll take care of this. Give my regards to Jorjina."

"I will."

The rain we'd received made our unpaved, normally dusty roads damp and muddy; the slop sucked at my sneakers with each step. Luckily my umbrella shielded me from the downpour that had developed as I walked, but my once pristine sneakers were the color of the mud beneath them. I sighed, knowing that Lehi would rather I wash my shoes dozens of times before replacing them. I was so busy focusing on my shoes, however, that I almost missed the man staring at me from the unfinished construction project to my right.

Burt Jameson.

I'd managed to dodge Burt since starting my job with Jorjina Black. Lehi had staked his claim with me on our initial walk to the house, and since then, Burt had stayed away from me.

But today was the exception.

"Miss Brinley," he called from the covered porch of the partially built home. Before I could trudge through the muddy road to turn the corner, he'd hoisted himself over the railing and made his way toward me.

"Elder Jameson, please." I shook my head furiously, pinching my eyes tightly as the rain pounded around me. "I-I can't speak to you. It's not right."

"I'm sorry. I promise I won't ask about Rebecca."

I stared at him in confusion, until I remembered their four children.

"How are my boys? Are they all right? Are they adjusting?"

Burt Jameson had seven other children to support with his first two wives, but I knew that didn't change the love he felt for the children he shared with Rebecca.

"They're well." I bit my lip, determined not to become emotional. "They struggled a bit in the beginning, but they're doing better. They really are."

"That's good."

He shifted his weight, his boots sloshing in the mud. The rain poured down, pasting his graying hair against his skull. Nervously, he raked his fingers through the long strands, pushing them away from his forehead. His pale skin had aged rapidly since the last time we'd spoken. I knew he was miserable. But I also knew there was absolutely nothing I could do about that. Rebecca had made her choice. Yes, it was the wrong one, but she'd made it.

Rain dripped from his bushy eyebrows as he lifted them at me and asked, his voice cracking, "Is he good to them?"

I knew what my answer should have been. It should have been an honest representation of Lehi Cluff's paternal role. He'd screamed at each of the boys, had slapped their faces on occasion. He'd even given the eldest the silent treatment for several days after a disagreement. His treatment of Burt's sons was deplorable.

That was the honest answer. But I'd caused enough trouble already.

And the truth was, telling Burt about the pain his children were dealing with wouldn't change a thing.

Not one thing.

So, I kept sweet. I harnessed my emotions and told a lie to make Burt feel just a tiny bit better.

"Yes, he is. I'm sure that they love and miss you every day. But they're thriving, Elder Jameson." When he sighed at my response, I said it again. "They're thriving."

He closed his eyes and nodded as raindrops streaming from his forehead to his caterpillar eyebrows, down his crooked nose and landing on his parted lips. "Now, I must go."

"Wait, plea—"

"Elder Jameson, I *have* to go. This isn't right." When he didn't move, I said what I needed to say to change his position. "And *the prophet* is expecting me."

When I said that word *prophet*, Burt took a step back. That word carried power—power and fear and responsibility. Burt glanced around us, taking in our surroundings before stepping to the side to let me pass.

"Good-bye, Miss Brinley. And thank you."

"You're most welcome," I whispered, turning my face before he could see my lips tremble.

I stepped quickly through the mud, my heart thudding inside my empty chest as I made my way to the home of Jorjina Black.

"You'll catch your death! Get inside!" Jorjina whooped, her frail arm holding the screen door open for me.

"I'm sorry about the mud."

She shrugged off my apology. "You're the one who has to clean it. Why should I worry?"

A clever wink let me know she was only teasing. I'd come to depend on that wink. Jorjina's sense of humor wasn't what you'd expect from our version of royalty. She was clever and quick-witted, even sarcastic at times.

I'd noticed that when the prophet joined us for tea, checking in on us from time to time, her demeanor changed. She stiffened in his presence and refrained from her normal clever remarks. Those were the mornings when her eyes lost their luster, their youthful glow.

She was different around her son. And if Jorjina Black couldn't be herself around the prophet, what chance did the rest of us have?

Luckily, the prophet hadn't joined us in several days. It was just Jorjina, me, and a cake that was waiting to be baked.

"Clarence told me your news," she said casually while stirring the chocolate batter.

"Oh." I paused, not sure how to respond to that. I'd come to enjoy my time with Jorjina, and didn't want her to send me away.

"I hope you'll still continue on. For as long as possible, that is. I've gotten quite used to you."

She winked. And my lips curled into a satisfied smile.

"I'll stay as long as my husband will allow."

It was the truth. When my fake pregnancy reached its inevitable end, I'd be able to continue my work with Jorjina. Over the past weeks, my time with her had become my escape. A few afternoons per week, she'd insist I leave her alone, that I'd allow her to rest in private. For this reason, I'd started to carry my cell phone inside my brassiere, beneath my long underwear and dress. It was undetectable, but allowed me to contact Porter whenever the opportunity arose so we could be together.

We'd make love in his bedroom, and then he'd stroke my hair and sing me songs as I laid my head against his chest. It was heavenly.

And then as the dinner hour approached, I'd dress and return to the comforts of Jorjina's home.

She never asked me where I went. Part of me wondered if she knew, if she had some sort of mind-reading abilities. Porter said that was ridiculous, but then showed me websites that listed people who called themselves "psychics," claiming to be able to predict the future and read minds. It astounded me.

One afternoon, Porter had to work late, but I still had to leave Jorjina's home as was expected of me. I couldn't return home, or Leandra would certainly tell Lehi about the breaks I was given by Jorjina, and the time I had with Porter would certainly become a thing of the past.

So instead, I'd walked to town and sat in the coffee shop below his apartment. I'd used some of the money Porter had given me months earlier in the drugstore to purchase a cup of tea, and I'd sat in the corner, watching the patrons as they sat nearby.

I'd grown used to the way that my dress, lack of makeup, and hairstyle had attracted attention. It no longer fazed me and I was able to blend in as best I could. And so, for those two hours, I'd sipped my beverage and watched the people around me. I watched people type furiously on their tiny computers. I watched as husbands and wives talked about their children. And I watched as a large group of women argued the merits of homeschooling.

In a word—I was fascinated, completely and utterly fascinated by the tiny shop and the people it attracted. If I could have stayed there longer, I would have. I'd make myself comfortable in my tiny booth, nibble on a muffin, and watch the world pass by.

That was the only time I'd ever visited that coffeehouse, but I started to imagine myself there with Porter with my hair up in a loose ponytail, wearing shorts and a T-shirt rather than my heavy, oppressive dress, and I'd have a purse with an embroidered owl strung across my chest.

That daydream filled my thoughts as Jorjina brought me back to the present.

"That makes me happy. I like you, dear." Jorjina's thin fingers stroked the top of my hand in a kind, maternal fashion. "And I hope you'll be here for as long as you can."

"Me too."

"But I'm a realist. I know that in several months you'll have a little one to attend to, and that son of mine will replace you with another inadequate and unfriendly woman who will burn the eggs."

I chuckled as I poured the batter into the greased pans, shaking my head. "I'll teach her, if you like. So she gets them just right."

Jorjina paused, leaning her body against the counter. "You'd do that for me?"

"Mm-hmm." I nodded emphatically. And it was the truth.

"Well, how about that," she whispered, staring off into space.

"I'm sorry?" I asked, confused.

Her brow knitted for just a slice of a moment. Before I could react, she shook her head briefly before looking me dead in the eye. "Oh, nothing. You're just growing on me, is all."

I wanted to be comforted by her words. But I wasn't. All of my stolen moments with Porter seemed in jeopardy. I felt on display, exposed and vulnerable.

Could it be that my "honor" of working for the prophet's mother was nothing but a ruse? Was Lehi spying on me? Was the prophet?

My heart raced as I placed the cake pans in the oven, avoiding my employer's gaze as I set the timer. Then I turned to the window to focus on the rain that continued to pour from the sky.

Jorjina's shoulder brushed against my arm as she moved to stand next to me, and placed her hand on top of mine. "You're safe here." Her eyes were solemn, pleading. "I promise you. No matter what."

She squeezed my and nodded, urging me to believe her. But I couldn't, and I struggled to compose my features. I had no idea what to believe.

Could I trust her?

Could I trust *anyone?*

When I was younger, everything was simple. I knew my place in the world. I knew my role, my duty, my destiny within our community.

But that was no longer my reality. I was breaking every rule, challenging every belief that I'd once held dear. And the woman I'd grown attached to over the past several weeks was sending me mixed messages, confusing me.

And I had no idea what to do.

My brain told me to hide everything inside, not to trust, not to feel.

Keep sweet, keep sweet, keep sweet.

And my heart . . . that part of me wanted to believe in her, to believe that she'd grown as attached to me as I was to her. My heart wanted so desperately to believe that someone knew my secrets and supported me just the same, someone inside the compound, someone living the life I was expected to live.

But was that even possible?

And was I a fool to believe that the mother of the prophet himself could be that person?

Mentally I chastised myself, a similar refrain running through my mind:

I'm a silly girl.

A foolish girl.

A stupid girl.

And yet my heart continued to win, no matter how much my brain raised cautious pleas.

I could no longer stifle the screams.

They were coming.

chapter 20

"I THINK SHE KNOWS." My words came out in a harsh whisper as I inhaled deeply, out of breath from running to town.

After leaving Jorjina's, I was desperate to talk to Porter. Once I'd passed Samuel and the other guards at their small tower, I'd run the rest of the way to Porter's apartment. Without knocking, I let myself in, knowing the door would be unlocked. Inside his living room, I paced back and forth, fretting and working myself up into a panic while Porter stared at me in confusion.

"Knows what? About you and me?" His forehead wrinkled as he attempted to keep me rooted to one place, but I couldn't stop moving.

"Yes."

"That's impossible."

I shook my head sharply, hugging myself as I strode from the door to the couch and back again. "No . . . she knows. She *knows.*"

"Brin, slow down." Porter pressed the palms of his hands on my shoulders. "Talk to me. Tell me what happened."

"I'm in trouble." I brushed past him, my head spinning. "So much trouble."

"You're safe here," he said, his voice stern, and a chill ran down my spine.

"That's exactly what she said. Word for word." I stared at Porter, trying to process what Jorjina had meant by those words. The world was closing in on me, and I was certain I was being punished for all my sins against Heavenly Father, for my transgressions against my husband.

"The prophet's mother?" he asked.

I nodded, finally standing still, staring him in the eye. "She said I was safe with her."

We stood in silence.

"She knows, Porter. I feel it in my bones."

"Okay, stop." He walked to the couch and sank into the cushions, then placed his head in his hands. "So, what . . . you think she's, like, telling the fucking prophet everything you're doing? You think she's some sort of spy?"

I shrugged. "I don't know." My chest felt heavy and I struggled to breathe, then the room began to spin around and around. I was having a panic attack.

Porter jumped up and caught me just as my legs gave out, keeping me from tumbling down to the dirty carpet. He wrapped his arm around my waist and led me to the bedroom.

"Lie down, put your feet up."

I closed my eyes and attempted to slow my breathing. Porter sat next to me, clutching my hand in his.

"Stay here . . . with me."

My eyes opened quickly, and the panic accelerated within my chest. "I can't."

Porter pursed his lips and looked away. "Brin . . . what is it you see in me? I mean, what is this about?"

Despite the pressure in my chest, I sat to face him. "I don't understand."

"I mean, what do you see in me?" He peered at me wide-eyed, his expression distressed and vulnerable.

"I—"

"That's what I was afraid of." He stood and took my place pacing the room.

"What do you mean?" I asked, still confused.

"Is this just a game to you? Am I a game?"

"How can you say that to me? You're everything! Absolutely everything!"

I moved to the edge of the bed, trembling. How could he think that? Every morning I started the day with thoughts of Porter. Every night when I prayed to Heavenly Father, I prayed for Porter—for his happiness, his well-being, his health, and the strength to conquer his addiction.

"Then why won't you stay? I'm offering you a place to be away from all of them, and you won't take it."

"I'm not ready."

"Why? Why not?"

"Because I'm married! I can't just stay here and never go back."

Panic filled my chest at the thought of leaving behind the only life I knew for a man I'd only known for a few months. Yes, I was falling for him. Yes, he was constantly on my mind and in my heart. But how could I know that he was ready to commit to me? To provide for me? That was a huge burden to carry, and I couldn't expect that of him. Not yet.

"He's *not* your husband, Brinley. No matter what the prophet 'revealed.' He has one wife and that's Leandra. You're not bound to him unless you choose to be. Period."

He was right. Legally, Lehi had no claim to me. It was a celestial union, a marriage of faith. And clearly mine was fading fast. I stared at him, acknowledging how correct he was with that statement.

Porter's eyes bore into mine, and part of me wanted to unbraid my hair, to strip myself of my long, heavy dress, and make myself at home in his apartment. But I knew I couldn't do that.

"I risk everything to come here. You have to know this isn't a game."

Porter looked away and crossed his arms in front of his chest, building a wall between us.

"Porter, please." My fingers grazed his elbow and he flinched at my touch. When I gasped, he closed his eyes tightly. "You're everything to me. You could never be a game."

"What do you see in me?" he asked, his voice small. His body seemed to crumple into itself. I'd never seen him like this.

"You're kind and you're strong," I began, stroking his shoulder with my fingers. "You protect me and you make me laugh. I never laughed before I met you."

"I believe that." He chuckled under his breath. "What else?"

"You have this tough exterior, but for me . . . for me, you're gentle, sweet." His expression softened and he covered my hand with his own. "And no one, *no one* on this earth makes me light up like you can. No one makes me feel the way you make me feel. And I'm starting to think no one else ever could."

"Then why?" He paused and his brows drew together. "Why won't you stay?"

"I'm terrified, Porter. So terrified that if I stayed here with you, you'd grow tired of me, and then where would I be? All on my own. I'm not ready for that."

"What makes you think I could ever get tired of you?" His thumb traced the curve of my chin.

I shrugged my shoulders and stared at the floor. "You've only known me for a few months. You might change your mind. You can have anyone you want . . . anyone without this," I pulled on the end of my braid, "or this," I yanked at the fabric of my dress. I choked back the tears, but they streamed down my cheeks. "What if you decide I'm not worth it? Then where will I be?"

He was silent, and for a moment I worried that he'd agree with me. That I'd just given him a reason to turn his back on our time together, to turn away from us completely. But instead, he took me into his arms.

"You're right, Brin. I could have someone out here. I could. But that's not what I want. I want you. Only you."

"Why? I don't get it! All I do is mess up your life! You should be with someone from the outside world. Someone you won't have to bend over backward for, someone you can hold in your arms as you sleep. Someone who doesn't have a husband waiting for her! Someone who isn't damned to hell!"

I sobbed into his chest and he stroked my back.

"God, you break my heart when you talk like that." He stroked the top of my braid. "He's not waiting for you. He doesn't even notice when you're gone. You know that, right?"

"I do."

"And you're not damned. If anybody's damned to fucking hell, it's the one everyone calls the prophet. He's a sick fuck who plays with your lives for his own twisted purposes. He controls every single one of your lives. It's disgusting."

"I-I'm starting to see that."

"We need to get away. Just the two of us. Somewhere where we can just be us, ya know? Where we can be alone and not worry about Cluff or the fucking prophet or any of that bullshit."

"That's impossible," I said.

"No, it's not. I told you before, there's always a way."

Wriggling out of his embrace, I fought the panic that stirred within me. I needed air. I crossed the room, pulling at the latch of the window. The breeze streamed in and I inhaled deeply, feeling my pulse calm ever so slightly.

Porter stood his ground, watching as I placed my hands on the rail of the window.

Inhale, exhale. Inhale, exhale.

"If Jorjina knows, if sh-she knows and sh-sh-she's spying on me—" I couldn't look at him. The panic inside me wouldn't allow it. My stuttering had returned, and I was mortified.

"Then what do you have to lose?" The plea in his voice demanded the proper response. But I didn't have one.

"Nothing?" I paused, finally making eye contact. "Everything?" I shook my head, not knowing the answer.

Porter moved close behind me, placing one hand next to mine on the window ledge as the other gently caressed my waist. "You're already on borrowed time. If she tells the prophet, there's no way you'll be able to stay. You *have* to know that."

I shuddered in response, my feet rocking slightly . . . back and forth, back and forth. I couldn't soothe myself, couldn't make my body calm.

"Please, let's go away. Just us, away from all of this bullshit. I know the place. Just trust me, please."

"I-I . . ." My limbs shook and it was difficult to swallow. I wanted to indulge my fantasy of being with Porter without worry, without my braid, my dress, my stifling long underwear. I wanted it so badly.

Porter pressed himself against my back, tucking his chin into my neck. "I'll protect you. Please believe me."

"I do, I—"

"Just trust me. Please, I need you to trust me. If you can't, then we're over before we started."

I turned to face him. "My trust in you is not the problem. It's them . . . all of them."

"Then let's figure this out." He pressed his forehead to mine. "They don't deserve you, Brin. They don't."

"Maybe I don't deserve *you*—"

"Stop. Don't even say that. That's the biggest pile of horse shit I've ever heard. You're the best part of my life. You're the reason I wake up every day, the reason I get my ass to work. Hell, you're the reason I haven't gotten high in months. It's all because of you."

"Oh," I said, surprised at the effect I'd had on him.

Porter placed his hands on each side of my face, angling my chin so that our eyes were locked in a steady gaze. "Don't ever say that again, all right? I won't tolerate it."

I nodded, tears running down my face and onto his knuckles. My mouth went dry as his blue eyes pierced mine. Relief coursed through me, and I relaxed at his touch.

"I need to say something, and you have to hear me," I begged.

"Anything." Porter's lips formed a straight line, and I could feel his body stiffen.

"Please don't doubt my feelings. Ever. I'm not ready to leave, I'm not ready to be discovered, but that doesn't change my feelings for you. You're always on my mind, so much it's unnerving."

He nodded as a sigh left his mouth. He pressed his lips to mine, his hands still gripping the sides of my face. "God, I can't get enough of you."

Our kisses grew more urgent, his tongue stroking mine, his hands moving to the buttons of my dress. I brought up my hands to assist his and soon the dress and long underwear were tossed across the room. Porter hoisted my legs around his waist and backed me into the wall, the curtains blowing in the breeze. The slightly toxic smell of paint traveled through my sinuses and I flinched as the cool texture of the wall tickled the hot skin of my back. I linked my feet around Porter's lower back as his lips traveled to the base of my neck, planting demanding kisses against my skin, sending me into a frenzy.

I craved him, all of him.

"I want to please you." My hand cupped his hardness.

"What? No—" he started to protest.

I'd told Porter about my honeymoon, and because of that awful experience he hadn't allowed me to pleasure him in that way. But today, I wasn't taking no for an answer.

"I want to try . . . for you. Don't say no," I said boldly, pressing a finger to his lips.

He released me from his grip, slowly lowering me to the floor. We shifted our bodies, and I pressed his shoulders against the wall. Porter swallowed hard before releasing a sigh.

Ever so slowly, I unzipped his jeans, tugging them to the floor. My eyes locked with Porter's as I removed his boxer shorts. He was ready for me. Completely ready. Before he could protest, I'd taken him into my mouth, teasing his tip with my tongue.

"Oh God . . ." Porter murmured.

My eyes never left his as I moved up and down on his length, savoring the feel of him inside my mouth. Unlike my experience three years ago, I enjoyed this. The pulsing of my private area continued, and moisture collected in my panties. I was ready for him.

Porter tugged at the base of my braid, pulling my mouth from him. "Not like this," he said, his eyes dark.

"But I—"

"Shhh," he whispered, pressing a finger to my lips and lifting me to my feet. "I need to be inside you."

I cracked a smile, knowing just how much my body craved its own release. But instead of walking me to the bed, as we'd always done in the past, Porter turned me so that I faced the open window. He tugged at the curtains, giving us privacy.

"Hold on to the windowsill."

I did as I was told. Instead of his directions intimidating me, as Lehi's always had, they excited me. Adrenaline created pathways through my system as Porter yanked my panties to the floor. He walked away for just a moment, but returned with a condom. After opening the package and sliding it down his length, he entered me from behind. My body tensed slightly, having never experienced anything like this position in the past.

"I'll go slow," he assured me, gliding in and out of me in a gentle rhythm. "I'd never hurt you."

"I know," I responded in a hushed tone. "Don't hold back."

With that whispered invitation, Porter quickened his pace. He slipped one hand in front, his fingers circling my most sensitive spot as he pumped behind me, and I moaned at the touch of his fingertips. Pleasure built within me as I approached my release. Porter's forehead pressed against my neck and the heat of his breath spurred my excitement.

My knuckles turned a ghostly shade of white as I gripped the window frame, my body preparing for the orgasm building within me.

"Come for me, Brin," Porter moaned. "You're so close, I can feel it."

The gravelly tone of his voice, combined with the intoxicating strokes of his fingers pushed me over the edge. I seized around him in ecstasy, screaming his name out the open window before collapsing onto the ledge. Porter continued to thrust inside me before finding his release. He gripped my braid as he came, groaning through gritted teeth.

Together, we fell to the floor, the heat from our bodies cooled by the breeze that billowed the curtain.

"God, you're amazing," he said before kissing the top of my forehead. "Was that okay for you? Not scary or anything?"

"Not at all." I shook my head. "I liked it."

"Good."

We lay in silence for several minutes before, at my request, Porter played the mix of CDs he'd created with me in mind. Bob Dylan belted out "Shelter from the Storm," and without even realizing it, I began to sing along. I loved that I was learning the lyrics—they were heartfelt, loving, and full of passion.

They reminded me of Porter. He was my shelter from the storm that was my life.

"I know what to tell them," I muttered, finally hearing the answer inside my head.

"What are you talking about?" Porter asked, obviously confused.

I'd noticed over the weeks we'd been physically intimate that after we'd made love, my brain was on high alert. It was sharp and keen, full of ideas. Porter said his head was "mush" after making love to me. So I was used to conversations like this—me having a sudden idea or revelation, and Porter confused by my burst of self-proclaimed genius.

"You wanted us to get away. For a weekend."

"Oh, right. Of course, yes." He stroked my arm so lightly that goose bumps rose.

"Jessa. I'll tell them she needs me."

"She's the sister who had the—"

"Miscarriage, yes. I'll tell them she had another, and that my mother is too sick to help."

"Is it safe? Will Lehi contact her husband or something?"

"No," I said, "that's why it'll work. Lehi doesn't like Kurt and vice versa. It should work fine. Besides, what you said was true. If I'm on borrowed time, what does it matter? If Jorjina is spying on me and reporting back to the prophet, then my days are already numbered."

Porter pulled away, pushing up on his elbow and peering into my eyes. "Are. You. Sure?"

"Yes. I want to be with you, and not just for a few stolen hours. I want to fall asleep in your arms, wake up the same way. I want, even if only for twenty-four hours, to feel like I'm really yours."

"You *are* mine. Always." A single tear fell from Porter's eye. Rather than wipe it away or get embarrassed as I'd expected, he simply pursed his lips and shrugged. There was nothing else to say.

chapter 21

JORJINA WAS FURIOUS.

And panicked.

For just a moment, she knew the girl could see through her—see the truth. But not all of it. Not nearly all of it. Nevertheless, she worried that the damage was done. That she'd tipped her hand in a moment of vulnerability. She wanted to reassure her, to help her understand. To assure her that she had no intention of turning her back on Brinley for her son's benefit.

Those days were done.

For four years, Jorjina had been forced to play a part in a ruse against the women of the compound. Each time a new helper would be assigned to her, Clarence would sit his mother down and explain the conflict at hand—what information was needed, what secrets were demanded. And for four years, she'd played her role.

But not anymore.

She was done being a pawn, done playing a part in the twisted games of her son. Done manipulating the innocent lives of those around her.

Heavenly Father did not condone manipulation. Their god did not want her to lie, to exploit, to expose the weaknesses of others. In no way did her son's methods exemplify the role of a true prophet.

Her husband had been different. Walter Black was a true prophet, a leader who loved the members of their community and stayed true to his word, no matter the consequences to himself. He believed in the goodness of his people, in the path to celestial heaven. He walked the walk and talked the talk.

He was truly a good man. A man you could believe in, a man you could follow through the gates of Heavenly Father.

Clarence, however, was an entirely different story.

Even at the age of seven, Clarence showed signs of being selfish, manipulative, and untrustworthy. Jorjina remembered the lies he told on a daily basis, all self-serving, of course. He'd lie to his siblings and about them. He'd lie to make himself look better in his father's eyes. And no matter the punishment, no matter how red his little bottom became from the spankings Jorjina was forced to give him, he never repented. He never learned his lesson.

He felt entitled to his lies, to his abhorrent behavior . . . after all, he was the oldest son of the prophet. And at an early age, the very bright boy had learned that he would, in time, take over that role for his father. In time, the entire compound of ten thousand residents would be under his advisement, under his control.

When Clarence turned twelve years old, Jorjina discovered that he'd been stealing from not only his parents, but from the other sister wives and children as well. While completing routine house cleaning, Jorjina had decided to rearrange the storage in her sons' bedroom. Clarence shared a room with two of his younger brothers, but had claimed the majority of the closet as his own. When Jorjina accidentally dropped a pair of socks on the floor of the closet, the lid of a large shoebox was nudged open, and her eyes widened in disbelief.

When she knelt down and opened the box fully, she discovered hundreds of dollars in cash, house keys, watches, prayer books, and several small diaries stolen from his sisters. Jorjina was aghast at the selfish and sneaky behavior of her son. The thought of him becoming prophet ran chills down her spine. And so she confronted Walter.

"He can't be your successor. He just can't." She held the open box for Walter to inspect. After sifting through the stolen belongings, he closed his eyes tightly and sighed.

"I'm afraid there's nothing to be done. He's the oldest. It's the way of our community. My hands are tied."

"What about Paul? He's a good boy. Or Joseph . . . either one of them would be adequate for the job."

Walter's forehead wrinkled in consternation. Jorjina knew he agreed with her, that Clarence was not capable of truly leading the people of their faith. But he expected her to keep sweet, to force her emotions down below the surface. He told her that when the time came, he would confer with Heavenly Father and make the proper decision.

Ten years later, however, he died suddenly without ever telling his sons, or Jorjina, who his successor would be.

In accordance with tradition, Clarence had assumed the role of prophet a mere two minutes after his father was pronounced dead at the local hospital. Jorjina had wailed as she clutched her husband, taken entirely too soon. But when she looked up at Clarence, tears clouding her eyes, she didn't see any sign that her son was in mourning. Instead she saw a twitch of satisfaction in his expression. It didn't surprise her, but it sickened her just the same.

That was more than ten years prior to the present day in her kitchen, where the young Brinley had turned a ghostly pale and closed herself off to Jorjina. Her heart ached, knowing that the friendship she had attempted to build with the girl was in jeopardy, knowing there was absolutely nothing she could say to make Brinley trust her intentions.

None of the other young women had recognized, or even suspected, that the prophet was using Jorjina to learn their secrets. After several weeks, each of them had become comfortable enough to entrust Jorjina with their deepest private thoughts and emotions. And each time, it pained Jorjina to then share that information with her son.

Luckily, many instances were minor—nothing to cause a reassignment or discipline of any kind. Because of this, Jorjina and the prophet had been able to continue the underground method of retrieving information about families in question. She thought for sure when Burt Jameson's wife, the girl who constantly burned her eggs, was reassigned to the Cluff household, that this job of hers would come to a screeching halt. She'd assumed that Rebecca would inform her new sister wives that Jorjina was, in fact, the person who had revealed her secrets to the prophet. But that hadn't happened.

Rebecca, a tall woman with a full head of auburn hair, had been kind and well-intentioned with Jorjina, and they'd built a friendship on the surface. For some reason, Jorjina never felt fully comfortable with Elder Jameson's third wife. But regardless of that, she'd done her best to fulfill her duties to her son by encouraging Rebecca to share the details of her life while they walked through the vacant park on a lonely Wednesday afternoon. Rebecca had arrived that morning with bloodshot eyes, her vulnerability hanging from her sleeve. Over the years, Jorjina had developed quite the "poker face," as her late husband had called it. Rebecca, however, had none.

That day, Jorjina knew the time had come for her to learn the secrets of the Jameson household. And so she pushed for Rebecca to confide in her. She made no promises of keeping said secrets; she couldn't handle telling outright lies. But she attempted to make Rebecca as comfortable as possible as they walked through the park, the sun shining brightly above them as they made their way along a winding path.

"You know you can talk to me, dear," Jorjina had said. Rebecca bit down on her lower lip and Jorjina knew she wanted to talk, to release her pent-up frustrations and emotions.

"It's just, well, my sister wives dislike me."

"How could they dislike you? You're such a sweet girl," Jorjina said sweetly.

Rebecca shook her head abruptly. "They do, and it's my fault. It's completely my fault. I ruined their family the moment the prophet pronounced us man and wife."

Jorjina had taken Rebecca's hand in hers and stopped walking. "Talk to me, dear. You'll feel better, I promise."

It wasn't a lie, not technically, anyway, but it felt like one. A wave of guilt rolled through Jorjina. She didn't want to do this anymore. Destroying lives was not her chosen path in life.

"Burt and I . . . we have this . . . connection. It's magical, when we're together. I'm sure that sounds ridiculous, but—"

"No, not at all. Walter and I had the same thing. He was taken with me, and I enjoyed that. I cherished it."

"I do too. But my sister wives, they won't talk to me, they won't *look* at me. I've been married to Burt for twelve years, and I feel like I'll never truly be part of the family."

"Is it that bad?"

Rebecca shrugged her shoulders. "The worst part is . . ." She hesitated before wiping her misty eyes. "That I feel like his mistress."

"Bite your tongue, girl," Jorjina had said with wide eyes. She hadn't expected anything as serious as this.

"It's true, I do. Yes, we're married. Yes, I was revealed to the prophet as the third wife, but what he feels for me, he doesn't feel for them."

“Has he told you this?”

“Yes, ma’am.”

“And how do you know he doesn’t say this to all of you, as a way of making you feel special?”

Jorjina knew of men in their community who told little white lies to their wives, “secretly” revealing them to be his favorite in order to keep them all content within the confines of their plural marriage.

“I know because . . . because, the other wives have accused me of stealing his time, stealing him away from them, from their hearts.”

“I don’t understand.”

“He doesn’t want to sleep with them anymore. He makes excuses, tells them he’s tired or not feeling well.”

“Oh, that does sound serious.”

“They’re angry, they both want more children. They feel cheated out of their life’s purpose.”

“Does Burt understand that what he’s doing is wrong?” Jorjina pressed, needing to get all the pertinent information before reporting back to Clarence.

“He doesn’t care. He says I’m the only one who matters to him. He’s even mentioned leaving the compound . . . just us and our boys.”

“Oh my.” Jorjina’s jaw dropped. Clarence had suspected favoritism, but defection? No. Even Clarence would be surprised when Jorjina divulged the secrets of the Jameson household.

Rebecca pressed her hand to her mouth. Jorjina changed tactics, suspecting that Rebecca knew she’d told her too many of their secrets.

"It's all right, dear," she'd whispered to Rebecca. "Let's go back to my house. I'll let you sit in my armchair. You can rest your head, rest your thoughts."

"Oh, okay," Rebecca muttered, hanging her head.

Within days, Rebecca had been reassigned to the Cluff household. Since then, Jorjina had been plagued with guilt and remorse. She wished that she had misdirected Clarence's suspicions. But she felt it would have been only a matter of time before one or both of Rebecca's sister wives reported Burt to the prophet.

Jorjina had enjoyed a few peaceful months with no helper to speak of. She'd been able to lounge on her back patio, listening to the birds sing from the wall of the compound. She'd hoped that Clarence's conniving ways would catch up to him, that no more helpers would be assigned to her home.

But on a day when she least expected it, Clarence informed her of a new helper. And in a moment of irony, that new helper was one of the very sister wives she'd assumed would be aware of her underhanded behavior. A wife of Lehi Cluff.

But Brinley knew nothing of Rebecca's earlier position as her helper. And not only that, the two women had bonded . . . truly bonded. Jorjina genuinely liked the seventh wife of Lehi Cluff, despite the fact that she despised Brinley's husband.

Lehi reminded Jorjina of her son, Clarence. Both were selfish, narrow minded, and expected their wives to be completely subservient to them in every possible way.

Walter hadn't been like that. Despite being the most powerful man in their compound, Walter was interested in the opinions of his wives. Each week, they'd have extensive family meetings where he not only welcomed his wives to offer him feedback on the household, but he demanded that if they were too intimidated to share during the meetings, that they made time to tell him one-on-one. He knew he couldn't make them all happy at once, but he did his very best to maintain harmony in his household. The happiness of his wives, his children, his *family* meant something to him.

Once he had passed away, she realized just how lucky she had been to have such a considerate husband. Now she was surrounded by men like Clarence, like Lehi, who had no appreciation for their wives or children.

Men who did not deserve sweet and gracious young women like Brinley.

Jorjina saw something in Brinley—something she wanted to encourage, to nurture. She wanted to give Brinley every opportunity to explore the world on her own terms. Never before had Jorjina offered to allow a helper to have a daily break. That was specifically something she had offered to her newest helper. She could only imagine how unappreciated Brinley was by Lehi Cluff. And although it was against the doctrine she held so dear, she was tempted to encourage Brinley to leave the compound, to leave the religion, the faith.

Jorjina was old. She'd lived her life, but when she spent time with Brinley she was reminded of just how many young women were sacrificing theirs. And she cared too much for Brinley to lose decades of her life to a man who didn't appreciate her.

She wanted to help her. But after her slipup in the kitchen, she wasn't sure that could ever happen.

Brinley no longer trusted her. And she had no idea how to regain that trust.

But she was determined to do her very best to do just that . . . Clarence be damned.

chapter 22

THE PLAN WAS SET into motion. In just a matter of hours, I'd have an entire night away with Porter. More than twenty-four hours away from the compound, the Cluff household, and my role as the seventh wife of Lehi. For one night only, it would just be Brinley and Porter. That was all.

I was so excited that my thoughts were bouncing around inside my head. Calming myself enough to talk with Lehi had been challenging. For just a moment, I thought that maybe he'd express concern regarding my supposed pregnancy, that perhaps he wouldn't want me exerting myself by traveling to Jessa's home across the compound, or assisting her with too many things in her home. I had a speech prepared in case it was necessary.

It wasn't.

"How long will you be gone?" he asked, feigning interest. It was a Saturday morning, and the children surrounded my husband in the common area of the home. The boys played a rowdy game of tag while two of the girls assisted Brenda with her knitting project. He removed his glasses and pinched the bridge of his nose.

"Just one evening," I said. "Her husband is away on a job, and she needs support."

"And your mother? She can't help Jessa for one night?"

"She's still not well and there's no one else. I'm sorry, but she nee—"

He shook his head. "It's fine. But check with Leandra regarding your chores."

"Yes, sir," I said. "And thank you."

"Mm-hmm." He grunted, turning his attention back to the children running freely around the common area.

Quickly, I went to speak to the first wife regarding my responsibilities. As my feet crossed the threshold into the kitchen area, I could hear Lehi scolding two of the boys for being too aggressive with each other. I shook my head at the irony.

"Overnight?" Leandra screeched.

"Yes." I remained stone-faced, determined not to let Leandra get to me. I had permission from Lehi and that was all I needed. "Lehi has given me his blessing. I just need to know if there are any chores you'll need me to complete before I leave."

Leandra's hands pressed into her hips as she glowered at me. I raised my chin in defiance, showing her I would not back down to her. Not anymore.

Instead of protesting, however, she simply offered a dismissive wave of her hand. "No. The other wives will pitch in."

"Thank you."

"Be home by lunch tomorrow."

"All right," I answered, turning to walk away from my scowling sister wife.

"That's not a request," she snapped. "I expect you to be here when lunch is served."

Keep sweet. She's not worth it. Keep sweet. She's not worth it.

"Yes, Leandra."

Smoke filled the kitchen and Leandra shouted, "Rebecca, your eggs are burning! Honestly, girl, they are the easiest things to cook! How do you manage to constantly burn the eggs?"

I walked to my room to retrieve the one suitcase I owned. It was old and blue, given to me by my mother the day of my wedding to Lehi. I'd used it on my honeymoon for our evening at the seedy motel, but hadn't touched it since. Dust had collected on it after three years on the top shelf of my closet.

I was going to make new memories with this suitcase. New memories with Porter.

And I couldn't wait.

A look of confusion crossed Tiffany's face when I entered the free clinic. She had been hunched over the desk, handling never-ending paperwork, and when she saw me, I noticed her lower her gaze to check the calendar, knowing I wasn't due for another batch of pills for at least two weeks. The goofy grin on my face revealed that I was up to something. Her lips lifted into a smile as I approached.

"You look different," she said, looking me up and down.

I had no real response; I knew she was right. I brushed at the warm skin of my cheeks, knowing that they were glowing in anticipation. All I could do was widen my grin.

"Things are good, I guess." Tiffany smirked and placed her hands on her hips.

"Yes," I admitted. "But I need your help."

Tiffany shook her head, looking slightly annoyed, then crossed her arms in front of her chest. "Why does that not surprise me?"

Right then and there, I realized that the only time I visited my cousin was when I needed something from her. Shame washed over me, making me feel small and petty.

"I-I'm sorry, Tiffany. I should come by more, just to see you."

"Whatever, it's fine." She flipped her short hair behind her ear before glancing down at the suitcase at my feet. "Oh my gosh, are you . . . are you leaving? Like, for good?"

"No."

"Oh." Her brightened expression dimmed to one of conflicted concern. "Then, um, what do you need?"

"I-I want to surprise Porter. We're spending the night together, and I don't want to look like . . ." I pinched at the fabric of my dress. "Well, I don't want to look like this."

"Are you serious?" Her smile widened into a toothy grin as she clenched her teeth. "That's awesome!"

"I was hoping you could loan me some clothes. I'd return them, of course."

"Of course." She glanced back to the other employees at the desk before taking a quick look at her wristwatch. "I'll take a quick lunch break. We can go to my apartment and I'll send you on your way."

"Are you sure it's okay?"

"Are you kidding? I'm so proud of you right now, I can hardly stand it. Just give me a sec."

Tiffany walked back to speak to another employee, gestured to me, and then reached under the counter to retrieve her purse.

"Follow me," she said with a smile. There was a bounce to her step that I'd never seen before.

We walked two blocks to her apartment, which was situated above the drugstore. We climbed the three flights up to her small residence.

"It's a studio, so it's tiny," she admitted as we walked into the one-room apartment. "But it's all mine."

I took in the deep red and white curtains that hung from the windows, feeling drawn to their bold color, a color not allowed on the compound. Tiffany was embracing her freedom and expressing her personality through her decor. Her couch was a deep plum color and several posters hung from the walls. I wasn't sure what they represented—movies? Bands? I didn't know, but was curious.

"I love it." And I did. I was taken with her tiny home, and for the first time wasn't afraid of what it represented. Instead, I was fascinated.

"So . . ." Tiffany walked to a small white dresser and removed several tops of assorted colors, placing them on her bed. "You can borrow whatever you want. Depends on what you're most comfortable in."

I reached out to touch the soft fabric of a pale yellow tunic. It was modest, but delicate and pretty.

"May I?" I asked, holding it up to my chest.

"Of course."

"Can I use your bathroom?"

"Don't be silly, just change here." When I bit my bottom lip, Tiffany rolled her eyes. "I'm not looking at you or anything."

"All right."

Removing the dress that felt like it was stitched together with twenty pounds of fabric, I stared at the other items she placed on the bed. A pink sweatshirt, jeans, skirts, and a tiny black sweater. When I'd finally removed my dress and long underwear, I tried on each piece, finally opting for the tunic and jeans.

"You look awesome."

"Thank you," I said, turning my body as I glanced at my reflection in the mirror. I was taken aback at how pants felt on my body. The jeans hugged my thighs and flared slightly at my ankles. I'd always felt that we were required to wear our bulky dresses to reinforce our femininity, but I was wrong. I felt more feminine in that pair of jeans than I had in my twenty-two years wearing nothing but dresses.

"What about your hair?"

I closed my eyes and inhaled, exhaling softly through my mouth. It was time.

"Will you change it for me?"

"Do you mean style it?"

"Yes, please."

Tiffany crossed to me and removed the rubber band holding my hair in the thick braid. Her fingers sifted through the thick layers, allowing the strands to loosen. My scalp tingled as the hair was released.

"Do you want me to cut it?"

I gasped.

"Never mind," Tiffany said with a laugh.

"Not yet," I said, grasping a handful of hair and holding it close. "I'm not ready."

"I get it," Tiffany conceded, stroking my hair gently with her fingertips. "I chopped mine off immediately and I kinda wish I hadn't."

"Why's that?"

She shrugged. "I guess it felt like an act of rebellion, not freedom. Now when I cut it, it's freedom. I'm making a choice *for* myself, not *against* the prophet or my parents or whatever."

"That makes sense."

"Wait as long as you like. I shouldn't have asked that, I'm sorry."

"It's all right."

"Let's see here," she said, pulling my thick locks into her hands. "What if I curl it? I can give you some loose waves. It'll be gorgeous."

"I trust you."

An hour later, I found myself in front of Porter's door, feeling unsure of myself and of my appearance. I had no idea if he would approve of the changes I made.

When I'd taken one final glance in Tiffany's full-length mirror, I was astounded at the look Tiffany had created. The tunic was loose enough that I didn't feel too on display for the men who passed me on the sidewalk, yet the jeans hugged my thighs in a way that made me feel sexy—and I wasn't sure how I felt about that. I needed to see Porter's reaction to feel validated.

I needed to know if I belonged in his world. Because we both knew he'd outgrown mine.

The door opened and Porter stared at me in silence. Pressure filled my chest as I waited for a reaction, then I immediately began mentally chastising myself. He must have been less than impressed with the changes I'd made to my body, my hair, my clothing.

"I-I'm sorry, I'll . . . I'll go back . . . I'll change." Humiliated, I clenched my fists, hating that I was showing so much vulnerability, first with my appearance and then my stutter.

"What?" Porter grabbed my elbow. "No, *no*, Brin. You shocked me, but I love this. You look so natural, so . . . different. It's like I'm seeing you with new eyes."

"Oh." I cleared my throat. "I was worried. I thought you hated how I looked."

He pulled me close, running his fingers through my newly wavy hair from root to tip. "First of all, no way. That's impossible." He chuckled. "Secondly, have you looked in a mirror? You're freaking hot."

I glanced down shyly, my shoulders rising in modest happiness. "Thank you."

"Did you do this for me?"

"No. Well, yes." I hesitated. "I did it for both of us."

He pressed his lips to my forehead. "I'm so glad you did." He wrapped his hands around my waist.

I peered into the long hallway, feeling bashful. "Should I come in?"

"Well, actually, I have a surprise for you," he said. "Just give me a minute, okay?"

Porter grinned in a way that I'd never seen before. He seemed giddy. Was it my outfit? The fact that he could finally run his fingers through my hair as he'd been dying to do for weeks? Or was it the surprise he mentioned? Regardless, he had my full attention. Knowing that I could cause such happiness in Porter made me fall even more for him.

"Ready?" he asked, dragging the old suitcase behind him.

"You're using it," I said, gesturing to his dusty case. The smile ran away from Porter's face and I immediately wanted to pretend I'd never drawn attention to his choice in luggage.

"For this? Absolutely."

"This?" I asked, puzzled once again.

"You'll see. Come on, Brin."

We drove for over an hour with the radio blasting and the windows rolled down. For just a moment, I was tempted to unbuckle my safety belt and hang my feet out the window, but I didn't have it in me. Not yet, at least.

Porter turned the car onto a gravel road that almost resembled the compound. Hesitation and comfort, in equal measure, rose in my throat. I had no idea where we were going, but I was eager to find out.

Finally Porter turned at a tiny yellow mailbox, and pulled the car into a dirt driveway in front of a small cottage.

"Where are we?" I asked, peering at the tiny house. It was in the final stages of construction, framed and roofed and sheathed, the windows and doors installed, but it wasn't yet complete.

Porter stopped the engine, removed his key, and looked me in the eye. "Home."

"What?" I asked, slightly panicked. Had Porter just said we were *home?* What and where exactly was home?

"Well, mine, anyway. Let me show you."

Pebbles crunched under my sneakers as we walked through the dirt to approach the porch of the tiny residence.

"But you live in your apartment . . . don't you?" My heart was racing. I didn't understand.

He opened the door to reveal an empty living area. Unpainted drywall lined the small room that was about the size of my bedroom at the Cluff house. I could see and smell the wood of brand new kitchen cabinets as Porter led me into the kitchen. The countertops had been installed, but the room hadn't been painted and there were no appliances yet.

"About a year ago, my boss bought this land, all of this. And then his wife dropped a bomb on him. She wanted a divorce."

"Okay."

"He was going to build her dream house. But when she left him, he couldn't even hear her name, let alone deal with this." Porter gestured around the house. "So, he offered the land to me. Instead of a bonus. I took it, I mean, who turns down free land?"

"Wow."

He continued to tell his story as we walked through the small one-bedroom cottage. Pride brightened his expression as he showed me the living room, kitchen with dining area, and a bedroom with an adjoining bath.

"So on Sundays, I come here to clear my head. I bought a bunch of lumber from him, and I've been working slowly. And for a while, I didn't do anything at all."

"You didn't? Why not?"

He pursed his lips and shrugged. "Not motivated, I guess. But that all changed when I met you."

The pumping of my heart accelerated and butterflies swarmed my belly.

"Did you know I've been clean for two months?" he asked, taking my hand.

I knew he'd been doing his best, but I'd avoided mentioning timetables for fear of frightening him or setting him up for failure.

"No, I didn't."

"That's because of you, Brin. You're my motivation."

My cheeks burned and I squeezed his hand before he continued.

"I've been building again, and it's actually pretty awesome. I come out here, blast my music, and work my ass off, and then I go home to my loser roommates and pass out." He scratched the back of his neck and laughed. "I can't stay there. I'll never stay clean if I do, even with you in my life."

I flinched. I'd hoped that his feelings for me would and could be motivation enough for him to stop killing himself slowly with drugs.

"It's the God's honest truth, unfortunately. They're a bunch of miserable guys all huddled together eating garbage, playing video games, watching porn . . . and out of sheer boredom, they get high. I know because I was one of them. I have to get out of there."

"That's wonderful, Porter. I'm so proud of you. And this place—"

"I know it's nothing compared to the mansion you live in now. But I have three acres here. One day, it'll be more than this. It'll just take time."

"You didn't let me finish. I was going to say this place, it's beautiful. Truly beautiful."

"It will be."

Hours later, we were lying on an air mattress as candles flickered, painting shadows on the walls of the bedroom. A half-eaten pizza and an empty wine bottle sat on the floor next to us.

"You know," Porter murmured, "you've become pretty feisty."

"Feisty?" I asked, shocked. I pushed onto my elbow. "What on earth . . . ?"

"Calm down," he said, sitting up. "I just mean, you know, you're not afraid to take control in the bedroom. I like it. I like it *a lot*."

I knew what he was talking about.

That night, perhaps influenced by the wine I'd used to wash down my dinner, I'd initiated sex between us. Not only that, though, I'd been on top for the first time. It was exhilarating to have Porter beneath me, his eyes wide, his hands clutching my breasts as I moved above him. He'd given me plenty of orgasms, but that one was pretty spectacular.

"You bring it out in me, I guess."

"Nah, you're just a vixen." He winked.

I was starting to get used to his sense of humor. It was what Leandra would call inappropriate, but to me, the less I judged, the funnier it became.

When I swatted him with the back of my hand, he pretended to flinch as my hand made contact with his bare skin. "And you're a—a . . ."

"I'm a what?" he pressed. Porter knew that name calling was not something I was used to, or at all comfortable with.

I'd planned to call him a jerk, but instead, I had to tell him what I was really feeling.

It was time.

"You're a dream." My cheeks turned hot as I looked down at the blanket draped across my bare chest. His presence in my life was like a light . . . a beacon of hope. The prophet was constantly talking about following the light, following the way of our Lord. But up until meeting Porter, my life was so dark, so dull, and so serious. I was told about light, told about beacons and hope and faith, but had never experienced them.

But Porter made me feel all those things. He was quite literally a dream come true.

"And you," he murmured, placing a hand gently behind my neck, "are my heaven."

I was stunned.

In our religion, heaven was the ultimate destination, the place we worked so hard to earn. For Porter to say I was his heaven here on earth left me speechless. Utterly and completely speechless.

"How can you say such a thing?" My curiosity was getting the better of me. I couldn't just accept a compliment of this magnitude; I had to *understand* it.

He took a deep breath. "The compound . . . that place is my hell. It represents all of the awful things that I'll have to live with for the rest of my life. But you, you're my heaven. My new beginning, my paradise. Does that make sense?"

Completely overcome with his confession, I pressed my lips to his, deepening the kiss immediately. I moved to straddle his stomach, then leaned over to plant kiss after kiss on his face, his neck, and his chest before finally accepting the most breathtaking compliment of my life.

"Yes, it does." My eyes welled with tears. "Thank you."

Porter pushed to a seated position, holding me steady in his lap so that my legs wrapped around his waist, and my heels pressed into the muscles of his back.

He swallowed hard, his eyes wary as he said, "I'm in love with you."

I'd be lying to myself if I said it didn't scare me. But I felt the same way and I needed to express it, but somehow those three words didn't seem adequate.

Porter apparently could read the worry on my face. "What is it?" he asked, shifting slightly.

"I'm not sure I can form the words. Love doesn't seem like enough. You're just . . . you've changed my life."

"And you've changed mine." He still looked confused as his fingertips slid down my cheeks.

"I love you in a way that I didn't know I could," I finally said, and Porter smiled and released a sigh. "And I love you in a way that I never will again."

He cupped my face in his hands, his expression pained. "We have to do this, Brin. You and me. Please don't say no. I'm begging you."

"I know," I said, smoothing his hair with my fingertips as I nodded. "I'll never say no to you again."

The screams in my head had arrived.

And I welcomed them with open arms.

chapter 23

"HOW ARE YOU FEELING?" Jorjina Black asked me. We were sitting at her dining room table, waiting for our cherry pie to finish baking. Jorjina had been hesitant to try my mother's specialty dessert, claiming that chocolate was the one and only gateway to her heart. But I'd insisted, wanting to share the recipe with someone who appreciated sweets as much as Jorjina did.

To say that I was apprehensive around her would be accurate. I was. But I enjoyed her company, and was feeling slightly relieved that when I'd begrudgingly returned to the Cluff household after my night away, no one seemed to even notice that I'd been gone. Lehi wasn't waiting for me, and Leandra wasn't jumping to confront me about my secrets or my whereabouts.

Could I trust Jorjina? I wasn't sure. But I was required to spend my days with her, so decided to make the very best of it. And that included making my mother's famous cherry pie.

"I'm fine." I crossed my hands over my abdomen, as was expected of me. According to the calendar, I was about to begin my second trimester, so I played the part. "My morning sickness is calming down. Hopefully that's not a bad sign."

"It's time. Soon you'll enter the gorging phase." She cackled, then took a sip of her tea.

"Gorging?"

"Sure." She threaded her fingers together, leaning her hands on the mahogany table. "Food tastes exquisite in the second trimester. No more crackers for you, girl."

I smiled, wishing I could trust this woman. She was so unlike Leandra or any of my sister wives. She felt like family.

But family doesn't spy on you—or report your behavior to the prophet.

"Listen," she said, a serious look taking over her face. "I've made a decision, and you're not allowed to object, because, well . . . just because."

"Okay . . ." I dug my teeth dug into my bottom lip, wondering what she could possibly mean.

Jorjina rose to her feet, removed a wad of bills from her pocket, and held them in the palm of her hand. "Stand up."

I did as I was told. And when I did, she shoved the money into the pocket of my dress.

"Jorjina, why—?"

She shook her head and grasped my hands. "You've been with me for weeks, day in and day out. You deserve to be paid."

"I can't accept this." Pulling away, I dug my hand into the pocket and clutched the money. "This job is an honor, it's—"

"Stop." The wrinkles in her forehead deepened, punctuating the severity of her tone. "I want you to have this. I'm an old woman, Clarence takes care of me. I have no bills, no worries, and nothing to spend my money on. I'd like to spend it on you."

"But . . . but Lehi takes care of me, as well," I replied, playing along with my role as a happily married woman and mother-to-be.

"He doesn't need to know about this. This money is *yours*, do you hear me?"

"Yes, ma'am."

"Don't you dare hand it over to Cluff. Promise me."

Hearing her refer to Lehi that way ran chills down my spine. I was intrigued, to say the least. The expression on her face was sincere, and I could feel her desire to protect me. She reminded me so much of Aspen. They both seemed to want to protect me from harm, to keep me safe.

"I promise."

Our eyes were locked as we stood there, frozen for a moment. My mouth was agape, and I had no idea what else to say to express my gratitude. I broke our gaze and reached for my chair. But before I had the chance to sit, Jorjina wrapped her arms around me in a tight hug.

"I want the best for you," she murmured against my hair. "Please believe me."

"I-I do," I whispered.

She pulled back, her hands gripping my shoulders. "No, you don't." She shook her head hard, her eyes tearing up as she spoke. "You think I'm tricking you. But I swear to you, on the grave of Walter, that I'm not. I want to help you."

"But why?" I didn't understand why Jorjina would pledge her loyalty to me rather than her own son.

"I told you I've grown rather attached to you and that was the truth. You're a good girl. And I know that man doesn't deserve you."

"Lehi?" I asked.

"Well, yes. Who else would I be talking about?" Her cocked to the side like a bird as her eyes narrowed.

I froze. And my heart raced.

Beep. Beep. Beep. The oven timer broke the tension of the moment.

Quickly, I scurried to the stove, avoiding Jorjina's prying eyes. She was most certainly on to me. I removed the pie from the oven, then kept my back to Jorjina as I ran water to wash dishes that had piled in the sink.

"Is there . . . someone else?" Jorjina crossed the room and stood next to me as my shaky hand gripped the rolling pin, covered in flour and dried dough.

"Of course not!" I shrieked, still avoiding her gaze. "I'm a married woman. I'm expecting my first child. What kind of person do you think I am?"

As loudly as I protested, though, I was certain she could see through my performance. I clung to my lies, but my burning face and shaking hands gave me away.

"I think you're a lovely person who is stuck. Stuck with a husband who will never love you. Stuck with sister wives who will never appreciate you. And stuck in a community that will continue to stifle you until the day you die."

I dropped the rolling pin and turned to face her. "How can you say that? Your husband was the prophet!"

"I know, I know," she said, pacing the kitchen. "I know Walter would be ashamed of me. I know it."

"You barely know me, Jorjina."

My voice cracked as I leaned against the porcelain sink, holding on for dear life. Jorjina stopped pacing and turned to me with her hands on her hips. Her white hair fell from the poof of her bangs, but she didn't notice. She was disheveled, frustrated, and seemingly desperate for me to hear her.

"I've been on this earth for a *long* time, dear. I *know* you. I see you for who you are, for what you have to offer this world."

"To serve the prophet, my husband and Heavenly Father—"

"Perhaps." She nodded. "But then again . . . maybe this isn't the place for you."

The temperature of her kitchen seemed to rise within seconds. The neckline of my dress became damp from the sweat glistening on my clammy skin. I didn't know what to say, what to believe, who to trust. Did Jorjina think I was damned?

"Why do you say that? Do you think I'm not good enough to be part of the chosen?" I was careful not to raise my voice against my employer, but found myself more confident in demanding the answers I needed.

"No, dear. Absolutely not. If anything, it's the other way around."

I gasped. Audibly.

"Things were different," she went on. "Years ago, when my husband was still with us. He was different. He was kind, he cared for and loved every single person of our faith. He was a man of God, and of his word."

"What are you saying? That your son . . . that he's not?"

I knew the answer, just as I was sure most people in the compound knew that Clarence Black was not a kind man, or a loving man. He was not a protector of his people. He was a protector of his role as prophet. But I had to see Jorjina's face. I had to know her response to that question—it would tell me everything I needed to know.

"Yes." She hung her head in shame. "That's what I'm saying."

"And the money?" I asked, removing it from my pocket. I didn't have to look at the bills to know that I was holding an outrageous amount of money for a twenty-two-year-old woman of our faith.

"I want to give you every opportunity to go. If that's what you want."

"And if it's not?"

"Then it doesn't matter. All that matters is that I've given you an *option*. And my heart can rest with that knowledge, that I did the right thing."

Before placing the money back into my pocket, I purposely counted the bills. One by one, I flipped each bill between my fingertips until I reached the end. Jorjina stayed silent, her eyes on me as I counted. The tension in the large kitchen was evident as I raised my gaze to meet hers.

"Eight hundred and seventy-three dollars?" I screeched.

"Yes." She hung her head. "It's all I had."

I placed the bills on the counter. "No, I can't."

Jorjina lunged for the counter, snatched up the money, and stuffed it back into my pocket, her nose just inches from my own.

"Yes, you can and you will," she snarled. "If you don't, you'll regret it for the *rest* of your life. Let me help you, Brinley, please."

My hand wrapped around hers, squeezing hard. "Why? What's in it for you?"

"Peace of mind? Redemption?" She pulled from my grip and waved her arms wildly in the air.

"Redemption? Why do you need to be redeemed? You're the mother of the prophet!"

Jorjina stepped back, took in a deep breath, and wiped the sweat from her forehead before she spoke in a calm, soft tone. "I've sinned against the women of this community. My behavior was beyond wicked and I *need* redemption, Brinley. I need it more than you could ever understand. Please, take the money. Take the money and let me rest at night knowing I did all I could to help instead of hurt . . . for once."

"For once? But—" My jaw dropped as I flashed back to the scene in the kitchen two days prior. Leandra yelling at Rebecca burning the eggs.

Everything was starting to make sense. Everything.

The girl who burned the eggs. The one Jorjina mentioned months before.

It was Rebecca. Rebecca was reassigned after working here, after helping Jorjina.

She was being *watched*.

Gut instinct told me that Jorjina was telling the truth today. Her confession was clear. Her trembling hands, her tear-soaked face told the story of her regret, but obviously that had not always been the case. She'd been the prophet's informant for months, perhaps years.

"You're safe here," Jorjina whispered. "I swear it. Please, Brinley. You have to believe me. You're safe."

"I believe you," I said, taking her hand in mine. "I do."

She wrapped her arms around me and sobbed into the crook of my neck, her wails loud enough to wake her cat who slept in a ball on one of the kitchen chairs. He stood, yawned, and glared at me.

I shrugged at the cat as I held Jorjina close to me, murmuring soft words and running my fingers up and down her back in soothing motions. No matter what story her past might tell, I knew she was taking a stand, changing her direction and fighting for me. And I respected her for that. But there was no way I'd reveal my secrets.

I was going to leave the compound. This much was true.

But I was going to do it on my own terms. No one else's.

Just mine.

chapter 24

IT WAS LEANDRA'S IDEA.

Months earlier when Rebecca had returned to the Cluff house with puffy eyes and balled-up fists, Leandra had pulled her aside to the fabric room and insisted that she share what was bothering her.

It was Brinley. And Rebecca's former husband, Burt Jameson.

Rebecca had seen them talking on the street corner. She said that Brinley had looked upset, and although Rebecca couldn't see Burt's expression, she told Leandra that she no longer trusted Brinley and her intentions toward Burt, herself, or anyone in their community.

Leandra was surprised at how easily Rebecca could be convinced to talk about what had happened, especially since it was taking quite a while for Rebecca to initially warm up to her. Leandra had blamed Brinley for that, and now she was feeling justified in her intuition.

She was a bad seed, and now Rebecca saw it too.

"You must tell the prophet. It's your duty as a member of this family." The anger in Rebecca's face turned to intimidation and fear. Leandra wasn't surprised by that reaction; many responded that way to the prophet. But not Leandra.

Yes, to Leandra the prophet was a smart, powerful man who could make or break the lives of those in the community. But she knew that she could use that to her advantage.

Leandra had a history of staying on the good side of the prophet. Her mother had been the original housekeeper of the Black household. For years, Leandra had watched her mother serve the prophet. When she was fifteen, Leandra had begged her mother to allow her to assist her at the large home of the prophet. Her mother had rejected her requests several times, until one day she was too tired to resist. She'd allowed Leandra to join her on Saturday mornings, and soon they became a team, scrubbing, mopping, and dusting the home of Walter and Jorjina Black.

Her mother was grateful for the assistance, and Jorjina Black was impressed with the young Leandra, often saying that she felt she'd make an excellent wife to one of the many men in the community. Leandra didn't want to be just any wife, however. She wanted to be a first wife. To her, there was no other rank more supreme than the first wife of a man of substance, a man with close connections to the prophet himself.

When she was sixteen years old, Leandra knew she wanted to marry Lehi Cluff. He was just a few years older than she, and his father was a close advisor to the original prophet, Walter Black. She studied Lehi, knew he was in good standing with the prophet, and knew that he had the potential to become an important elder of the church. All he needed was an exceptional first wife.

While in the company of Jorjina Black, she found ways to drop hints about Lehi. How handsome he was, how resourceful he was in his role as foreman of the prophet's construction company on the compound, and what a devout follower he was of Heavenly Father.

Jorjina would nod without a smile, and encourage Leandra to prepare herself for marriage. After all, by the age of sixteen, many women in their community were doing just that—becoming wives. Becoming the glue that held families together.

When she was seventeen, Leandra and Lehi were married in a small ceremony. She beamed and couldn't keep her eyes off her new husband, the man who was going to give her purpose, give her standing in the community . . . right alongside the prophet.

For over twenty years, Leandra and Lehi had a strong partnership, one not based on love, but appreciation. He respected her abilities in running a household, her unique ability to make the other sister wives fall in line with her wishes.

Until Brinley, that is.

Brinley stuck out like a sore thumb from the very beginning. She was nineteen, older than many of the others had been when they'd joined the family. Lehi dismissed it, insisting she was a sweet girl who was eager to please the prophet and to join them all in the celestial kingdom. But Leandra wasn't convinced. Something was off about the seventh wife of Lehi Cluff. Leandra just couldn't put her finger on it.

Until, that is, the day she convinced Rebecca to share her story with Clarence Black, their current prophet. She was hoping the prophet would hear Rebecca's story and reassign Brinley immediately. Perhaps she'd be sent to another compound, maybe one in Texas where many of the prophet's siblings resided. The logistics didn't matter to Leandra.

She just wanted Brinley gone, and she was determined to see it through.

No matter the consequences.

And so, she'd walked with Rebecca to the house of Clarence Black. One of his many wives answered the door and allowed them to enter, escorting the two women to the prophet's office where he delivered his sermons via loudspeaker. It was also the place where he conferred with Heavenly Father, as well as church elders.

The prophet welcomed the two women into his office, but expressed his surprise that Lehi had not accompanied them, as was customary.

"I apologize," Leandra had begun. "He's at work and won't return until this evening. And I'm afraid this is urgent."

"Oh." His head snapped back slightly. A pen balanced between his two index fingers as he leaned back into the soft leather of his armchair. "And what is the emergency at hand?"

Leandra turned to Rebecca, who then cleared her throat. "It's Brinley, our sister wife."

"And what about her?" the prophet asked, his brow furrowed. There was nothing dismissive about his body language. Once he'd heard the name, he'd sat up straight in his chair, his eyes boring into Rebecca's. Leandra knew they had his full attention.

"I saw her speaking to Burt." Rebecca cleared her throat again and corrected herself. "I mean, Elder Jameson." He was no longer her husband. It was no longer appropriate for her to refer to him in such a casual way.

"And what were they saying?" the prophet asked, crossing one ankle to rest on his opposite knee, that pen still balanced between his fingers. He moved it toward his mouth, back and forth . . . slowly, ever so slowly.

"I-I couldn't hear them," Rebecca stammered. "But Brinley was visibly upset. I can't help but feel as if they are planning something."

"Why do you say that?" the prophet pressed.

Leandra knew this was his way. He didn't say much but asked many questions, allowing his subject to connect the dots, place the pieces of the puzzle together, make the connections for him.

"Because, he . . . ." Rebecca hesitated for a moment before closing her eyes and continuing. "He wrote me a letter. And Brinley delivered it."

"What did the letter say?" The prophet pursed his lips tightly, and Leandra drew in a heavy breath, feeling weighed down by the tension in the air.

"He wanted me to leave with him."

Rebecca hung her head and Leandra gasped. She did not know the extent of Brinley's history with Burt.

The prophet placed both his feet on the floor and slammed the pen down on his mahogany desk.

"And abandon his wives?" he snapped.

Rebecca flinched. "Yes," she whispered, staring down at the floor.

"I see."

The room was silent for several seconds. Leandra shifted in her seat. She didn't regret bringing Rebecca here, not for a second. But she was uncomfortable with the tension in the room. She was used to controlling the tension, and this time the control was out of her hands. She didn't like feeling powerless. Not one bit.

"I am going to confer with Heavenly Father in this matter," the prophet said, leaning back in his chair and regaining his composure, his voice modulating into his usual monotone. "But rest assured I will follow through. It may take some time. I need to investigate the situation more thoroughly. And I'll need to see that letter."

The two women glanced at each other. Leandra was unsure of what that meant. She knew it was not her place to question the prophet, but the words left her mouth before she could stop them.

"Will Brinley be reassigned?"

"Miss Leandra, I hesitate to take such drastic action, especially since the Cluff household has already been altered these past few months."

Leandra nodded, biting down on her lip. She knew she was being scolded, no matter how nonthreatening his words might have been. Leandra glanced at Rebecca, who had several tears rolling down her cheeks. For a moment, Leandra felt sorry for Rebecca and for the upheaval she and her sons had endured. But her faith was undeterred and she knew it was for the best. Rebecca would heal and the boys would benefit from the influence of the Cluff family's standing within the community.

"Trust that Heavenly Father will give me the knowledge to make the right decision in this matter."

"Yes, of course." Leandra remained in her seat, hands folded in her lap, waiting to be dismissed by the prophet. She glanced again at Rebecca, whose leg was bobbing up and down. Her nerves were clearly getting the best of her. It was obvious that, despite her anger, Rebecca still cared for Burt Jameson, and that the anger she felt earlier that day was being replaced by fear.

But what was done was done.

"Thank you for the visit today." The prophet rose to his feet, and Leandra and Rebecca followed suit. "Give my regards to your husband. I'll be in touch."

Leandra and Rebecca nodded in silence, then walked to the front door of the Black household.

"That was a mistake."

Rebecca hadn't said a word for two blocks. Leandra shook her head at the misguided eighth wife.

"Pish posh," she snapped, knowing that their visit with the prophet was entirely necessary for the survival of the Cluff name. She couldn't allow a foolish twenty-two-year-old girl to tarnish the reputation she'd spent decades building and maintaining. "Do not speak a word of this to anyone but Lehi. And make sure you deliver the letter as the prophet requested."

"Yes, Leandra."

"I'm serious." Leandra planted her feet and glowered at Rebecca. "Brinley and the other wives can never know about this."

"I understand. I have no intention of saying anything to anyone."

"Good." Leandra nodded. "Keep it that way."

chapter 25

PORTER HADN'T ANSWERED my texts. All day.

I wanted—no, *needed*—to tell him about my experience with Jorjina that day. I needed him to know that I was contemplating packing my things, contemplating leaving the Cluff home. I just wanted the green light. I needed to know that I had a place to stay.

But he wasn't answering.

The blue suitcase called to me from my closet.

Go.

Do it.

Be brave.

Just go.

But I couldn't, not without talking to Porter first. While I waited to hear from him, I removed the pile of money from my pocket and placed it inside the front pouch of the suitcase. I sorted through the dresses in my closet—blue, green, lilac. They were all the same, and they were items I would never wear in the outside world. Jorjina's money would see to that. I'd be able to buy new clothes, and help Porter with the cost of groceries until I was able to find a job. Perhaps Tiffany could put in a good word for me at the free clinic. I'd be a loyal worker, earn my own money, and make my way in the world.

My mind continued to spin as I pondered what else to pack. Certainly not my dresses or long underwear. I looked around my bedroom, searching for items I didn't want to leave behind. The trinkets from Aspen's children, those would come with me. They'd remind me of the sister wife who actually cared about my well-being. I'd miss her, miss her instincts and her honesty. But she wasn't enough to keep me here. I needed Porter.

The photographs of my family called to me from the wall. I couldn't pack them yet, or else Aspen or the other sister wives would be aware that something was amiss. But I made a mental note to pack them when the time came.

I pulled the phone from my pocket. Still no texts from Porter. Perhaps he was working on the house.

Whenever I thought of the tiny cottage, I got goose bumps on my arms. The thought of living there, just Porter and me, delighted me to no end. When I daydreamed, I envisioned an endless loop of possibilities playing out in my head like a picture book.

Maybe we'd paint the walls a beautiful sea green, and he'd chase me around the living room until he caught me, pulled me to the floor, and wiped fresh paint on the tip of my nose. I'd pretend to be upset and swat him on the chest.

We'd make love in the empty room, reveling in our privacy, in the home we were creating together. Maybe I would teach him to cook my famous apple dumplings, show him how to peel the apples and roll the dough. He'd flick bits of flour at me as I instructed him, distracting me with his humor, then he'd grab me by the waist and hoist me up on the counter. My bare legs would wrap around his waist and I'd kiss him hard before insisting we get back to baking the dessert. Maybe we'd . . .

Boom.

What was that?

I gripped the corner of my dresser, wondering where that loud noise had come from.

Boom.

There it was again. It was coming from the window. I'd left it open slightly since a thunderstorm had begun earlier in the evening. I sent up a quick prayer to Heavenly Father that Porter was on the other side of the glass.

Knock. Knock. Knock.

Someone was at my door. I had to decide—window or door? Window or door?

I chose door. I had to.

Aspen was standing on the other side. "Did you hear that?" she asked, peeking over my shoulder into the room.

"Yeah, I did. I think it was a raccoon."

"A raccoon? No, I don't think so. That seems very unlikely."

"It was. I watched as it pounced toward my window," I lied, "practically scared me to death. But it's gone now, it ran away."

"Oh." She hesitated, narrowing her eyes, still looking past me. "All right. If it comes back, let me know."

"Of course."

Closing the door after Aspen, I locked the latch and returned to the window, throwing it open and facing my fears head-on.

A pair of familiar knuckles gripped the window sill.

"Porter, what are you doing?" I shrieked, pulling on his forearm, helping him into the room.

He was a mess. His hair, his skin, his clothing—all soaked from the rain. But not only that, something was off. Something was horribly wrong.

"What's going on?" I asked as he hoisted himself over the window and crouched on my floor, wrapping his arms around his knees. But he didn't answer, didn't speak a word. Instead, he pulled me down to the floor, his hands gripping my wrists like a vice.

"Porter, you're scaring me."

Still, he said nothing. His body slumped until his head rested in my lap, his arms wrapped around my waist. And then it happened.

Porter Hammond cried.

He hiccupped and he sobbed, soaking my dress with his tears. Again and again, I pleaded with him as I stroked his sopping wet hair.

"Porter, please . . . tell me what happened."

But he didn't respond and each time I asked, he simply tightened his grip on my waist. I was terrified for him, for us. I didn't know how to help him, didn't know how to care for the man I loved. Not unless he told me what was the matter.

Something had ripped him apart. Something or someone had done this to him.

Finally, he let out an agonized whisper. "I don't know what I was thinking."

"About what?" I asked, trying desperately to understand.

"I shouldn't have done it." He choked on his sobs. "I should've known better."

"I don't understand. What did you do?"

Was he referring to me? His love for me? I was completely bewildered by his behavior. And I had no clue how to support him.

"Never," he said between sobs, "never again." His fingers dug into my waist and I flinched at the throbbing pain. But I welcomed the pain. The pain told me that his regrets had nothing to do with me, with us.

No, this was something bigger. Something much bigger.

My mind was a whirlwind. Even though I was confident that his devastation had nothing to do with me, I still had no idea what he was talking about. I'd never seen him like this, so unglued; even when he was coming down from the meth, he wasn't like this. This was an emotional response, not a physical one.

But from what?

"Porter, I can't help you unless you talk to me. I can't make anything better."

"You can't," he whispered. "No one can. It's done. I'm done."

"What?"

He sat up with a start, his eyes wild as they bored into mine. He spoke so quickly and urgently, I almost couldn't process his words.

"You have to leave this place, Brin. You have to go before it destroys you. Stay here any longer and it will. I know it."

I nodded. "I know."

If only he knew just how ready I was. But not like this. I couldn't leave with him like this. This Porter scared me. And as much as I loved him, I couldn't go anywhere just yet. I could hold him, support him, nurse him, and love him. But I couldn't leave with him. Not yet.

"You have to let me in." I stroked his cheek. "You have to tell me what's going on. Tell me, Porter, please."

He stared at me. His eyes were thoroughly bloodshot; tears and rain combined to soak his cheeks. He pressed his eyes shut and shook his head violently before sinking back down to rest his head in my lap. Shivers took over his body from the cold wetness that permeated his clothing.

"I need to warm you up," I whispered before shifting to retrieve the quilt folded at the foot of my bed. Porter moved with me, his arms still wrapped around my waist. Spreading the blanket around him, I rubbed his limbs and back, hoping to spread warmth throughout his body. Within minutes, his shivering had subsided and his breathing had evened out.

He was asleep.

I leaned back against the wall, thinking. I couldn't wake him, yet I couldn't leave him alone on the floor of my room. So instead, I closed my eyes and drifted to sleep with Porte's head in my lap.

When I woke the next morning, the damp blanket was draped on my legs, but the weight of his body was no longer pressed against mine.

Porter was gone.

chapter 26

TWO DAYS. And still no word from Porter.

I'd sent countless text messages with no reply.

Perhaps he was finished with me after all? His words echoed in my head . . . *I'm done, I'm finished.* Perhaps he couldn't bring himself to say good-bye?

I had no idea what to think. Leandra and the other sister wives were filling my days with endless chores, making it impossible for me to sneak away. During my time with Jorjina, I was still wary and cautious to sneak away to see him. And if I were being honest with myself, I was too afraid to go regardless of my situation.

Perhaps he was sending a very clear message, one I was unable or unwilling to see. Perhaps he wanted to be left alone . . . for good. That thought made my stomach churn. The idea of life without Porter was unbearable in and of itself. But life stuck in the Cluff household? Stuck, just like Jorjina had predicted? That would be unbearable.

I couldn't let that happen.

No matter what, I had to leave this place, even if Porter was no longer one of my reasons for leaving. I couldn't give up on him, though, no matter how timid I was due to our current circumstances, no matter what the consequences might be. I loved him, truly loved him, and wanted him in my life. And I knew I had to see him. I had to overcome my fears and sneak away.

And so I did.

With my heart racing, I threw open my bedroom window and perched on top of the sill. There were several feet between the window and the nearest branch. Could I do it without breaking a leg?

I didn't care. I had to try.

With a single deep breath, I threw myself at the tree, grabbing the thick branch with desperate hands. The bark dug into my palms and I grimaced at the pain. My legs dangled and a breeze blew through my skirt, pushing it from my body. With renewed strength and purpose, I used my hands to walk me to the trunk, then wrapped my arms around it and slid carefully down to the ground.

With my purse over my shoulder, I set off to see him. I had to get answers. No matter the consequences.

Charlie answered the door. Dark circles sat beneath his eyes. He was high, or coming down from one. I could only hope that Porter hadn't joined him.

Did you know I've been clean for two months? I remembered those words and prayed that Porter was still clean.

"What do you want?" Charlie demanded, the muscles of his bare arms bulging as he spoke.

"I need to see him. Is he here?"

"Maybe."

I had no clue why Charlie was treating me with such disdain, but he wasn't my concern. Porter was.

For the first time in twenty-two years, I rolled my eyes. I pushed past Charlie, calling Porter's name as I walked through the kitchen and into the living area.

There he was, slumped on the couch wearing just a T-shirt and boxer shorts. He glanced my way, but didn't move.

"Go away, Brin," he muttered, focusing his attention on the army game one of his roommates was playing. Machine guns blasted from the television, and bodies flailed with blood splattering across the screen. Disgusting.

"I need to talk to you."

"No." He wiped his hand straight across his entire face, and right then I knew.

He was coming down from a high.

No. No. No. No.

"I'm not taking no for an answer." I planted my feet and hooked my hands on my hips.

"Is that so?" Unsteadily, Porter rose to a seated position on the couch. His eyes widened and then shut as he pressed his head to the back of the cushion. Part of me wondered just how coherent he was.

"Yes. Let's go to your room."

"Oooh," he said, his words dripping with sarcasm. "Someone's feeling feisty, huh?"

"Stop it," I said through gritted teeth. I was in no mood for his inappropriate humor. This was not the time or the place.

His roommate, Darren, snickered from the chair.

Without hesitation, I turned to him with daggers in my eyes. "Quiet. This isn't about you."

"Control your woman, Porter," the overweight boy said with another snicker.

"Shut the fuck up, douche." Porter stood and walked to his roommate, his hand making contact with the top of Darren's head. Darren tossed his remote control across the room and stood opposite Porter, pushing him square in the chest.

"You wanna step to this, you fuckin' pussy?" Darren screamed.

"Yeah, motherfucker, I do!" Porter yelled, inches from Darren's face, not backing down. "You don't fucking talk to her like that, you hear me?"

Darren glowered at Porter, but was visibly intimidated. Porter wasn't backing down and Darren knew it.

"Whatever," Darren said, his voice lowered. "Keep her the hell away from me, all right?" He retrieved the remote control from the other side of the room and returned to his chair.

"Fuck off," Porter snapped, then took me by the hand and led me to his bedroom.

He locked the door behind us and pressed one hand against the wood, glaring at me. The other sat on his hip. His skin was covered in scrapes and bruises, presumably from climbing up and down the tree outside my window.

My own dress had two large grass stains from the trip I'd just made down the tree, when my knees made impact with the earth. The palms of my hands were scraped and burned from the bark.

"Why are you here?" he demanded.

"Why are *you* so angry at me?" I asked, and reached to take his hand.

He pulled it away immediately, then let out an intimidating laugh. "Who says I'm angry?"

"Are you high?"

I refused to go around in circles as he avoided what was really going on. I needed to know which Porter I was dealing with—Clean Porter who loved and adored me, a man with ambition and goals. Or Meth Porter—the Porter who hated the world and withdrew into one gigantic ball of anger.

"Maybe," he said, looking past me.

Clearly, that really meant yes. Disappointment filled me from the top of my head to the tips of my toes, along with disappointment and despair. Where was the man I'd fallen in love with?

He was gone, leaving someone else in his wake. Porter was nowhere to be found.

"You're possessed," I told him. "And I can't go any further with you when you're like this."

"I'm not possessed, Brin. It's called an addiction." He rolled his eyes. "Never mind, think what you want. I'm going to hell anyway, right?"

"No." I reached again for his hand. This time he didn't pull away. "I don't believe that."

"Why not?" he demanded.

"Because your soul's too beautiful for hell."

"That's total and utter bullshit, and you know it . . ." His voice trailed off and he broke our eye contact.

"No, it's not. Now, please tell me what happened."

My head raced with possibilities, and it ripped my heart apart that every single scenario involved his addiction. Did he owe someone money? Did he steal again? What had he done to cause himself such pain and despair that he'd start using again? I pushed my anger down within my gut, angry with him for choosing drugs over us, angry with him for falling into old habits.

Wasn't I worth more than that?

"I *don't* want to talk about it." He pulled his hand away even as I fought to hold on. He then flopped onto his bed and rolled to his side, staring out the window.

"We have to, Porter. If we have any chance of making this work, you have to let me in."

I sat down next to him and stroked his side, trying so desperately to calm and soothe. His muscles tensed beneath my fingertips.

"I can't . . . not this."

"I was ready to pack my bags, to *leave* Lehi, to leave the compound, the only life I've ever known. I was going to leave all of it."

He turned over and his eyes were wide. "You were?"

"Yes."

"And now?"

"Well, I certainly can't stay with *you*."

"Why the hell not?"

"Because clearly I can't count on you. You promised to get clean . . . and you're not. And then you avoided me! You couldn't even take a minute to text me."

"I couldn't."

"Why? Did you lose your phone?"

"No."

"Then what?"

"I was too high." He hung his head and looked away.

"Right." I grimaced at the idea of Porter so high that he was physically unable to type on the keys of his phone. "And now we're back where we started, aren't we? What happened to the man from last weekend? The man who showed me a house? The man who wanted to get out of this place?"

I threw out my arms, wildly gesturing to his disaster of a bedroom littered with dirty laundry, food wrappers, and soda cans.

"I just . . . I screwed up, okay?" His voice cracked in desperation.

"Fine, you messed up. But that doesn't change anything." I tapped him on the shoulder to make my point. "You *have* to be honest with me, even when you're hurting like this."

"I'm not *hurting*. I'm pissed off."

"Fine," I said. "Then tell me what you're so angry about. Who made you so *mad* that you came crawling through my window in the middle of a rainstorm?"

His eyes filled with daggers, pointed directly at me. But I wasn't about to back down.

"C'mon," I pleaded. "You know I'm on your side. Don't push me out of your life. Don't make me walk away. Because I will, right here and now. I'll walk away and never come back."

I rose to my feet, demonstrating how serious I was. It took every ounce of strength within me to even threaten such an action. If he allowed me to leave, I'd be devastated.

Hooking my hands on my hips, I said, "I have other options when I go, ya know. I can stay with Tiffany. I'm sure she'd let me, all I have to do is ask."

He scoffed at me. "That's ridiculous."

"Oh, really?" I asked, then turned toward the door. "I'm not bluffing, Porter. I'll leave that place with or without you."

"Okay, okay."

Porter pushed himself to a seated position and took my hands in his, his fingers twitching with nervous energy. His pulse beat like rapid fire through his hot skin.

"Don't go anywhere, all right? I'll tell you. I'll tell you everything."

chapter 27

PORTER COULDN'T GET his mother out of his head. The last time they'd seen each other, the last time they'd spoken, it had been gruesome. The absolute worst day of his life. The day she dropped him on the street corner with a hundred dollars in his hand, a suitcase full of clothes, and absolutely no idea how to function in the outside world.

But he missed his mother. So much it physically hurt. With Brinley's presence in his life, he'd not expected to be dragged back to the compound where he'd spent the bigger portion of his young life. But dragged back he was.

He was a man devoured by love, in love with a woman he wasn't supposed to have. And he knew he was going to burn in hell—of this he was certain, but he no longer cared. She'd brought happiness into his dreary, dark life. Brinley inspired him to be better, to be a man she'd be proud to call hers. For her, he'd move mountains, he'd change his act, get clean once and for all, finish building his house and move away from the roommates who dragged him down. He'd be better for her. A much better version of himself.

But he hadn't expected this.

He didn't expect that his intense feelings for Brinley would make him curious—curious about his mother, and if she missed him as much as he sometimes missed her. He didn't expect to find himself standing in front of Samuel at the gates of the compound, bribing him with fifty bucks so Sam would turn a blind eye and allow him to knock on the door of his parents' home. He'd been bribing Sam for months on Brinley's behalf, but this time it was for himself. He had to face his past, face his demons, face the parents who no longer acknowledged his existence.

There he stood, trembling as ice-cold raindrops fell from the sky and onto his bare arms. Should he knock? Ring the bell? Or should he accept that his family had moved on without him?

He despised them, but at the same time he ached for them. And he had no idea what to do.

Before he had the chance to make a decision, the porch light turned on and Porter's entire body stiffened in response. No longer a choice to be made, he had to face whomever would answer the door in just seconds.

It was his younger brother, Matt; they hadn't seen each other in years. Matt had grown at least three inches taller than Porter and now towered over him in the doorway, a scowl upon his pimply face.

Porter wasn't at all intimidated by the size of Matt; instead, he stood tall and demanded that Matt get his mother. He needed to speak to her. When Matt refused, Porter yelled past him into the house.

"Mother!"

"She doesn't want to see you. You no longer exist," his brother hissed.

"I'm right here, right in front of you, asshole. Of course I exist."

"Not to us," Matt said with a snarl. "Look!"

His brother gestured to a family portrait that hung in the hallway behind him. Dark blue ink was scribbled across Porter's face, as if he could simply be erased from existence. Porter stood on the porch, his shoulders slumped as he stared at the photo.

Alice Hammond rounded the corner of the hallway and locked eyes with her son. She looked just as he remembered her, with maybe a few unfamiliar wrinkles and a little more gray in her hair. But her face was just as he remembered. The face of someone he trusted with his life.

"Porter," she whispered before shooing several of his siblings away from the door. When they left begrudgingly, it was just Alice and her son, face-to-face for the first time in years.

"You can't be here," Alice said, her head shaking back and forth.

"Was it really this easy?" Porter asked, gesturing to the photograph.

His mother hung her head.

"What? You just pretend I was never here, that you didn't carry me for nine months? That you didn't nurse me as a baby?"

"Stop it, please," Alice begged, her eyes filling with tears.

"No, I need to know!" Porter glowered at the woman who had raised him, the woman he loved more than anyone else in his world. "I need to know how you could throw me out like a piece of fucking trash!"

"Watch your language!"

"Are you kidding me? You tossed me aside and you're going to correct my fucking language?"

Alice winced, then cried out, "Profanity is not allowed in this house!"

"Where's Dad?"

"My *husband* isn't here this evening."

"Ah, with another wife, I see." Porter sneered, crossing his arms in front of his chest. "Do you enjoy sharing him, Mother?"

He couldn't imagine giving his heart to another woman now that Brinley possessed every fiber of his being. He wanted her and only her. Her happiness meant more to him than his own. He had no idea how his father, and the other men on the compound, could dole out their love in that way. In fact, he was pretty certain that they didn't. They were doing what was expected of them, just like the women of the compound. And for that, he felt sorry for them.

When Alice didn't answer his crude question, they stood in awkward silence. Porter wanted to believe there was a shred left of the kind woman he knew for the first years of his life. The woman who held him in her arms when he scraped his knee. The woman who baked him his favorite dark chocolate cake on his birthday each year. He had to know if she was still inside the woman before him.

"I had to see you," Porter whispered. secretly wishing his mother would reach for him, to take his hand or pull him into her embrace. But she didn't. She stood several feet from him, cold and stiff.

"I'm sorry," she muttered, breaking eye contact and crossing her arms in front of her terry bathrobe, her hair still up in the traditional braid. "But you shouldn't have come."

"Mother, don't you miss me?" he pressed, desperate to know the answer.

"No." Her eyes bored into his, and he knew. She had no regrets. She stood by her decision to remove him from the Hammond family.

Once again, he was wounded. He was the young boy standing on the street corner, watching his mother drive away from him. Watching her withdraw her love.

"You were supposed to love me," Porter cried. "More than Father, more than the prophet. I'm your child."

"You *were*." Alice's words were cold, calculated, rehearsed. "You *were* my child."

Her words stung more than anything had in Porter's life. But before he could even attempt to recover from the pain of her words, she continued. He braced himself as she began to speak.

"But now you're just a stranger. A stranger who needs to leave my home."

Porter's teeth clenched so tightly his jaw ached. Her words shocked and destroyed him. Seething, he replied, "You were supposed to protect me from the evils of the world, not become one of them."

Alice swallowed hard, covering her mouth with the back of her hand. Porter didn't care. He wanted to hurt her, to cause her pain the way she'd caused an insurmountable amount of pain for him and his life in the outside world.

"How do you live with yourself?" Porter shook his head, fighting back the tears that were building. He couldn't let her see the emotion that was expanding within his chest. "You're a despicable human being, and I'm better off without you."

"Leave, please," his mother begged.

He knew he'd affected her. He'd finally broken through her tough exterior to expose her lies, her hypocrisy, her selfishness.

"No problem," he snapped before punching the front door. His knuckles made contact, denting the wood. "I'm outta here!"

Porter heard the door slam behind him. He knew that in just a few short hours, his mother would block out their entire interaction, as if it had never happened. His decision to confront her was a disastrous mistake. He didn't think it was possible for his mother to wound him more than she had years ago in his father's truck.

But she had. Her cold reaction to him standing in her doorway destroyed him. The way she looked at him, the cutting bite of her words. Now, more than ever before, he knew he was an orphan in this world.

Alone.

And then his phone buzzed from the pocket of his jeans.

With tears burning his eyes, he trudged through the mud to seek out the only person he could trust. The single, solitary person who actually loved him. Who wasn't ashamed of his existence. The only person in the world who understood him and loved him just the same. Despite his faults, despite every shitty decision he'd ever made in his lifetime.

She was the only one who mattered.

chapter 28

My mouth dropped open and guilt attacked my body like a swarm of vicious wasps. As Porter finally revealed what had happened that night, my heart plummeted to my feet. I'd doubted him, thought the worst of him when he needed me the most. I could only hope he'd forgive me.

"Is it my fault?" I asked.

"You've never even met my mother, Brin. How could it be your fault?" His eyes were dull, lifeless, as shell-shocked as if he'd survived a war.

"I mean, the reason you went back. Was that because of me? Because you thought you had to or something?" I couldn't quite process why he'd made the decision to see his mother again.

"Of course not. I just—being with you, it got me thinking. And since I've been clean . . . or, I was, anyway." He groaned. "When I'm clean, my thoughts go back there. I don't know why."

"I'm sorry. I feel awful that I bring you back there, you know, in your head."

"None of this is your fault," he said, wiping a tear from his eye and clearing his throat. "I know I'm not her son anymore. I just wish she loved me as much as I still love her."

"You still love her?" My heart broke in two.

He chuckled, but it came out sad, melancholy. "Against my better judgment, yes."

"They don't deserve you," I whispered, rubbing his thigh. "Not one bit."

He pressed his lips into a fine line as he shook his head. Then he took a deep breath as he avoided my eyes. "My brain knows that, but . . ."

"But what?"

"What if it's true, Brin? What if I really am damned?"

"Don't even say that!" I snapped, jerking my body away when he attempted to hold my hand.

His expression softened and he trailed his fingers down my cheek. "I told you, you're my heaven. If I burn when I die, that's fine. I'm a selfish man and I want my heaven now."

"And I told you, you have a beautiful soul. You're not going to burn."

He shrugged, releasing a sigh. "You're the only one who seems to think so."

"You need to think so too. How can you love me if you don't love yourself?"

His hands fell to his lap as he pondered my question. "Loving you is just . . . it's the simplest thing I've ever done. Loving myself? Totally different story."

I shifted to rest my head in his lap. He wrapped an arm around my shoulder, pulling me closer. "I'll prove it to you. I'll show you how deserving you are."

"I'm a junkie," he muttered. "You deserve better."

Shaking my head, I gripped his bended knee. "No. I deserve a man who will love me, protect me, and cherish me. A man who would climb through my window to give me a way to communicate with him. A man who will put me first."

"Sounds like quite the guy." He chuckled, stroking my hair. "I'll let you know if I run into him."

"Silly man," I said with a roll of my eyes, and continued to massage his knee. "You're all I need. You know that."

"You know what my biggest fear is?"

"Tell me."

"That one day you'll agree with my mother."

My muscles went rigid and I recoiled, pushing up to my knees, facing him head-on. "Never. Do you hear me? I could never see you the way they do."

"Who's to say you won't?" His eyes were vacant again, as if he were already mentally preparing for my exit from his life. "You were ready to leave earlier."

"I was trying to make a point. You're always telling me to stick up for myself, to stick to my guns, as you say. That's what I was doing. But if you think that even for a second I *wanted* to leave, then you don't know me at all."

He closed his eyes tightly, releasing tears that fell from his cheeks. He nodded, again and again, and I could only hope that he was finally hearing me. That he was hearing how much I truly cared for him. This wasn't about sex, and it wasn't about rebellion. This was about a woman loving a man so much she'd do just about anything to prove it.

"I love you, Porter," I whispered, crawling into his lap and wrapping my arms around his neck. I nuzzled my head into the crook of his neck, feeling his heart thumping wildly in his chest.

"I love you," I whispered. "I love you."

Again and again I said the words, urging him to believe me. Urging him to believe that he was worthy of love, of love that was reciprocated, of love that was real and honest. Love that was right in front of him.

He finally spoke, the raspy voice that always gave me goose bumps. "I'm going to spend the rest of my life proving my love to you," he finally said.

"Show me now," I whispered, feeling bold.

No verbal response was needed. Porter's strong arms wrapped around my bottom and he hoisted me in the air, placing me on my back, then he kissed and licked my neck as he stripped me of my heavy garb. Instinctively, my hands went to his boxer shorts. I removed them quickly before he was even finished with the first two buttons of my dress.

"Someone's eager," he teased.

"It's your fault. You've done this to me." I laughed, running my fingers through his silky hair.

"I've created a monster, huh?" The life was returning to his eyes, and it filled me with relief and endless amounts of adrenaline.

"Yes." I nodded. "And I need you. Right now."

Porter stripped my dress from my body, removing the long underwear and undergarments. For the first time, I ripped the condom packet open and rolled it onto him. He exhaled loudly as I did.

"I'm impressed," he said with a tilt of an eyebrow.

"Make love to me," I pleaded. I needed to connect with him, to feel the weight of him on my chest. And I wanted it to last as long as possible. "Go slow."

Porter's eyes never left mine. Gently he entered me, gliding in and out in a gradual and deliberate motion. His elbows dug into the mattress, just above my shoulders, and I wrapped my legs around his waist. Pressure built within me almost immediately and with each stroke, it continued to build. With each kiss, each tender smile, I was pushed further toward the edge. I reached down to grip Porter's bottom, my fingers digging into his skin. He released a moan, his lips curling up in pleasure.

"Hurry, Brin, I can't . . ." He groaned as he pumped into me. "I can't wait much longer."

Curling my body toward his sent me over the edge and I cried out, throwing my head back into the pillow beneath me. Porter continued to thrust several times before groaning and collapsing onto my chest. Instead of rolling to his side, Porter remained above me. His fingertips traced soft lines from my forehead to my chin as he studied my face.

"You have two tiny freckles above this eyebrow."

"I do?" I played along. Of course, I was aware of them. When you spend your life not wearing makeup, you become quite aware of each and every facial feature you possess.

"Yeah." He smiled before kissing the freckles. "They're beautiful. Just like you."

"I think you're beautiful too."

He paused with a subtle smirk. "You mean *hot*, right? Guys don't want to be *beautiful*."

"Yes, *hot*," I replied, forcing the word from my mouth. I'd grown used to the slang of the outside world, but there were certain words that still felt odd to say. Porter told me that I was "hot" quite often, but it wasn't something I was comfortable repeating.

"Hey," he said, his eyes turning serious. "Did you mean what you said earlier? About being ready to leave?"

"Yes. I'm absolutely certain. I can't stay there."

"That's awesome. Seriously, the best thing you've ever said." His grin turned boyish, giddy.

"But I can't stay with you, not if you keep using."

"You'd seriously live with Tiffany instead of me?" His tone turned hateful quickly, a symptom of coming down from the high. I hated that I knew the pattern, recognized the mood swings, but I did. Despite my desire to soothe him, I had to stay firm.

"Yes, I would."

"And if I get clean? For good?"

"Then I'd want nothing more than to live with you, in the house that you're building."

"Okay, then," he replied, his voice calmer. He rolled to his side and perched on his elbow. "I can do it. I promise you, Brin."

"Don't promise me," I insisted. "Promise yourself. Do it for *yourself*, not me."

"All right," he said, and nodded.

"And I'm *leaving* for me. I don't belong there. I see that now. Finally."

"Thank God. I've been waiting for this day," he said. "Seriously."

"Me too," I said with a smile. "Me too.

Walking home, I was in such a daze and lost in my own thoughts that when I reached the front door of the Cluff house, I didn't even recall how I arrived there. I thought of lazy mornings with Porter, my legs resting in his lap as we read the morning newspaper while we sipped orange juice and feasted on pastries from the local bakery. No screaming children, no sister wives barking orders. Just him and me. Together.

My mind was so occupied with thoughts of peaceful days away from the compound, that I didn't notice the sullen faces of my family. The house was quiet, eerily so. But I didn't notice that either. Not until later when I heard the dreadful news.

When my shoes hit the tile of the entryway, Rebecca yanked on the sleeve of my dress and dragged me to her bedroom, jerking me inside the room and slamming the door behind her.

"What did you do?" she demanded. Her cheeks resembled the skin of two plump tomatoes. They were damp with tears, but I had no idea why.

"I don't understand."

"He's gone," Rebecca choked out.

"Who? Who's gone?"

"Burt," she spat out, her nostrils flaring. "He's gone."

Admittedly, Burt Jameson hadn't taken up my thoughts in quite some time. I'd accepted Rebecca's choice. I'd accepted her swollen belly and her ambivalent attitude toward my presence in her life. But seeing her body language, her agony, I knew something horrible had happened.

"He left?"

She shook her head vigorously, her lips twisted as more tears fell from her puffy eyes.

"No, you foolish girl." She sneered. "He's *dead*."

Dead. Gone. Buried.

Visions of Burt with lifeless eyes permeated my brain, and I scrunched my eyes tight to make them stop.

"What?" I cried out in shock, then reached for her hand. Despite her cold exterior the past several months, I still yearned to comfort my sister wife and former friend. But she yanked her hand away, holding it close to her chest.

"W-what happened?" I stammered.

"They found him hanging from the beams." Her tears overpowered her vocal cords and she began to sob, sitting on the edge of her bed and hanging her head in her hands.

"I don't . . . I don't understand."

"He killed himself, Brinley!" she screeched. "He hung himself in the house he was building! The workers . . . they found him."

"Why?" I asked. But it was a question that didn't need to be asked. We both knew the answer.

"Because he couldn't be with me! He left a note. He couldn't go on . . . wouldn't live his life without me."

"Oh no."

My entire body felt as if I'd been hit by a speeding train. I knew he was miserable . . . I did. But what more could I have done? Could I have saved him?

"He *knew* I was pregnant. How did he *know* that, Brinley?"

A gasp left my lips. Was she blaming *me* for Burt's death?

"I-I didn't . . ." I stammered, "I didn't say a word! I promise you!"

"I don't believe you." She was seething, glowering at me, but I didn't understand her wrath. Yes, I'd spoken to Burt when he'd approached me. But I wasn't deceitful, nor did I seek him out to share information regarding Rebecca's new life with Lehi. And I didn't understand why she thought that I had.

"Leandra showed me the note! He knew I'd moved on, that I was pregnant. And he couldn't go on." Rebecca stopped, stared off into space, and whispered words, presumably from the suicide note. "*I can't go on without you. I'm a pathetic man.*"

"He wasn't pathetic," I argued.

"I didn't used to think so. But to be willing to leave his wives, his children? I don't know what to believe anymore."

"You said Leandra gave it to you? How did she—"

"Burt's other wives gave it to Lehi. They were hoping he'd help pay for funeral services, but he refused. So, there'll be nothing but shame and embarrassment for them."

"Why would Lehi pay—"

"Because," she screamed, "they said it's my fault! It's all my fault. And Lehi's responsible for me now."

"Oh."

Rebecca paced the floor, her words cracking as she walked. "You've done *nothing* but meddle since I joined this family. Why did you have to push?"

"I swear to you, Rebecca, I didn't tell him *anything*. Yes, he pulled me aside a few weeks ago. But he just wanted to know about his boys, that's all. I promise you."

"Weeks ago? How many times have you spoken to him?"

"I-I don't know. He'd approach me, ask me questions. I didn't know what to say—"

"He knew! He knew I was pregnant." She pushed herself up from the bed, threw her hands up in the air, and stormed toward me.

"You're showing!" I exclaimed. "It's obvious to the *world*, Rebecca. Someone, anyone could have told him."

"No, *you* told him. I know it, I feel it in my bones. Months and months ago, you gave me that note. The note he wrote. Anyone else would have destroyed it. But not you."

"He loved you," I said softly. "It was obvious in every expression, every word he spoke to me. And you missed him too. Of course I gave you the letter. How could I not?"

"Don't you understand? It wasn't your place!"

"You loved each other! I just wanted you to be happy. I didn't want you to move on with Lehi if there was still a chance that you could be happy."

"Don't you understand? I had no choice!"

"That's not true." I shook my head back and forth with vigor. "We *always* have a choice. You could've met him under that tree. You could have run away, given your boys a future with two parents who loved them. But you didn't."

"That would have been sinful . . . and selfish."

"Abandoning the one you love so you can get to heaven is selfish, not following your heart."

She scoffed, looking me up and down. "You're still seeing him, aren't you? The angry boy who lives above the coffee store."

I wasn't expecting her to mention Porter. He had nothing to do with any of this.

"That's not *any* of your business." I crossed my arms in front of my chest and glared at her.

"Oh, please." She sneered, wiping the top of her nose with her hand. Then she stopped, clutched her belly, and stared at me with wide eyes. "Just whose child are you carrying, Brinley?"

"Don't be ridiculous," I said contemptuously, attempting to dismiss her accusation. But I couldn't let my eyes meet hers. I could feel her studying me as we stood in silence.

"*Is* there a baby?" she pressed, and my stomach dropped to my knees. "I mean, my belly is here, clear as day, and yet you haven't even started showing."

Again, I was silent. But inside I was screaming.

No! No! No! No!

Rebecca can't find out, she just can't!

Her anger was evident in every inch of her body. If she told Lehi, I had no idea what would happen.

"You're a wicked, wicked girl," she shouted. "You meddle in other people's affairs, and you abandon Heavenly Father to indulge in selfish sins of the flesh! But I never thought you'd fake a pregnancy to carry on an affair with an outsider!"

"You know nothing about me, or my feelings for Porter." Despite trying to calm my voice, my words still came out harsh. I wouldn't let her call me wicked. I knew well enough now that I was far from it. "You're lashing out at me because of your own horrible decisions."

"Horrible decisions? I was proving myself to the prophet, to Heavenly Father," she wailed. "I gave up my one true love!"

"Because you were scared!"

"No! Because I needed to prove that my love for Heavenly Father was, and will always be, more than anyone . . . even Burt." Her eyebrows drew together as she stared at me in confusion. "Isn't yours?"

That answer was simple. Without hesitation, I said, "No. I love Porter more than anything. More than my own life. And I'd never turn my back on him. I love him too much to do that."

Visibly shaken by my words, Rebecca wrapped her arms around herself, and her eyes widened in shock before narrowing in condemnation. "Then I will pray for your soul."

Months ago, those words would have destroyed me. They would have caused me to question everything I'd ever believed, every action I'd ever taken, and every word I'd ever spoken. But on this day, I was strong enough in my conviction, strong enough in my actions, and strong enough in my own words.

"I don't need your prayers." I pulled my shoulders back and held my head high. "I have my own."

I walked out her bedroom door, knowing my time in the Cluff household was coming to an end. I couldn't trust that Rebecca would keep any of her assumptions to herself. I had to make a plan, and quickly.

chapter 29

THE CRISP COTTON COLLAR of my mint green dress was slightly bent. Each time my fingers pressed it down, it jumped back up. It was determined to resist any changes I tried to force upon it. In years past, I would have taken the dress off, sprayed the collar with starch, and ironed it until it fell in line with the rest of the dress. But not today.

Today, I allowed the rebellion of my dress to inspire me.

Today was the day, my last on the compound. It had been six days since my confrontation with Rebecca, and although I wanted to believe that she'd refrain from telling Lehi about Porter, I couldn't trust her. Instead, I had to act quickly—to say my good-byes and leave this place.

I had two good-byes that I needed to make, to Aspen and Jorjina.

The trouble was that I had to say my farewells carefully, so as not to raise any flags or to arouse suspicion, even though these were the very women I was closest with. I had to do it, though. I had to thank each of them for their kindness, their love, and their desire to protect me within the confines of our community. Aspen was surrounded by little faces when I approached her in the common area. Ruthie was seated in front of her, Aspen combing her hair before styling it in its proper braid. I pulled at the bottom of my own braid, moving it to hang just next to my bent collar. The irony wasn't last on me as I held the intricate braid in my hand, knowing today would be the very last day in which I wore my hair this way.

"Good morning," she said absently, as if this morning was just one of the thousands of mornings in which she planned to greet me with those words. She had no idea that tomorrow I'd be gone.

"How are you today?" I asked, perching myself on the sofa, watching as she effortlessly weaved her daughter's hair into the perfect style.

She grunted in response to my question, holding an elastic band between her teeth. "Another day." She tapped Ruthie's shoulder when she finished her hair. Ruthie climbed to her feet, thanked her mother, and placed a kiss on her cheek. "Next."

Her youngest girl, Sheena, then took Ruthie's spot and the ritual was repeated.

"I'm going to Jorjina's."

I wasn't sure what else to say, not knowing how to say good-bye to Aspen without her knowing it. I had no idea how she'd react. Would she scream and shout at me, demanding I stay? Would she quote from *The Book of Mormon* until her face turned a sickly blue? Jorjina had hinted that this might not be the place for me, but Aspen hadn't. I had to tread carefully.

"Be careful what you say to that woman," Aspen whispered through clenched teeth after glancing around the room.

My stomach flipped. "W-why do y-you say that?"

Had something happened? Was there something I didn't know about Jorjina? Something new? Something upsetting?

Aspen gestured for me to come closer, so I slid to the floor, my knees touching hers. She glanced down at the contact, and I pulled back slightly.

"Rebecca was her assistant. Just before she was reassigned."

"Oh." Relieved that this was something I already knew, I schooled my features into an approximation of surprise. Aspen couldn't know what had transpired in Jorjina's kitchen and that I already knew this information.

"I think she feeds information to the prophet," Aspen continued while I remained stone-faced, but nodded along. A look of irritation crossed her face. "Anyway, just be careful."

"I will. She's a kind old woman, though. You'd like her."

I firmly believed that Aspen and Jorjina had more in common than they had differences. They were both strong, steadfast women of the "weaker" sex who wanted to protect me like one of their own children.

Unfortunately, Aspen had no intention of considering a possible kinship with Jorjina Black. She rolled her eyes before sending Sheena to play with her siblings, then glanced at me.

"I know something is different with you," she said. "I can feel it. But I can't help you if you don't trust me."

Her words shocked me to my core. I knew Aspen was observant, perceptive, but I thought I'd managed to remain the same Brinley while in the Cluff household. Apparently not.

I said nothing, unsure how to respond. I couldn't tell her. I couldn't.

Aspen's mouth fell open and her cheeks turned white. "Don't you trust me?"

"Of course," I finally answered.

"Then?" Aspen demanded, her voice shrill.

I shook my head slowly back and forth. "You've always been there for me, Aspen." I took her hand in mine. "I just wanted to thank you for that. Thank you for protecting me, teaching me, even when I resisted."

"You're scaring me," Aspen said softly, and took a ragged breath. She tugged on my hand, pulling me closer. "Talk to me."

I had to soothe her, to calm her nerves. I had to deceive her one last time—for her own safety and mine.

"There's nothing to say, I promise." I paused before realizing I had the best possible excuse. I'd done plenty of reading on this topic; it was time to utilize it. I pressed my hand to my abdomen. "It must be the pregnancy. I've been so emotional these days."

"Of course. Well, that makes sense, doesn't it?" Aspen smiled then, a fake smile showing too much teeth. That smile gave me goose bumps; Aspen never faked happiness. On the surface, she was accepting my excuse. But what was hiding beneath that facade?

Her fingers released my wrist and they did, I felt her letting go of me, of us.

Memories. So many memories rocketed through my brain, like a show on Porter's television. Aspen checking on me after my horrific honeymoon with Lehi. Aspen guiding me through life in the Cluff household—the day to day, the mundane, the necessary. None of my other sister wives had bothered, allowing me to figure everything out on my own. But Aspen took pity on me, and gave me endless tips to help me through each day as a wife in the house of Cluff. Aspen protecting me from Leandra's wrath on more occasions than I could count. Aspen assisting me with my sick mother.

In that very moment, I realized just how much I would miss my sister wife. For three years she'd accepted me, even when she clearly had no patience for my mistakes, my naïveté, and my youth. She'd accepted me, loved and defended me, even when I didn't deserve it.

I would miss her terribly.

Overcome with emotion, I rose to my knees and pounced on Aspen, wrapping my arms around her shoulders and squeezing her tightly. Initially, her response was wooden and unresponsive. But after several seconds, I felt her muscles relax, and she warmed to our embrace. Her hands wrapped around my back and rubbed my back gently, as I'd seen her do so many times with her children.

"Wow, you really are overemotional in your second trimester, aren't you?"

Tears slipped from my eyes and landed on the shoulder of Aspen's dress. Her words made me pull away, and I wiped my eyes with the back of my sleeve. "Sorry, I—yes, I guess I am."

"It's fine." Aspen stiffened once again, pulling away from my arms.

I released her, rose to my feet, and wiped my eyes once again. "I-I'm going to be late. I'd better go."

"Have a nice day and remember what I said." Aspen turned away and wiped at one of her eyes.

Even though I knew she would never admit it, she'd been touched by our moment together. She cared for me immensely, of this I was certain.

Jorjina was especially mild mannered that day. She said nothing when I was fifteen minutes late. She shrugged off the toast I burned and didn't blink an eye when I forgot to put the teakettle on.

My mind was racing and my thoughts jumbled, planning my escape since it was imminent. I'd pack my suitcase; the eight hundred dollars was already tucked inside the front pouch. The trinkets from Aspen's children were necessary, as well as my undergarments and toiletries. I'd considered taking my wedding band from Lehi, knowing that I could possibly trade it in the outside world, either for money or some other goods. But I'd never get past my guilt. The ring belonged to Lehi and any wife who might come after me. So, it would be left on my dresser. When Lehi inevitably discovered I was missing and had left my ring behind, he would know that I was gone forever.

Packing my room would only take a few moments. But to leave without suspicion would require my waiting until everyone had gone to sleep. That would give me ample time to contact Porter with my phone, and it would ensure that Tiffany would be at her apartment after a long shift at the free clinic.

"Your head is in the clouds," Jorjina said, yanking me from my thoughts.

We were standing at the counter. The pot roast we'd prepared for dinner steamed from the ceramic dish. I shook my head, trying to startle myself back into the present moment.

"Penny for your thoughts."

Her crow's feet were extensive, and when Jorjina was concerned, it only magnified the creases in her skin. At that moment, Jorjina's wrinkles seemed to travel past her temples to cover her cheeks. She was worried about me. About me and my thoughts.

"It's best if we don't talk about it."

"I've told you before, you can trust me. I've done terrible things in the past, but you're special to me. I'd never do that to you."

"I know, I just—it's better if we don't . . ."

"I see." Jorjina nodded, stabbing slices of the roast and placing them on a plate. The sadness of her expression sent a stabbing sensation right to my heart. I'd miss her, and quiet moments like this. Normally I'd assist her in preparing her supper before leaving to eat with the Cluff family. But today I was compelled to alter my plans.

"May I . . . um, may I eat with you tonight?" I reached for the cabinet, but waited for her permission before retrieving a plate.

"Yes, of course. I'd be delighted." Jorjina waved me away from the cabinet, grabbed a plate and placed it on the counter, then scooped a heaping portion of the roast. A giant, giddy smile crossed her face as she dug with the serving spoon. "Carrots, my dear?"

"Yes, please, but let me help—"

"No. Not today. You're my guest and you must let me serve you."

"All right."

I enjoyed this feeling; it was as if I were her guest of honor. No one in the Cluff household cared if I was present for a meal or not. No one *wanted* me near them. But Jorjina, she was different. Slowly, I was starting to trust her. And I knew that if given more time, I would have shared my secrets with her, but there simply wasn't time to do that.

I had to be smart. I needed to leave the Cluff home in the middle of the night, and be sure to leave no clues behind. If she'd already shared my secrets with the prophet, so be it. But deep within my heart, I knew that wasn't the case. I knew it with every fiber of my being.

Jorjina and I laughed and talked as we feasted on the pot roast, Jorjina praising my skills in the kitchen, especially considering my young age. She knew I had paid attention during my younger years, and appreciated my efforts. When our plates were scraped clean, I offered to wash her dishes before leaving. Oddly enough, even though I was excited to make my exit, I was dreading saying good-bye to one of the only friends I had.

"No, don't be silly. Like I said, you're my guest. Besides, if I'm too tired to do it, you'll have something to keep you busy in the morning." She pursed her lips together, biting down on her lower lip. Her eyebrows shot up toward the ceiling as she stared at me.

I swallowed hard, not knowing how to respond. But I didn't have to. Jorjina placed her hand over mine and squeezed. "Thank you for having dinner with me."

"You're welcome," I managed to choke out. My voice was hoarse, my throat dry.

"You know," she said slowly, then released my hand. She perched her chin in her hands and gave me a sad, but tender look. "If you were to ever take my advice and leave this place, I'd pray for you."

I paused and embraced her hypothetical topic of conversation. "You would?"

"Of course. You're a treasure of a girl, Brinley. I see bright things in your future." Her crow's feet seemed to diminish, her smile taking over the landscape of her worn, yet still beautiful face.

"Really?"

"Absolutely. You will shine brightly, my darling. I just know it."

My eyes blurred with tears, and I mimicked her posture, perching my chin in my hands. "Well, if I did . . . hypothetically speaking, of course . . ."

"Of course," she said, urging me on with a smile.

"You'd always hold a special place in my heart. Always."

Jorjina closed her eyes and nodded her head before clearing her throat and rising to her feet. "Well, off you go. I'll, um, I'll see you in the morning. Bright and early."

"Bright and early," I repeated, standing to face her. Taking two small steps forward, I wrapped my arms around Jorjina, resisting the urge to squeeze her too tightly. She was more fragile than Aspen; I had to be gentle.

"Thank you," I managed to say, fighting the storm of tears that threatened.

I left Jorjina's house and made my final walk back to the Cluff household, unable to wipe the grin from my face. Soon I'd be packed and waiting . . . waiting to exit this life and start anew. I began to take inventory as I entered the house and closed the front door behind me.

I needed to retrieve my phone from the closet and send a text message to Porter, letting him know that I'd made my decision. I needed to finish packing my suitcase, brush my teeth, and wait, wait, wait until the time was right.

When I walked past the kitchen, Brenda glanced up from the sink and nodded stoically. Piles and piles of dishes rested in soap suds beneath her hands. Normally I would have offered to assist her, but tonight I was no longer willing.

Tonight was about me. About my future. About everything I had to look forward to.

"Good night," I simply said and she nodded in response. A sense of peace spread throughout my body, throughout my brain, calming the racing thoughts. In just a few short hours, I'd be free.

But that all changed when I opened my bedroom door to find my husband and his first wife standing in my room. Leandra held my purse in her hands and Lehi stood with his arms crossed, his cheeks bright red, his chest heaving and his nostrils flaring.

And everything changed in an instant.

chapter 30

Months earlier . . .

LEHI WAS BONE TIRED when the prophet requested a meeting. He'd been on several job sites, supervising young idiots who were too weak to carry a two-by-four, and too stupid to know it. His job was an exhausting one, but it allowed him to support his large family. He owed his position of prominence in the company to the prophet, and so he had learned that when the prophet requested a meeting with you, you didn't say no. You accepted, you obeyed, and you fulfilled your duty to the one and only voice of the Lord.

"Come, sit," the prophet had said. His hair was silver like Lehi's, but it was shorter, more polished, as was his appearance as a whole. Lehi spent his days on construction sites; his hands were calloused, his skin rough and dry. The skin beneath the prophet's eyes didn't sink or hang like Lehi's. Even though the prophet was balancing over thirty wives, he never looked exhausted.

Lehi wondered how the prophet was able to accomplish that. Lehi could barely handle the eight wives he'd been given; he couldn't imagine having dozens and dozens of women demanding his time and energy.

"Two of your wives visited me yesterday, and I must say that I'm quite concerned, Elder Cluff. Quite concerned, indeed."

Lehi had expected this topic of discussion. Both Leandra and Rebecca had informed him of their meeting with the prophet. He knew of Burt's contact with his youngest wife, and he also possessed the letter in which Burt had begged Rebecca to leave with him.

Lehi was indifferent toward his newest wife, Rebecca. He knew her heart was unavailable, but it didn't bother him in the slightest. He had made peace with the fact that he would never be involved in a love affair with any of his wives. Instead, he chose to appreciate them for their best qualities.

Leandra was a force to be reckoned with; she was strong and she kept the house running in an impressive manner, which reduced his stress. In the bedroom, he secretly called her "Captain," referring to the tight ship she ran in the Cluff household. But Leandra was also domineering and demanding, and she exhausted him with her constant demands and complaints.

He remembered the day when he'd truly started to love Leandra, back when they'd been married for three years and shared only two children. Since then there were moments—small ones—where he felt complete, as if they could be content with just the two of them. But Leandra's constant focus on their status as a family was exhausting and drained his heart of any true romantic feelings.

Her determination for the Cluff family to be held in the highest regard was difficult for Lehi during those days, but that was no longer the case. He'd witnessed firsthand how much more comfortable, how much *easier* life in the compound could be if your family was in good standing with the prophet. And Lehi had no intention of losing the status he and his family had attained. They'd worked for decades to achieve it, and he would fight with everything he had to maintain it.

And so, his indifference toward his eighth wife was not the issue. She was his now, and he was responsible for her actions, good or bad. Burt wouldn't let go, and in addition to that, he was attempting to coerce Rebecca to leave their community. The shame that action would bring upon both families would be catastrophic.

"Yes, they informed me," Lehi responded, referring to his meeting with his first and last wives. He reached into his pocket and retrieved a tattered envelope. "Rebecca said you requested this letter."

"Yes." The prophet's face was devoid of emotion. He extended his hand over his desk, retrieving the letter from Lehi's hand. He studied the simple piece of paper before returning it to its envelope and handing it back to Lehi. "You may keep that."

Lehi was puzzled. He didn't feel a need to keep the letter. To him it was a stab at his masculinity, at his standing in the church. That this man would attempt to steal his newest wife was insulting, to say the least. Nevertheless, he stuffed the envelope back into his pocket, vowing not to return it to Rebecca. She needed to forget Elder Jameson, and the sooner the better.

"I'd suggest that you keep an eye on this situation. Make sure that Rebecca is not coerced into acting on such devilish behavior."

"Rebecca has been nothing but gracious and willing to adapt to her life with us."

"I'm pleased to hear that." The prophet leaned back in his armchair, folding his hands together over his midsection. Relaxed, yet stiff. "The Cluff family has always been a model for the community. I'd hate to see that change."

"I agree. Please be assured that I'll do everything that I can to maintain that."

"I'm certain you will." The prophet shifted his weight and planted his feet on the floor, standing and placing one hand on his desk while scratching at the stubble on his chin with the other. "Which leads us to your seventh wife."

"Brinley." Lehi nodded.

"I must tell you that I'm puzzled as to what to do."

"I understand." Lehi was hesitant to make his plea. Instead, he would allow the prophet to steer the conversation and respond accordingly. That was what the prophet preferred. There was no questioning Clarence Black, but over the years Lehi had learned how to make requests without insulting the prophet.

"I'm not sure how involved Brinley is with Elder Jameson," the prophet said. "She delivered the letter. This much we know."

"Yes."

"Tell me your impression of the girl."

Lehi cleared his throat. This was his opportunity, but he had to be careful. "She's kind, obedient, and an essential part of our family."

"If she's so obedient, then why did she deliver that letter?" the prophet asked, his voice rising. Lehi could feel the bite in that retort.

"Of that I'm not sure. But it is possible that Brinley did not know of the contents of the letter. Perhaps, she thought it was for the boys—"

The prophet waved a dismissive hand. "That doesn't matter. She should have destroyed the letter. It was insubordination of the highest order."

"I understand."

"Listen, all wives are to know their place. Every single one. And every man must be cognizant of that, as well, and must treat them equally. Rebecca was removed from the Jameson household for that reason."

Lehi nodded. "Yes. I strive to do that in my home."

The prophet narrowed his eyes, perching himself on the corner of the desk and peering at Lehi. "I'm considering reassigning Brinley. There are several men in the Texas compound who are in need of additional wives. She could be relocated. Perhaps then she'd learn not to be swayed by men such as Burt."

Disappointment spread through Lehi, and he was no longer sure that a plea would be appropriate. Brinley was the most beautiful of all his wives, the one he enjoyed the most in the bedroom, and so he'd wanted to ask the prophet not to reassign her, to allow her to stay in his home. But he feared the prophet would accuse him of favoritism if he were honest regarding his intention.

"You must do what you see fit, but I would be most appreciative if you'd allow her to remain in our household." Quickly, Lehi thought of a half truth to sway the prophet without revealing his true motivation. "She's quite helpful with the children and her sister wives."

"Interesting," the prophet responded, and Lehi could feel cynicism in that one word. "Your first wife doesn't seem to agree with you. Perhaps there is some discrepancy here."

"I-I don't understand."

"She seemed quite eager for Brinley to be removed from your home."

Lehi's mouth was agape as he heard this bit of information. He knew that Leandra was frequently annoyed by Brinley, which was to be expected given the large age gap between them. But he never expected that Leandra would want to see her reassigned. He had no idea what to say in response, so said nothing.

The prophet considered for a moment, then said, "I'll take care of this. She'll be given an honor, a position assisting my mother in her home. She'll begin on Monday. I'll gather information and make a decision posthaste."

"Thank you."

Thank God.

Lehi was determined not to lose Brinley. He enjoyed his time with her more than any of his other wives. She was the only wife who had cooperated on their honeymoon. Leandra had slapped him across the face when he'd turned on the TV. Others had cried, one had even choked and then vomited on his penis. But Brinley, she'd cooperated, and Lehi had even managed to convince himself that she'd enjoyed it.

She was the only wife who wore makeup in the bedroom without question, without making Lehi feel guilty about his needs. Furthermore, her movements in the bedroom lately were turning him on. She was coming into her own, becoming more sexual, and that aroused Lehi to no end. When he came with Brinley, he came *hard.* He looked forward to nights with her more than any of his other seven wives. He couldn't lose that time. He wouldn't.

Each wife played a role. Leandra managed the home. Brenda assisted with managing the finances. Aspen had the memory of an elephant and could always assist Lehi in remembering important dates and events for the family. Brinley—well, Brinley was his release. He'd fight to keep her in that role.

No matter what.

chapter 31

THE SCREECH OF Leandra's voice broke the silence in the room, but did nothing for the tension. Although she was a tiny woman in stature, her booming voice could alert the entire compound. And part of me wondered if it would.

"You filthy little whore," she screamed, dangling my purse accusingly between us. "How dare you?"

I said nothing in response. There was nothing left to say, and so I listened. I took the abuse in the hopes that they'd say their piece and leave me be. Leave me to abandon this place where I never quite fit in.

"Did you honestly think you could get away with this, you foul, wicked girl?"

Her shrill voice assaulted my ears. I glanced at Lehi, and although no words came from his mouth, he was visibly shaken, obviously enraged. His chest continued to heave in and out. His cheeks were a deep tone of scarlet and his nostrils flared wide.

As I continued to watch him, memories flashed through my brain, causing my fear to build. Memories of Lehi slapping the children, and Lehi shouting at Leandra behind closed doors. Unlike Leandra, Lehi was not tiny, dainty, or small in stature. He was large, muscular, and dangerous. I watched him carefully from the corner of my eye as I attempted to turn my attention back to Leandra.

While my attention had been on Lehi, Leandra had been digging through my purse, invading my privacy. My pulse quickened as she removed an item from the bag. The cell phone.

"These contraptions are *not allowed in this house*!" She crossed the room and shoved the phone in my face, so close it almost touched the tip of my nose.

The door creaked open and Aspen entered. My heart raced.

Did Aspen have something to do with this ambush? The idea of her betraying me was more than I could handle.

"I'm sorry to disturb you," Aspen said, "but is everything all right?"

"It seems Brinley has been keeping secrets from the family," Leandra spat out. "Lots of secrets." She then waved the phone in Aspen's face.

Aspen looked at the phone, then looked searchingly at me. Did she want a reason, an answer?

"Did you know about this?" Leandra narrowed her eyes at Aspen. "Do you have one too?"

"What? No, of course not! Brinley, doesn't have a phone!" She turned her attention to me. "Tell them that's not yours!"

I stayed silent, unsure of what to say. No matter which words I chose, they'd all lead back to deception. My deception.

"It most certainly is hers!" Leandra shrieked. "She has messages on this thing. Hundreds of them! With someone named Porter."

"Porter?" Aspen's voice was shaken. "Brinley, who in the world is Porter?"

I swallowed hard. Then the tears came, brimming from the corners of my eyes.

The color drained from Aspen's face. "Who . . . is . . . Porter?" she demanded once again.

“I wanted to tell you,” I said, my voice cracking.

Aspen looked away, looked to Leandra. And just as I had dreaded, I lost her. Lost her support, her love, and her trust.

Leandra lifted her chin. “Apparently, he’s a man living outside the compound. Someone who knows all about us.”

“He used to be one of us,” Lehi growled. “His name is Porter Hammond, yes?”

I nodded, shocked that Lehi would remember Porter.

Leandra turned her attention to Lehi. “How do *you* know him?”

“He worked for me, on one of my construction sites. His parents removed him years ago. He was a bad seed.”

“Sounds familiar,” Leandra said with a sneer.

I didn’t care what they thought of me; I didn’t. But I couldn’t handle Lehi reducing Porter to such a foul name. “He is *not*!”

“Brinley, stop!” Aspen linked her arm with mine, pulling me close to her and farther away from our seething husband. She was obviously worried about my safety. Lehi’s anger was building and she probably feared that soon he’d express it.

“There’s more to her lies,” Leandra yelled, tossing the phone on the bed and reaching back into the purse. “How did you get this money?”

Leandra clutched the eighty-five dollars that I’d been saving for months, money from Porter. It all started in the drugstore, and since then he’d given me money whenever I’d accept it. For a moment, I was thankful that I’d chosen to hide the money from Jorjina. If Leandra found that, I had no idea what would happen.

“Are you stealing from us?”

"Of course not!"

"Then, what? Where did you get this?"

"Porter," I answered, unashamed.

"And what do you need it for?" Leandra demanded, but she obviously already knew the answer.

"I'm not going to answer that. It's not your business." I stood tall in defiance, my bravado hiding the fear that consumed my brain, my heart.

Apparently my defiance was the last straw.

"Our *business*?" Lehi roared, stepping past Leandra. He towered over me, and his rage made him a giant. His eyes bulged from their sockets. His fists balled up so hard his knuckles turned white. "*You are* my business. You're my wife! The mother of my child!"

"Not so fast," Leandra said, her voice wicked, mischievous. "My dear, there's one more thing in this bag. Something I neglected to show you earlier."

"What is it?" Lehi asked, annoyed.

And I knew right then, right there, that I was finished. I was done. I would never see Porter again. Or Tiffany. Or the light of day.

"Care to tell us what these are, Brinley?" Leandra held the small plastic disk in her hand, opening the lid to reveal ten pills remaining in the pack.

Her smug grin enraged me, but there was nothing I could do. My anger was moot. I was caught in their web, and there was no escape.

"Medication?" Lehi asked, confused. "You're on medication?"

"Lehi, dear, this is *not* medication. Brinley is perfectly healthy." Leandra strolled past Lehi, planting her feet right in front of me. "No, these tiny little pills *prevent* pregnancy."

"*What*?" Lehi roared.

Leandra pursed her lips and said, "Our little Brinley is on the birth control pill."

"Birth control pill?"

Lehi snatched the disk from Leandra's hand. After inspecting the half-empty case, he stormed toward me, pushing Aspen out the way and pressing me up against the wall. Hard. So hard, I thought my muscles might bruise on contact from his thick fingertips digging into my skin. The case dropped to the floor.

"How did you get these?" he demanded. "Why are you taking them?"

"Lehi, please," Aspen begged, pulling on his forearm. "Let her go. She'll explain. I'm sure she'll explain everything. Don't hurt her, she's pregnant!"

"You silly girl," Leandra said to Aspen, pulling her away from Lehi. "You do realize what this means, Lehi, dear." Leandra crossed her arms in front of her chest.

Lehi snarled, loosened his grip on my shoulders, and glared at his first wife. "What?"

"Our dear Brinley isn't pregnant. She never was."

And then it happened. Before I could react, the back of Lehi's hand smashed against my cheek, sending me flying against the nightstand. The corner of the furniture tore into my side and I screamed, then fell into the lamp, which tumbled to the floor, its light bulb shattering into tiny pieces. I stumbled to fall facedown on the quilt of my bed, until Lehi pulled me back into a standing position.

He slapped me again, catching my other cheek this time, and I fell onto the bed. Both sides of my face burned in searing agony. My ribs ached from the nightstand, my head spun, and I couldn't focus my eyes.

Again and again, Lehi yanked me up, pulling me to my feet before striking me again. My face, my belly, my ribs. Again and again, he punched me, yelling obscenities and cursing my name as Aspen pleaded with him to stop. A few sister wives tentatively entered the room, glancing at each other in horror while others gathered in the hallway, watching with wide eyes as the drama unfolded in the small room.

"You pretended to carry my child!" Lehi boomed. Another slap, and this time his wedding band cut the skin just above my eye. "You're going to burn. Do you hear me? You'll burn in hell for this!"

"Leandra," Rebecca said softly, "you promised! You promised she wouldn't be hurt."

"*I* promised nothing," Lehi said, throwing me to the floor. "*No one* deceives me like this! No one makes a damn fool of *me* and gets away with it!"

I couldn't see Leandra's expression, but even in my haze I knew she was feeling vindicated. Somehow she'd convinced Rebecca to spill my secrets, and made empty promises to get what she wanted. She wanted this. She wanted Lehi to be enraged. She wanted me on this floor, bent over in pain, blood pouring from my face.

She wanted all of this.

"You did this?" Aspen screeched.

"I-I didn't—" Rebecca sputtered as she tried to explain, but was interrupted.

"She did what she *needed* to do. This girl is wicked. And she needs to be purged from this family." Leandra's words sent a chill down my spine. Purged? I was going to be purged?

Lehi's foot collided with my stomach, a violent blow that knocked the air from my lungs. My knees jerked up in response. Instinctively I curled into the fetal position, a belated attempt at self-preservation. But I knew it was futile. Lehi would continue to beat me until I was within an inch of my life.

Of that I was certain.

"Stop him!" Aspen screamed, and I assumed she was yelling at my sister wives who had congregated in the room, watching Lehi abuse me. They stood there helplessly as I clung to my throbbing muscles, watching as blood pooled on the floor beneath me.

"No!" Aspen yelled. "You can't do this! I won't let you hurt her anymore!"

I curled tighter into a ball, covering my head with my hands, when I heard retreating footsteps. Someone had left the room, but I couldn't raise my head high enough to see who had gone, who had turned their back on me. My vision was fuzzy, but I could see several figures in the room. Leandra, Lehi, Rebecca, and Brenda. But I couldn't see Aspen.

Where was Aspen?

"Mommy?" a little voice called from the door. One of Brenda's children, I think. A fuzzy figure left the huddled group above me and shuffled to the door.

"Let's go. You can't be here," she said.

They left the room, but I heard the young voice again. This time I recognized her. It was Bonnie Jo, Brenda's nine-year-old daughter. She sobbed as she asked, "Why is Father beating Mother Brinley?"

Not only was Lehi placing scars on my body and my heart, but he was scarring the minds of his children who would remember this day. Bonnie Jo in particular would remember me beaten and bloody, lying on the floor while the other adults watched.

More footsteps, this time entering the room. I lifted my head to see. I hated the idea of another child witnessing the horrendous acts of their father. I recognized the shoes and the dress immediately.

Aspen.

She'd returned.

"Step away from her. Now!" Aspen yelled.

"This is not your concern!" Leandra snapped. "Brinley has sinned against her husband, against the prophet and Heavenly Father. And she must be punished."

"Lehi!" Aspen yelled, standing in front of me to block Lehi's blows. "Do not touch her."

"You don't tell me what to do! None of you! This is my home. My house and my rules. Do you hear me?"

And then I heard the sound of Lehi's hand making contact with skin. He'd slapped Aspen. I yelped to protest, but no words left my aching mouth.

When I looked up, I could see the blurry image of what appeared to be Aspen holding up some crumpled pieces of paper.

"I know what you did," Aspen said softly. "And if you touch her again, everyone will know. *Everyone*."

"Where did you get those?" Lehi demanded. "Leandra, how did she get those?"

"I found them in Leandra's room."

"How dare you!" Leandra shouted.

None of their exchange made any sense to me. But I listened, wanting desperately to know what Aspen had discovered.

"I wasn't going to do anything with them, not yet anyway. I was saving them until I could figure out the truth. But now you've shown the depths of your vile nature. And you've forced my hand. Forced me to reveal the evil nature in this room. In the two of you."

"Give those to me!" Lehi shouted.

"Even if you managed to pry them away from me, it doesn't matter because I have others. So many others. You must have practiced writing these quite a bit . . . had to get his handwriting just right, hmmm? Was it you, dear husband of mine? Or was it your first wife?"

"Shut your mouth, you wicked girl," Leandra screeched again.

"I know you're involved, you witch. Or these wouldn't have been in your room!"

"You sneaky girl, you wretched, wretched thing," Leandra screamed.

"You let her go," Aspen demanded. "Give me the keys to your truck. And you let her go."

"Or what?" Lehi said through clenched teeth.

"Or I'll tell the prophet."

All movement in the room came to a halt.

"I'll tell the prophet," Aspen repeated, "and you'll be gone. You'll never see any of us, any of your children ever again. Your home, your business, everything you hold dear. Gone. In an instant."

"You can't prove anything," Leandra cried out.

"The proof is right here." The papers crinkled in her hands. "All I have to do is say the word. Don't force me to reveal this, Lehi. Because I will. You *know* I will."

The room grew silent as Lehi considered Aspen's threat. I prayed it would work and that I'd escape the Cluff house alive.

"Wait," Rebecca whispered. "What . . . what are those? Is that—"

"Silence!" Lehi shouted and keys jingled. "Take her away." His words were rushed, sounding almost as if he were . . . *frightened?*

Aspen snatched the keys from his hand before Lehi continued. "But when you return, *all* of those papers, every single one, will be given to me."

Aspen nodded. "Understood."

"And if I ever find another, you'll be the one who's gone forever. Do you understand? I. Will. Kill. You."

I inhaled sharply at Lehi's threat, unable to imagine what he could have possibly done. I had to know. I just had to.

Aspen's arms looped through mine as she hoisted me from the floor by my underarms. My legs were too weak to stand, my vision was blurry, and the metallic smell of blood overwhelmed my senses.

"Someone help me," Aspen snarled. "Now!"

Rebecca joined Aspen and wrapped her arm around my waist, supporting my weight.

"I'm sorry, Brinley," she whispered. "So, so sorry."

"Porter Hammond. You know who he is?" Aspen asked.

"Yes. I met him months ago."

"Okay, while I drive, you need to make contact. Grab her phone. Call him, send a message, ask him for his address."

"I can do better than that," Rebecca said. "I'll take you to him."

chapter 32

"EVERYONE OUT!" Aspen screeched while she and Rebecca dragged me to the bed. Every bit of my body ached, burned, and pounded with pain. Lehi, Leandra, and the other wives left the room, and despite my pain, I was able to breathe. The danger was gone.

"My suitcase," I whispered to Aspen. "I need it."

"Where is it?" Aspen jumped to attention and ran across the bedroom. "In the closet?"

"Yes," I whimpered.

Aspen froze, looking back at me, studying me from head to toe. "Rebecca, fetch a first aid kit." Her face was solemn, downturned. "We're going to need it."

Rebecca ran from the room. While she was gone, Aspen retrieved my suitcase and placed it on the bed next to me. She scooped up my purse and its contents, placing it all in the case. Her hand smoothed down my disheveled hair and she tipped her head to the side, giving me a sympathetic smile.

"I'm so sorry this happened to you."

"You saved me," I said.

"Not quite." Aspen's fingers skimmed my temple, next to the cut that wouldn't stop bleeding. Her shoulders drooped and her spine bowed.

I grabbed her hand with as much strength as I could muster. "You saved my life," I said through my tears and cracking voice. "I'll *never* forget that."

Aspen looked away, sniffing and wiping at her nose. I knew she was fighting tears; she was never one to show emotion or weakness.

Rebecca entered the room and Aspen quickly wiped the tears from her cheeks. "Rest," she insisted. "We'll pack your things."

I submitted to her instructions and collapsed on the bed, trying desperately to ignore the pain. My wounds didn't matter; they would heal.

I was getting out. Finally.

And that was all that mattered.

Within minutes, my bag was packed with the bare essentials and my sister wives guided me to Lehi's truck. Every muscle screamed as they lifted me into the cab of the truck. I struggled to maintain consciousness as my mind tried desperately to escape the pain. My chest ached and my throat burned each time I swallowed. It hurt to breathe, and bruises were starting to form on my arms and legs.

Aspen climbed into the driver's seat, and Rebecca sat on the other side of me, next to the window. As we made our way into town, a stunning sunset filled the sky. I leaned my head back against the seat, wincing against the pain, as my sister wives argued. Oh, did they argue.

Aspen glanced at Rebecca. "Who is this Porter? And how on earth do you know about him and I don't?"

Poor Aspen was furious, although I knew she was really just hurt that I'd deceived her through lying by omission.

Rebecca looked away and shrugged. "I met him months ago."

"And . . . ?"

Rebecca brushed away Aspen's questions. Turning in her seat, she demanded, "You must tell me what you found, Aspen! What was written on those papers?"

"You answer my questions first."

"It was months ago . . ." Her voice trailed off.

"You said that already. Who is he? Is he good to her?"

Rebecca shook her head. "I-I don't know. I met him once, just once. Right after I joined the family."

"Oh, but you know where he lives?"

"It's a long story. Would you please, please, just tell me what was on those papers?" Rebecca's voice cracked.

Aspen snorted. "Are you joking? I owe you nothing! Nothing!"

"I know, but—"

"Where does he live?"

Rebecca glanced around, then said, "Um . . . turn right on Wilson Avenue. It's two blocks—"

"I know where it is," Aspen snapped. "I've lived here my whole life."

"Okay."

We drove in silence for several minutes, then Aspen cleared her throat and spoke. When she did, her voice was monotone, emotionless. "This . . . what happened to Brinley tonight, it's all your fault. You must know that."

"I know, I know, but—I have to know. You must tell me. I'll go insane if I don't know."

"Then go insane. Perhaps that will be your penance for doing this to Brinley."

"That's not fair," Rebecca whimpered.

"Nor is blaming Brinley for your domestic problems," Aspen snarled, her words laced with venom. "It's not her fault you were reassigned!"

"I-I didn't say it was!"

"Then why did you do this? Why? She could have been killed!"

Rebecca wailed in response, turning her body away, leaning her forehead against the passenger window and sobbing as though her heart were breaking. Normally, I would comfort her, but the pain was all-consuming. Besides, to be honest, Rebecca was not my favorite person at that moment. After all, she was the reason that Lehi beat me. She'd clearly given my purse to Lehi and Leandra, and set the confrontation in motion.

"I-I thought . . . I mean, I didn't know they would do that. I thought—"

"What? That she'd be reassigned?"

"Yes," Rebecca admitted. "Here's the coffee shop. His apartment is upstairs."

Aspen didn't respond. She pulled the truck onto a side street and turned off the engine.

"How do we get up there?" she asked once they were balancing my weight on the sidewalk, just below a lone streetlamp.

"Follow me." Rebecca pressed the button marked TRAVIS.

A moment later, Charlie yelled through the intercom, "Yo!"

Leaning toward the box, I said weakly, "It's Brinley. I need Porter." I moaned. "It's an emergency."

"Oh," he replied.

"Hurry!" Aspen screeched into the intercom.

Buzzz.

Rebecca held the door open and the two women carried me to the stairs. Slowly, we climbed, my knees weak, every step causing pain to shoot through my ribs.

The thunder of footsteps came rushing toward us. When I saw Porter and Charlie round the corner of the staircase, all my emotions came bubbling to the surface, and I began to cry.

"Brin?" Porter's head jerked back. He froze, staring down at me as his mouth fell open. Charlie nudged him, snapping him back into action. He ran down the remaining steps. Rebecca moved out of the way, and he wrapped his arm around my waist. "What happened?"

Charlie supported the other side of my body and they carried me the rest of the way. I sobbed as we walked. Porter demanded again and again for me to tell him what happened, but I couldn't speak for wailing.

"She's still in shock," Rebecca said. "But she'll be okay."

We entered the apartment and the men carried me to the couch. I lay on the couch with two pillows supporting my head and neck while Charlie scurried off to find their first aid kit.

Porter kissed my forehead, then studied my face. His face clouded as his anger built, and I knew that soon he'd explode.

"What the fuck happened to her?" he demanded, looking at Aspen, who'd grown silent in his presence. "And who the hell are you?"

"My name is Aspen."

"The pain-in-the-ass sister wife?"

"Porter!" I grimaced, knowing that Aspen didn't deserve that title. Not one bit. "Stop. She saved me."

"From what?" he asked, kneeling down beside the couch. "Who did this to you?"

"It—it's a long story," Aspen answered.

"I'm serious, Brin. Who the fuck do I need to destroy? Was it Lehi? Did he do this to you?"

I nodded through my tears. Porter's face hardened and his breathing grew ragged. He'd reached the end of his fuse.

"Rebecca," Aspen said, her voice controlled, somber. "Clean Brinley up. I need to talk to Porter."

"I don't have time to talk," Porter said, jumping to his feet. "I have to go."

"No!" I screamed, attempting to sit up. Searing pain shot through my ribs and I fell back to the couch.

Rebecca rifled through the first aid kit that Charlie handed her, then applied antiseptic to my cuts. I winced at the pain as Porter paced.

"He has to pay for this, Brin. I'm not gonna let him get away with it!"

Aspen stood opposite Porter. "It's taken care of."

"The fuck it is! I'm gonna fuck him up so bad he'll wish he'd never touched a hair on her fucking head!" Porter's chest heaved, the skin of his face and neck splotchy.

"Listen to me, please," Aspen begged. "You can't go back there. You'll only make things worse."

"I'm not afraid of that asshole. I'll fucking kill him!" Porter shot toward the door of the apartment.

"Listen to her, man," Charlie said, jumping up from his seat and blocking the hallway that led to the door.

"Get out of the way!" Porter yelled, shoving Charlie in the chest.

"No." Charlie softened his tone, going for calm. "If you go back there, you'll regret it."

"What the fuck do you know about *anything*?" Porter demanded, turning his fury toward his roommate, pushing him aside and storming to the front door. He gripped the handle and ripped it open, the doorknob punching a hole into the drywall it slammed into.

"You're making a mistake!" Charlie yelled, chasing after Porter. He grabbed his shoulder, yanking him back into the apartment.

"Porter!" I yelled, alarmed. My mind conjured up visions of Porter . . . Lehi, dead beneath Porter's feet. Porter in handcuffs, slumped over in the back of a police car. Porter never returning to me, never being a part of my life. I'd be here, in the outside world, finally. But he wouldn't be here with me. The thought sent daggers through my fragile heart.

"Look, man," Charlie yelled, his grip on Porter fixed and determined. "You've wanted her for months—you've wanted her here, wanted her to be free."

"So?" Porter looked past Charlie and met my gaze.

"So, she's *here*, man. She's what matters. Not him. Not *any* of them." Charlie shook his head as Porter's eyes remained on mine, his expression softening just a touch. But it was enough. "Just . . . calm yourself down. Focus on her, man. Focus on Brinley."

"Please," Aspen said, stepping in front of Charlie. "I made a deal. Brinley's free and that's all that matters. Let us deal with the consequences."

"And then what?" Porter's eyes were crazed, manic. "Then tomorrow he beats the shit out of you too? No, not on my fucking watch!"

"Porter, please!" I wailed from the couch. "Don't go back there. Stay with me. I *need* you."

He froze, then glanced back at Charlie and Aspen before crossing the room. He sat on the edge of the couch and stroked my hair.

Charlie spoke next as he and Aspen moved to hover over Porter and me. "Does her husband know about Porter?"

"Yes," Rebecca answered.

"So, he's probably waiting . . . he's waiting for you, man. Don't you see that? He's waiting for you to come pounding on his door. He'll fuck you up and then the cops will haul you away."

"I don't care," Porter said, still looking into my eyes. His face crumpled, and his eyes filled with tears before he pressed them shut. Tight. So tight. But they still escaped.

I squeezed his hand. "I do," I whispered. "Stay with me."

He shook his head with fervor. "He can't get away with this, Brin."

"He won't," Aspen replied. "Trust me. He won't."

"I don't believe you."

Porter rose to his feet and stomped out of the room. The rest of us stared at one another in silence. Silently, I prayed that he wasn't retrieving a weapon from his bedroom.

When Porter returned, I sighed with relief. His hands were still empty, but they were balled up tightly as his anger took over his body. He stormed through the room, throwing a solid punch at the wall, then roaring as his hand made contact with the drywall, a misshapen hole left in its wake.

"Porter!"

He turned and placed his other palm on the wall, then pressed his forehead to the surface, his eyes closed tight, his face in a hard scowl.

"I can't! I can't let this go. It'll kill me."

"And if you're in jail," I cried out, "rotting away in a cell, and I'm out here on my own? That'll kill *me*."

He wheeled around and said, "I have to do something, Brin." He shrugged, tears rolling down his face, and walked back to the couch to crouch down and stroke my hair. "You're mine. I need to protect you."

"Protect me *here*. Stay with me, protect me, *be* with me. You have to rise above this, Porter, or it'll destroy us both."

"Wait," Aspen said softly. "There is something you can do."

Porter turned and glared at my sister wife, unable to trust her yet since he'd only heard negative things from me about her nosy behavior, her constant correction of my mistakes. He didn't see the Aspen who had stepped between me and the hand of absolute evil. He couldn't possibly know how she had redeemed herself.

Aspen reached into her pocket and pulled out a crumpled piece of paper. "Hold on to this for me." She walked over and placed the ball of paper in Porter's hand, and when she did, Rebecca grimaced. I knew she wanted to leap across the couch to rip it from Porter's hands. "Guard it with your life. Lock it up somewhere."

"I don't get it. A piece of paper? What the hell is this?"

"My insurance policy. I'll ask for it when the time comes." A devilish smile lit up Aspen's face, as if she'd solved the ultimate puzzle, the ultimate game.

"Fine, okay." Porter stuffed the paper into his pocket as Rebecca closed her eyes and sighed.

"How will you reach us?" I asked Aspen. "I mean, when you need it?"

"I'll come here."

Porter and I shared a glance; we both knew his time in this apartment was limited. Then he said, "Wait, I have an idea. Do you have Brin's purse?"

"Yes, just a moment." Aspen unzipped the case, retrieving the tattered purse. The purse that contained all my secrets.

"Here," she said, handing the bag to Porter.

He dug through it and pulled out the phone. "Take this," he said, placing it in her hand. "My phone number is already in it. You can call me, text me, whatever. But this way you'll be able to reach me."

Aspen glanced at me. "And I can check on Brinley?"

"Sure," he said. "Of course."

"Wait," I said with a start, glancing back and forth between Aspen and Rebecca. "You can't go back there. Lehi, he'll . . . he'll make your lives miserable."

Aspen shook her head and smiled weakly. "We'll be just fine."

I wasn't convinced. My sudden fear of losing Aspen surprised me. Over the past three years, I'd relied on her, yes. At different times I'd resented her, feared her, and dismissed her. But faced with losing her, I felt as if a part of me were dying, as if one of my limbs were being removed from my body. Aspen had been my compass, my north star. She gave me boundaries, then pushed me when I didn't stay true to them. And she believed in my goodness. She believed in *me*.

"B-but," I stammered. "If you left, if you left the compound . . ."

Aspen shook her head. "No, Brinley. This life is not for me."

"You don't know that, you haven't—"

"I belong there," she insisted. "It's what I believe. It's where I belong."

"But I—" I choked on my words, sadness and grief filling me from head to toe. "If I'm out here and you're in there, then I'll be dead to you."

Aspen walked to me and placed a kiss on my forehead. "You're my sister," she whispered. "You'll never be dead to me. Never."

"Promise?" I asked, tears streaming down my cheeks.

"Yes."

Aspen wrapped her arms around me, careful not to hurt me. But I didn't care. I pulled her close, pulled her tight as the tears continued to spill from my eyes. She kissed the top of my head and said good-bye.

"We have to get back. I still need to deal with Lehi."

"Are you sure?" I asked, hoping once more that she'd change her mind.

She brushed me off, though, as I knew she would. Aspen was strong, determined, and independent. There was nothing I could say to force her to leave her faith. Despite the influence of the Cluff household, Aspen knew her place in the world. And that was to be a part of the chosen. To live in the compound and to serve Heavenly Father.

And I had to accept that.

"Brinley, I—" Rebecca said meekly. "I can never . . . apologize enough for what I did."

"You didn't know," I told her. "You didn't know what they were capable of. I understand. And eventually . . . eventually I'll forgive."

She nodded, her face twisting as tears fell. "Thank you."

Porter walked my sister wives to the door, thanked them for bringing me to him, and at Aspen's insistence, promised to remain at the apartment, no matter his urge for revenge.

"Let's get you to bed," he said, helping me off the couch and walking me to his bedroom. Carefully, he stripped me of my dress and long underwear as I sat on the edge of his bed.

I glanced around the room, astonished at how tidy it was. "You cleaned?"

"No big deal." He shrugged. "Just trying to clean up my act."

"I see," I said, smiling for the first time in what felt like an eternity.

"You won't be needing these anymore."

He tossed my clothes into the wastebasket. The heavy dress draped over the side of the can, toppling it to the floor. I stared at the can, lying on its side, knowing that I would no longer be weighed down by a garment of any kind. I would stand tall.

Porter dressed me in a soft cotton T-shirt and a pair of plaid boxer shorts. My body, despite the pain that I was still in, was enveloped in the peace these simple clothes provided. I stood in front of his mirror, stroking the bare skin of my arms as I studied my body. Purple bruises were forming on my legs. Bandages covered the gash on my eyebrow, and my hands that were cut by the shattered glass. But it didn't matter. None of it mattered.

Porter cleared his throat, taking my braid in his hands. "May I?"

I nodded, and Porter released my braid. His fingers weaved through the loosened strands, freeing my hair from its bonded state. Unimaginable relief swept through my body, my brain, my heart.

No more braids.

No more prophet, domineering husband, or sister wives.

I was *free*.

chapter 33

ASPEN WAS PROUD of herself. Not for what she'd done to protect Brinley. She couldn't imagine not rising to that occasion. She cared for Brinley, loved her like a sister. It was her duty, her obligation to protect her. No, she was proud of the armor she'd encircled around her when saying good-bye.

She couldn't let Brinley know that she was terrified.

Inside, Aspen dreaded seeing Lehi's face when they returned to the compound, hearing his venomous words. And the idea of laying with him to make another child was absolutely incomprehensible. She was proud that she'd placed a mask over her fear, given Brinley hope.

And she was satisfied that Porter would stay true to his word. He'd hold on to his copy of the note. She placed her hands inside the wide pockets of her dress, comforted by stroking the crumpled papers one by one. There were seven copies on her person, two inside her sock drawer, one in Ruthie's piggy bank, and three inside her mother's home. Aspen couldn't be too careful.

Rebecca had said nothing on the drive back to the house. But when they walked inside, Aspen was surprised to find Rebecca trailing behind her.

"I'm going to clean her room," Aspen said, and Rebecca nodded.

The two women stood in the empty room. Picture frames had fallen from the wall. The quilt on Brinley's bed showed evidence of the scuffle. It was rumpled crazily, with one pillow lying at the foot of the bed. Broken glass littered the floor at the base of the nightstand, and blood remained dark and sticky on the floor.

Aspen stared down at the blood and her brain flashed with snapshots of memories from earlier that evening. Brinley being slapped, kicked, and brutalized as everyone watched. Aspen had to know, she had to know why Rebecca would turn her back on her sister wife in such a despicable manner.

"Why'd you do it?" she asked, hanging a picture frame back on a nail jutting out from the wall.

"I . . . I don't know."

"Yes, you do. Just tell me. Stop pretending to be so innocent in all of this."

Rebecca's posture hunched and she played with the trinkets on Brinley's dresser. "I didn't get to be with Burt. I didn't get to be with the man I adored, the man I spent twelve years loving. And she was going to be with Porter. She was going to be happy, I could *feel* it. And it killed me. I was so jealous I could barely breathe."

"You're telling me that this was all about envy? All of it?"

"I can't speak for Leandra, or Lehi, for that matter. I don't know why they beat her like they did."

"I do," Aspen replied, eyeing the trinkets on the dresser. She moved to stand next to Rebecca and touched one by one the small gifts that were handmade by her children. They adored Brinley almost as much as she did. They would miss her.

Rebecca glanced at her. "Tell me, please. I'm begging you."

"Pride," Aspen said matter-of-factly. "Brinley shattered their pride. They tried to control her, but they couldn't. Clearly, she was too smart for them."

"I suppose you're right," Rebecca said. "Leandra was so focused on impressing the prophet. She wanted to maintain the Cluff name."

"Desperately," Aspen agreed.

Aspen knelt down to retrieve one of the trinkets that had fallen on the floor, a tiny butterfly made out of paper. She remembered the day Ruthie had given it to Brinley. It was the day she'd entered the Cluff family. Aspen had been suspicious and hesitant with Brinley when she first met her. Brinley was a sweet young thing, but she seemed terribly naive and Aspen wasn't known for her patience. Nevertheless, Lehi had assigned her to mentor Brinley and she had done so. For three years, she'd done her best to guide and care for Brinley as if she were one of her own.

And she'd miss that role. Looking back, it had truly been an honor. One she would cherish in the years to come.

Her thoughts were interrupted by Rebecca reading aloud.

"*I can't go on without you. I'm a pathetic man . . .*"

Aspen knew those words; she'd read them several times already. But they shouldn't have come from Rebecca's mouth.

"I don't . . . I don't understand," Rebecca said.

Aspen looked to Rebecca and gasped when she saw her holding one of the papers.

Rebecca looked up. "This isn't . . . it can't be. No. *No, no, no, no, no, no*!"

"How did you get that?" Aspen demanded, stalking toward her sister wife in a panic.

"It fell on the floor. You were hanging the picture and it fell out," Rebecca cried. "This is all my fault. All of it. He's gone and it's all my fault. They took him . . ."

"I'm sorry," Aspen said. What else could she say? It was the truth.

Rebecca's face turned ghostly white and she sank to her knees, clutching the note to her chest, wailing at the top of her lungs. "I should've met him that night. Under our tree. He must have waited and waited for me," she cried. "None of this would've happened. I could have saved him, I could . . . I could . . ."

Aspen wanted to be furious with Rebecca, she wanted to hold on to her anger for dear life. But as she watched her sister wife crumple on the floor, wailing in agony, she couldn't keep sweet. She couldn't ignore Rebecca. She had to comfort her.

"How could they *do* this?" Rebecca peered into Aspen's eyes, looking for an answer. "How could they be so evil?"

"I don't have all the answers. But there were over a dozen of these in her wastebasket. There's no mistaking what they did or how they covered it up."

"The note they showed me wasn't real, and I should've known. I knew Burt's handwriting better than anyone."

"You were grieving. You'd just lost him," Aspen said, attempting to make sense of the unimaginable.

"No, I lost him months ago, the day Brinley gave me that letter."

"Letter? There was another letter?"

"Yes. He wanted me to run away with him. He asked me to be his one and only."

"I had no idea," Aspen replied, trying to process the new information on Burt and Rebecca's love story.

"I turned my back on him, Aspen. I turned my back on the *one* man who loved me. The *only* one."

"Why didn't you go with him?" Aspen asked, curious. She hadn't gotten to know Rebecca in the way that Brinley had. In fact, she knew very little about Lehi's eighth wife, but she seemed to be learning more with each passing moment.

"I thought Heavenly Father was testing me." Rebecca wiped her nose as tears tracked down her cheeks. "I thought my faith, my love for him was being tested. And I wanted to prove it. That I could serve our Lord without question."

"I see," Aspen replied, and an ache stirred within her.

She understood Rebecca's desire to please Heavenly Father, to rise above her own wants and desires to serve the prophet and the community at large. And for the first time, she felt real sympathy for Rebecca. For just a moment she mourned Burt Jameson, the man who was the ultimate victim in Leandra and Lehi's sick games. The ultimate victim in their quest to be beloved by the prophet, to maintain their standing in the community and to avoid any dissension in their home.

To Lehi and Leandra, appearances were everything. Burt Jameson had muddied the waters of the Cluff family's pristine reputation and he had to be dealt with.

"I can't stay here," Rebecca whispered.

"But you're—"

"What?"

"You're pregnant . . . with Lehi's baby."

Rebecca's hands wrapped around the slight curve in her abdomen and she sobbed.

Aspen's heart was tugged as she watched Rebecca come to the realization that she was trapped. She wrapped her arms around Rebecca, allowing her to sob against her chest. Aspen's hands created large circles on her sister wife's back, attempting to soothe, urging her to calm.

"We'll figure this out. We'll get you out of here."

"Really?" Rebecca looked up hopefully, her eyes swollen and red.

"Yes. Both of us. If you can pull yourself together, I have an idea. Can you do that? Lehi is expecting us."

Aspen waited while Rebecca sucked in several deep breaths to calm herself. Normally her lack of patience would have gotten the best of her, but for this—for this, she needed Rebecca to be at her calmest. She needed her to be cool and collected.

After several minutes, Rebecca wiped her cheeks completely dry, took another cleansing breath, and spoke.

"All right, I'm ready."

"Both of you?" Lehi shouted, his arms crossed in front of his broad chest. Leandra stood at his side, glaring at Aspen and Rebecca, but Aspen was undeterred. She wouldn't surrender those forgeries. Not until she was satisfied with their bargain.

"Yes," Aspen said, her face made of stone. She wouldn't let Lehi know how intimidated she was. She couldn't. Or they'd never succeed.

"That wasn't our arrangement. I agreed to let Brinley go . . . that's it. Nothing more."

"The arrangement has changed," Aspen said. Her heart pounded madly within her chest. "Now we want more."

"How dare you," Leandra snapped.

"Consider the facts," Aspen said, laying out her argument. "You'll still have five wives and twenty-two children. It will be a smaller household, less mouths to feed, more room in the home."

"We don't *want* a smaller household," Leandra shot back.

"What you don't want is two wives living under your roof who despise you. One of them who knows your secrets, who *knows* what you've done."

"And you?" Lehi said, glaring at Rebecca. "Why do you want to leave?"

"I need a fresh start, Lehi. Please. Losing Burt, and now Brinley. It's just too much. I don't belong here."

Rebecca stared down at the hardwood, and Aspen knew why. If she looked at Lehi, she wouldn't be able to hide her rage, then Lehi would know his secret was revealed. And then they'd both be in grave danger.

"But you're carrying my baby! How am I supposed to request this? The prophet will never agree. Never!"

"We'll take the blame, Lehi. Tell him whatever you like. I'm sure the two of you can come up with something." Aspen's words were snide, meant to pierce, to remind Lehi and Leandra of what they'd done. "But you *must* have us reassigned. Send us to Texas, send us across the compound. Just tell the prophet that we must be removed from this household."

"There *are* wives needed in Texas," Lehi said slowly.

Aspen knew his wheels were spinning, considering the proposition. She knew she needed to push just a bit harder, to make sure he saw the benefits of this decision.

"We'll be far away. You won't be reminded of any of this. Of Brinley, of us. Of *Burt*."

Lehi inhaled abruptly, closing his eyes as he exhaled. He said nothing, so Aspen continued to plead her case.

"Once we have word that we're being reassigned," Aspen said convincingly, "you'll have the notes, every last one of them. Of that you can be sure."

"No." Lehi shook his head. "Rebecca stays. You may go, Aspen. But Rebecca must stay here."

Aspen was appalled. She threw her head back in disgust, knowing that Lehi was challenging her, asserting his power over her and all of the wives. Well, it wouldn't work. "No, that's not what I—"

"I don't care *what* you said. I will *not* request that she be reassigned." Lehi stepped toward Aspen, his nose almost touching her forehead as he bent down to speak. "You don't make the decisions in this house. I do. I don't care what proof you *think* you have."

"Then I'll tell the prophet. I'll tell everyone, I'll—"

"Stop," Rebecca said, placing her hand on Aspen's arm. "Aspen, no."

Aspen couldn't believe what she was hearing. Her eyes grew wide as she turned to Rebecca, trying desperately to understand. "What?"

"I'll stay." Rebecca raised her eyes to meet Lehi's gaze. "I deserve this. For what I did to Brinley, I'll stay. It's my penance from Heavenly Father. And I accept it."

"No, Rebecca, don't—"

"It's fine," Rebecca said, squeezing Aspen's hand as a tear slid slowly down her cheek. "It's how things are meant to be. You go. Start fresh. Embrace a new family and be free of this, all of this. Even me."

Aspen paused before asking, "Are you sure?" She wanted to give Rebecca every opportunity to change her mind. She wanted to shake her, to scream in her face, to insist that Rebecca would one day regret this decision.

"I thought I was being tested months ago, but this, *this* is my test. Right here and now." Rebecca took a deep breath before continuing, holding back tears as her voice broke. "I need to honor Burt, honor Brinley by staying here . . . staying and accepting my fate."

"It doesn't have to be that way," Aspen whispered. "You can have another chance, another start."

Rebecca simply shook her head.

Aspen's mind spun. She didn't want to leave her sister wife behind, caught in the clutches of Lehi and his evil first wife. She wanted to fight, to insist, to challenge Lehi enough that he would cave to her demands. But Rebecca had said her piece. Continuing to fight on her behalf would be futile.

"Fine. Rebecca will remain here . . . with you. But I demand to be reassigned."

Lehi nodded. "I'll speak with the prophet first thing in the morning. I'll tell him it's of the utmost importance."

Aspen gave him a curt nod and left the room to check on her children. Soon, she hoped they'd have quite the transition to make, and she needed to wrap her arms around her sweet babies, to tell them it would all be okay. Even though they'd have no idea what their mother was talking about.

She couldn't protect Brinley any longer, or Rebecca for that matter. But she could protect her children. She hoped they'd be safe and welcome in a new household, a new home. She wasn't one to embrace fairy tales or the concept of happily-ever-after, but she hoped . . . she hoped to be placed with a kind and gentle man. A man who would appreciate her sharp wit and remarkable memory. A man who didn't plot, connive, or control. A man who didn't lash out in anger. A man who stood by his word and insisted upon honesty. A man who was capable of love, who respected and cherished *life*.

A man . . . *not* a monster.

epilogue

One year later

MY NEW FAVORITE THING in the world was sunsets. Beautiful, glorious, calming sunsets. Each night, Porter and I would sit on our patio and watch the sunset, a cold beer in his hand, a glass of white wine in mine. We'd talk and laugh until that moment when the fiery orange orb slid just behind the mountains. In that moment, we'd be silent. Then Porter would reach for my hand, squeezing it tightly.

I'd lived with Tiffany for several months after leaving the compound. Porter respected my reasons. He had to get clean, for once and for all. I was terrified that the burden of playing nursemaid to my injuries would push him over the edge. So, instead I'd begged Tiffany to allow me to stay with her. Being a kindhearted person, she gave me her bed and slept on the floor next to me. She tended my wounds, iced my bruises, and kept me company when she wasn't working at the clinic.

Each night, Porter would visit. He'd sit with me and we'd talk about his day, about how the house was coming along, about how he'd resisted using with his roommates. He started attending Narcotics Anonymous. He made friends and quickly had a sponsor he could call in the middle of the night when he was feeling weak. He didn't want to place that burden on me, and I was grateful.

Each and every weekend, Porter stayed busy working on the house, getting it ready, making it perfect. Finally we drove to the small cottage one day, our fingers entwined on the front seat. A look of pride came over him as we strolled through the tiny house. The walls were covered in serene shades of blue and green, the carpet was fluffy and soft, and fresh flowers bloomed outside the kitchen window.

It was perfect.

Porter moved in immediately, saying good-bye to Charlie and the rest of his roommates. He was ready, truly ready for a new start, a new home.

I joined him three months later.

The money from Jorjina didn't go very far, and so we agreed that it was important for me to find work. I was nervous, to say the least, the day that I walked into the local grammar school for my interview as a study hall supervisor. I had no credentials, no formal education, and was shocked that they didn't laugh in my face when I applied. But that was the thing about the outside world; it constantly surprised me. And I'd surprised myself, as well.

Despite my assumptions about how I would carry myself in the outside world, I had yet to cut my hair. Tiffany's words had resonated with me; I didn't want my first haircut in twenty-three years to be about rebellion or revenge. I wanted it to be about independence, a fresh start, a new beginning.

And so, like any other evening, Porter and I were enjoying the sunset from our new patio. Porter was covered in dust from a job site, and I was still wearing my school attire and makeup, my long hair twisted into a tight bun.

"More wine?" Porter asked, holding the bottle over my glass.

"Trying to get me drunk?" I teased.

"You might *need* it," Porter said with a wink. "After all, our plans for this evening are a little . . . adventurous."

I giggled in response, taking another sip of wine, its sweetness easing down my throat as I pondered his words. He was right. But I was ready.

"I can't believe it's been a year," I said softly, then bit my lip, waiting for his response.

"Yeah." He grinned.

"I'm proud of you, Porter. So proud."

Porter had stayed clean since the day Aspen and Rebecca dragged me to his apartment. He'd made a decision to prove it to me, to prove he could clean up his life, his body, his mind, his soul.

And he'd done it. For three hundred and sixty-five days, Porter came to me willingly, proud of his sobriety, his self-restraint. And with each passing day, I fell more and more in love with him.

"Are you sure you're ready?" he asked, his eyes kind and unassuming. "It's okay if you're not."

"I'm completely ready."

"All right. I'll meet you inside." Porter grabbed his beer and walked inside the house. Stopping just before opening the sliding glass door, he paused for a second and smiled at me.

After finishing the rest of my wine, I rose from the table and entered the house. The walls were filled with framed photos of our first year together as a real couple. A year of healing, a year of second chances and new beginnings. The photos made me smile as I walked down the hall to the bathroom.

Porter stood behind one of our kitchen chairs, a pair of scissors in his hand, a pensive smile upon his handsome face.

"Are you sure? I can call Tiffany, I'm sure she could do a better job than I would." He rubbed the back of his neck, awaiting my answer.

"Don't be silly. I want you to do it. Only you."

I walked to the chair and sat down, then released my hair from its bun so it spilled down my back. Gingerly, Porter took it in his hands, draping it over the back of the chair.

Porter turned me toward the mirror, then said, "All right. Here goes."

I watched Porter in the mirror as he pressed his lips to the top of my head. This simple gesture solidified every desire I had to finally cut my hair. And it removed any doubt, any hesitation that remained.

I was ready.

My pulse quickened as Porter drew an invisible line just below my bust.

"Here?" he asked and I nodded.

Slowly and with deliberate movements, Porter opened the steel scissors and cut across my thick layers of hair. His tongue pressed against his top lip as he studied the angle of his cut, making sure the hair was lined up properly. I watched him in awe, at the lengths he'd go to take care of me, to nurture me, and to encourage my independence.

He'd never pushed me to do it sooner. He'd simply waited for me to be ready.

He snipped and snipped again and again at my thick head of hair. Soon the weight that I'd carried for twenty-three years was gone, pooled in a thick mass at my feet.

"Done," Porter said, looking rather proud of himself.

I stood, inspecting myself in the mirror. "It's perfect," I said, running my hands through my hair, amazed by how thin, how airy it felt slipping through my fingers. "Absolutely perfect."

"I've never seen you look so beautiful," Porter murmured, then placed a kiss beneath my ear.

"Really?"

"This may sound weird, so bear with me, but you look like *you*. The *you* I always imagined you'd be." He tilted his head to the side, then wrapped his arms around my waist. "You've always been beautiful, but now, now you're . . ."

"I'm free." I smiled, then turned to face him and kissed him gently on the lips.

"Yes. You're free." He lifted my hand and placed a sweet kiss on the back of it. "We both are."

Porter took my hand and led me to the bedroom, our bedroom. The old Brinley would have insisted upon marriage before living together. But everything in me knew this was the right path for us. I was in no rush to marry. Porter knew it, and I knew it. But if we did marry . . . when we did, things would be different.

I would be Brinley Hammond.

I would be the *first*.

I would be the *only*.

And I would *never* share.

acknowledgments

With each book I write, I am constantly reminded of the extraordinary support I have from fellow writers, readers, bloggers, friends, and family. This book was a long time in the making as the idea came to me over a year ago while driving to meet a friend for dinner. I pictured a boy and a girl meeting at a fence. The girl had a long braid and a traditional long cotton dress. The boy was angry and alone.

Thank you to Beth Ehemann who heard my idea months later when I was planning to start a totally different project and said (I have to paraphrase because my memory is not always the best!), "You need to write this book . . . now!" Thank you for all of the encouragement and awesome brainstorming that we did while this book was still an idea in my head.

A huge thank-you goes to Melissa Perea. MP was my muse, a brainstormer, a beta, a model, and a photographer! Thank you for everything you did to help me with this book—you truly went above and beyond. And another huge thank-you to Heather Bowser of Heather Bowser Studios for posing as my Brinley and for making all of the photos perfect!

Thank you to Regina Wamba at Mae I Design & Photography. I am so in love with the cover you have created with the photos taken by Heather. You made it absolutely perfect. I'm so in love with it and I loved working with you! You are creative, professional, and flexible! Thank you so much!

Thank you to Deb Bresloff for being a constant support—brainstorming, beta reading, and giving me so much encouragement through all stages of this book. I am so grateful!

For the rest of my awesome betas—I am so grateful for each and every one of you. You were each instrumental in helping me create this story. Pamela Carrion, Laura Wilson, Sally Bouley, Megan Kapusta, Allison East, Jennifer Merkley, Kim August, Jen Campbell, Lori Sabin, Erin Roth, and Sharon Cooper.

An enormous thank-you to Pam Carrion, my unofficial publicist. I can never thank you enough for everything that you do for me on a daily basis—running the Sister Wives group, arranging my blog tour and promo tour, assisting me with anything and everything to get the word out on this book. Thank you for being you.

Thank you to Janna Mashburn for always taking the time to create gorgeous trailers! And thank you for being an incredible person with whom I trust absolutely everything. I love you!

To my fellow authors who took the time to read or to brainstorm/chat with me about this project—Maggi Myers, Tiffany King, Tara Sivec, Jenn Cooksey, Michelle Warren, Melissa Perea, Beth Ehemann, Erin Noelle (my sprinting partner!), Mia Asher, Andrea Randall, Willow Aster, Jasinda Wilder, Karina Halle, AE Woodward, Claire Contreras, and Calia Read.

For the "Safe House"—your words of encouragement, your enthusiasm, and your support are absolutely priceless. I love you so much.

My editor, Pam Berehulke of Bulletproof Editing. I am so grateful for you and not only your talent in editing, but your professionalism, your sensitivity, and your kindness.

A huge thank-you to Charles Miles for introducing me to my agent, Jessica Watterson. It was such a selfless thing to do, and I will always be grateful to you for doing that for me.

Jessica and I are such a great team, and I feel lucky to call her my agent.

Speaking of which, thank you, Jessica Watterson, for all your support and excitement regarding *Wife Number Seven.* It is humbling and wonderful, and I'm so excited about this relationship that we are building together! You are a blessing!

Thank you to all of the bloggers who are participating in the blog tour/promo tour, who have read ARCs and taken the time to review. I appreciate you all so much!

Thank you to all of my readers, especially those in the Sister Wives Facebook group, who actively show their support for my writing and characters. You are all so awesome and I am so lucky to have you!

And thank YOU for reading.

about the author

Melissa Brown is a hopeless romantic living in the Chicago suburbs with her husband, Chris, and their two children. Aside from writing, she enjoys reading and baking. She also has a slight obsession with actor Henry Cavill. This is her fifth novel.

Connect with Melissa Brown online:

Melissa's Blog:

melissabrownauthor.blogspot.com/

Facebook page:

www.facebook.com/MelissaBrownAuthor

Goodreads Author Profile:

www.goodreads.com/melissabrown

Twitter:

@LissaLou77

also by melissa brown

Bouquet Toss

Champagne Toast

Picturing Perfect

Unwanted Stars

11677104R00214

Printed in Great Britain
by Amazon.co.uk, Ltd.,
Marston Gate.